LORD OF
LONELY VALLEY

**Center Point
Large Print**

**This Large Print Book carries the
Seal of Approval of N.A.V.H.**

LORD OF
LONELY VALLEY

PETER B. KYNE

CENTER POINT PUBLISHING
THORNDIKE, MAINE

This Center Point Large Print edition
is published in the year 2011 by arrangement with
Golden West Literary Agency.

Copyright © 1932 by Peter B. Kyne.
Copyright © renewed 1960 by
the Estate of Peter B. Kyne.

The text of this Large Print edition is unabridged.
In other aspects, this book may vary
from the original edition.
Printed in the United States of America
on permanent paper.
Set in 16-point Times New Roman type.

ISBN: 978-1-61173-106-4

Library of Congress Cataloging-in-Publication Data

Kyne, Peter B. (Peter Bernard), 1880–1957.
Lord of Lonely Valley / Peter B. Kyne. — Center Point large print ed.
p. cm.
ISBN 978-1-61173-106-4 (library binding : alk. paper)
1. Large type books. I. Title.
PS3521.Y5L67 2011
813′.52—dc22

2011005501

CHAPTER ONE

JANET CORLISS SAT FACING HER ATTORNEY, old Daniel P. Magruder, of Phelps, Chinn & Magruder, Metropolitan Trust Company Building, New York City.

Gazing past him, she caught through the window a glimpse of the Hudson River and the Palisades beyond; a United States Navy destroyer was slipping down the silvery stretch to the sea—and Janet sighed.

"I wish, Mr. Magruder," she said, "that I had been born a boy."

"In which event, I dare say, you would have been a doctor instead of a trained nurse."

"There are female doctors," she reminded him.

"No, I think I'd be an explorer. I'd go rolling down to Rio; I'd go places and have adventures; I'd sip life with a long spoon. I'd go to Mozambique."

"In heaven's name, why Mozambique?"

"The name sounds so alluring."

The old lawyer chuckled. His had been a very prosaic and unadventurous life. In thirty-odd years of practise he had not even risked contempt of court. "At your age I used to think that if I ever went voyaging, Janet, it would be to Surabaya. I

5

liked that name. Nice little succession of vowels to it."

"It can't beat Topolobampo, Mexico," she replied, and they both chuckled. "Seriously, though," the girl continued, "I grow weary of turning helpless human beings over in bed. My last case had delirium tremens and imagined he was standing in the intersection of Forty-second Street and Fifth Avenue. A troop of cavalry was charging up Fifth Avenue, the fire department with six fire engines abreast was coming down the Avenue, a herd of wild cattle was traveling west on Forty-second Street and a company of infantry with fixed bayonets was charging east on Forty-second Street. All converging on him. No wonder he screamed! My morale has been quite broken down."

"Well, you didn't really have to be a trained nurse, you know. You would insist on a profession."

"In case anything serious happened to me financially—of course. And I assure you nursing presents far better matrimonial possibilities than stenography." She permitted her violet eyes to rest humorously on Magruder. "Within the past three months two middle-aged men who have successfully wrecked their bodies while successfully laying up millions have asked me to marry them. Temptation like that is awful, Mr. Magruder. Each proposer baited his trap with the promise of a trip to Europe, where we could lazy around together and have a perfectly grand time."

"And you rejected both offers?"

"Mozambique or nothing for me." Her merry laughter filled the room. "When I go gypsying, Mr. Magruder, I'll go alone. No middle-aged ruin puffing stertorously at my side."

She rose and went to the window. "Oh, dear, I have spring fever. I always get my spring fever in the fall when the leaves begin to turn red and gold. I have it badly today. I want to go where life is different. I'm so fed up with this modern civilization I think I'd experience a distinct thrill if I could meet some man who, at fifty, would fight a bear-cat and spot the bear-cat the first three bites. I'm so weary listening to the prattle of amateur gin manufacturers, it would be a relief to meet the descendant of a long line of ferocious moonshiners who never betray the pride they experience in turning out corn whiskey that will give one a permanent wave."

The old lawyer laughed heartily. " 'Oh, would that we two were maying,' " he quoted. "I'm going to finish my business with you and chase you out of my office, or you'll infect me with spring fever, too. Before I do that, however, may I suggest that you're quite alone in the world, and if you feel like heeding the call of your wanderlust, why do you not go? Who is there to say you nay?"

"Go where?"

"Not to Mozambique, of course. But I can suggest a trip you might take—and to your profit. That country may be settled now, with a player piano, a radio, and a telephone in every home, but if the tales your grandfather used to tell me about it were fifty percent true, the passage of forty years may not have worn all the hair off it. Men were men in his day, and women stood for them."

"Where is this wonderful place, Mr. Magruder?" she asked soberly. "Perhaps women would still stand for that kind of men—if they could find them."

"I don't guarantee the men, but I know this land is rough enough to suit your heart's desire," the old lawyer replied. "Also you happen to own a sizable portion of it—and every one ought to know his own land."

"Oh, so you're suggesting I should go out and look at my land in Modoc County, in Northern California."

"I am. Something should be done about that land. All your grandfather ever did was pay taxes on it. According to him, it was worth that, but would some day be worth considerably more."

"The trouble with grandfather was that he thought he was going to live forever."

"Well, the land is yours now, Janet. The decree of final distribution in the matter of your grandfather's estate has been signed, and the executor has signed deeds to all the land, conveying title to you. All the bills have been paid, and I have a check for eight thousand and a few odd dollars for you. All you have to do is sign here on the dotted line and be off."

"But what shall I do with all that worthless land, Mr. Magruder?"

"I can't answer that for you, Janet. From this distance it looks like a frozen asset with zero temperatures likely to continue. In the probate of your grandfather's estate it was appraised at a dollar and a quarter an acre, which is the government price of desert land in the public domain. But your grandfather paid five dollars an acre for it in the late eighties, when land was a drug on the market. Which is my principal reason for suggesting that you go out there and investigate. The old man must have had a vision of sorts when he bought that land, and you may be able to see that same vision."

"If I do, I'll not stare at it more than forty years. He told me once his holdings out there gave him control of something, but for some reason he never managed to get to the point of exercising his control. I wonder why?"

"He told me about it once. A wild and woolly cattle king out there ran him out of the country. This person could shoot—and did. Your grandfather shot back but the other side was too strong for him. He didn't belong in that country anyhow. He was always a contrary man, however, so I imagine he hung on to those scattered parcels of land through sheer cussedness."

Magruder picked up a stack of deeds from his desk and shuffled them. "I have communicated with the county surveyor of Modoc County and discover that all of those holdings are surrounded by the public domain. In 1905, I think it was, all of that public domain was withdrawn from entry and included in the Modoc National Forest. Of course, since your grandfather acquired title in fee many years prior to the organization of the Modoc National Forest, he can not be dispossessed, but the Department of the Interior will be very glad to receive title to these scattered parcels of land, and in return give you an equal number of acres elsewhere in the public domain not included in any National Park, National Monument, or National Forest. Moreover, the land you would receive in lieu of your present holdings would be in one solid block instead of being scattered all over creation. Such a compact body of land, well selected, might be of ready sale and at a fair price. So I think it would be an excellent idea for you to work off your spring fever by going out to that country and estimating the situation. And while you are out there, you can record these deeds at the county seat. There is a law firm in San Francisco which attends to matters on the Coast for us, and I will give you a letter of introduction to them. They will handle your affairs if you desire them to do so."

"Today is the tenth of September," Janet mused aloud, "and Indian summer will be upon us in a jiffy. My spring fever always soars in Indian summer. Yes, I'll go. Show me the dotted line and give me those deeds. I'll have all my shopping done in a week. Then I'm going to buy a snappy little coupé and drive out to California. I'll drive leisurely, and I should get out there in three weeks—though if I find some nice place along the road I may stop there a while.

"Really, Mr. Magruder, I think you're a grand person for having suggested it. The more I contemplate it, the more captivated I am with the prospect. I'll give you my interest in Mozambique."

"Are you intending to travel alone?"

"Of course. Haven't I told you I'm tired of people?"

"But a young girl—"

"I'm twenty-two years old and I'm not afraid. Do please hurry, Mr. Magruder. Now that my mind is made up, I can not bear another moment of delay."

"You'll bear it and like it, young lady. I haven't completed my discussion of your land problem. Out of the twenty-two hundred odd acres you have one quarter section that, while the most

11

worthless of all the parcels, may prove to be of considerable value. A few months ago I received a letter addressed to your grandfather in my care. The tax bills on your grandfather's California property have always been mailed him in my care. This letter was from a man named Milo Landrum (make a note of that name), whose address is Modoc City, Modoc County, California. He asked if this quarter section of desert sand and lava was for sale, and if so, at what price was it being held. In answering I decided not to inform him that your grandfather was dead; I told him my client would be glad to receive his best offer for the land, that it was valuable because it is the key to a strategic situation and that, as a matter of fact, my client was not eager to sell, but might consider an offer based upon the strategic rather than the tangible value of the land.

"Upon receipt of my letter Landrum wired an offer of five thousand dollars. I replied that my client was not interested, and ever since Landrum has been raising the ante until now I have him up to fifteen thousand. Just a little game of business poker, Janet."

"Why, how lovely!" cried the delighted Janet.

"About twenty-five years ago your grandfather told me why he had bought this land: plain lust for vengeance against the wild and woolly cow person who ran him out of the country. And his ancient enemy had just written him, offering twenty-five thousand dollars for the property. It had cost your grandfather about eight hundred, I believe. I urged him to sell, but he merely cackled with pleasure and declared it was worth twenty-five thousand to make his enemy suffer and keep him from realizing on an investment that meant two millions or more to him."

"Who was this enemy, Mr. Magruder?"

"He told me at the time, but I have forgotten. All I remember is that the man's first name was Felix. He's probably dead now, but Felix is not a common name, and with that much of a clue you may be able to run him down if he is living, or his heirs if he is dead. He was a twenty-minute egg, according to your grandfather, and such men are not soon forgotten. He and your grandfather had a shooting scrape together in 1888. When you get out there, go to the local newspaper office and ask to look at their files. You'll probably find the story on the front page and thus ascertain the family name of that Felix person. If Felix is still living, or if he is not and you can locate his heir and that heir is interested in bidding against Landrum, why, all you have to do is to play one against the other until one of them quits—then close with the winner—that is, unless for the sake of sentiment you desire to keep your grandfather's grouch alive. As a lawyer I have discovered that there is never any profit in a grouch."

13

"Old Omar must have been something of a lawyer," Janet replied. "I'll take the cash and let the credit go. I'm to call on Milo Landrum in Modoc City and look up an ancient fire-eater known as Felix."

"And record those deeds when you get out there. I could mail them out to the county recorder, but I think you should make haste slowly. It might be to your advantage to delude your victims into thinking that you are merely the representative of your grandfather rather than the new owner. I'll mail you copies of the correspondence with Landrum."

When Janet had completed her business and made her adieu, Magruder gazed wistfully after her.

"How wonderful to be young and lovely and filled with good health and charm and humor and the thrill of adventure!" he soliloquized. "To be on the loose—instead of being old and tied to a business. Confound the duty complex!"

And having lost one client, he sat back to wait for another!

CHAPTER TWO

THE WILD HAY THAT WAS TO BE FED TO HIS cattle during the winter had been cut, raked, and stacked by September first, and now Raynor Lanier was busy irrigating the grass stubble before the frost of early fall should come to chill the soaked earth and retard the growth of winter pasturage. He must have a new growth of grass not less than six inches high to supplement the hay, if he was to winter his cattle successfully, and, since he was irrigating with Modoc Indian labor, whose loyalty and industry he could trust but not their efficiency, he had been out all day superintending the work himself. When he rode across the irrigated areas, he wanted his horse's hoofs to splash the water so high it drenched the rider's rubber boots, for then he knew his meadows were receiving the sort of soaking that, in combination with the warmth of the Indian summer days, would insure grass.

He had been out since dawn, and he had ridden far that day, starting at the concrete dam in Lonely Valley Creek, where the water was diverted and high-headed for ten miles through a ditch along the upper portion of Lonely Valley, in order that it might have a good angle of fall through the flood-gates along its length. That canal, twelve feet wide and six feet deep and running bank full, was a sight that never failed to thrill Raynor Lanier with the joy of possession. To him it was Nature's promise that all would be well with his little world for another year. And this water that spread out over seven thousand acres of meadow was all his, because every acre in Lonely Valley was his; and where there exist no adverse claimants to water, quarrels and litigations also are non-existent. There had been enough and to spare of that sort of thing in the history of the Lanier family, young Raynor reflected sadly, as his horse carried him at a fast running walk across the fat acres.

The spring of the sodden turf under his horse's feet added to the young man's feeling of contentment, for he loved this land of his with the fierce love of one whose very life lay rooted in it. He loved the aroma of it, the sunshine dappling the areas where already a tinge of green showed, and shining like heliographs on the water that accumulated in little depressions. Overhead flock upon flock of trumpeter swan and wild geese and ducks were winging south, urged by the instinct to find green winter fields and open lakes and ponds where food would be plentiful. Their cries filled the air; Lanier knew that as late as Christmas they would be flying over. In the dying pussy willows, sycamores, and aspens along the route of Lonely Valley Creek, from the high hills to its juncture with Lonely Valley Lake, grouse boomed mysteriously. In the fenced fields on the high ground beyond the hay meadows he heard the plaintive cries of little white-faced calves, born out of due season and, with their mothers, kept in Lonely Valley while the calves born in March and April were, with their mothers, far up on the summer range in the Modoc National Forest. Over all the land a faint bluish haze spread, obscuring it in places; over the haze the high, dark, timbered hills that surrounded the valley rose like sentinels.

"And this is my heritage," Raynor Lanier thought, as he drank in its beauty.

It seemed to him that he could never bear to leave it, since to him, as to his father and grandfather, it had always been a Land of Promise.

When the sun was an hour high, he rode home through the soft haze, pausing from time to time to gaze down over his empire to where the waters of Lonely Valley Lake lapped its western fringe; out across the lake, peaceful and shimmering until the waters appeared lost in space. He marked numbers of white pelicans hovering over its surface and from time to time dropping with the swiftness of tiny meteors into it, to rise presently with a fish.

"The unending warfare of all Nature," he

soliloquized. "Whether men or pelicans, all created things prey on each other, and the survival of the fittest is the supreme law."

When he came within sight of his headquarters, located on high ground well toward the northern end of the ranch, he was sensible again—as indeed he always was—of the pride of possession. His grandfather had been the author of the building plan—great log barns erected in orderly progression and so spaced that should one catch fire the others would be in no danger of destruction. Below the barns a large, circular log corral where his men broke colts in the fall; beyond that the horse pasture where the riding stock and the draft horses grazed; above the barns the bunk house and the foreman's log cottage; on a high knoll beyond the bunk house and cottage the fifty-thousand-gallon concrete tank fed from a giant spring and furnishing drinking water for man and beast as well as fire protection. And, some four hundred yards from the main ranch buildings, on a sparsely-timbered knoll and surrounded by a terraced lawn still faintly green in the desolation of winter, the imposing home his father had built in order that the third generation of Laniers might dwell in the midst of modern comforts and entertain his friends as a gentleman wishes to entertain. It was a handsome, rambling, bungalow type of house, built of selected, twelve-inch white-pine logs, cut in the fall, peeled, and seasoned all the following year to make them beetle- and worm-proof. Every two years the Laniers shellacked those logs, and the house glistened with an air of permanent newness.

As Lanier rode up a broad road topped with fine trap-rock to this house, the mood of introspection came upon him again. "It lacks a mistress," he said to himself. "What of the fourth generation?"

He did not know.

In front of the house he dismounted, turned his horse, gave the tired animal a slap on the rump, and sent him back down the road to the barn. Lanier removed his rubber boots, and an old Chinaman, in white apron and cook's cap, came out with a pair of slippers, into which Lanier stepped and walked stiffly up the steps to the veranda. From the veranda a man spoke.

"Good evening, Ray. I've been settin' here admirin' your view."

"Good evening, Landrum." There was a noticeable chill in the young man's tones, and the absence of the polite prefix of Mister—a usage which most cattlemen cling to long after time and intimacy should indicate its abandonment—accentuated the lack of warmth in his greeting. "Yes, it's a nice view. I never grow weary of it."

He stood a moment, gazing at his visitor. He knew that his Chinaman had purposely refrained from inviting the man into the house, and for a moment he was inclined to do the same. But the laws of hospitality may not be lightly evaded, so he added:

"There's a faint touch of winter in the air at sunset. Come in, Landrum?"

His visitor rose and followed him into the huge living room, where logs blazed invitingly in a six-foot stone fireplace. Landrum gazed about him, noting the thick Spanish rug, the heavy, comfortable chairs, the divan before the fireplace, the expensive combination of radio and phonograph in one corner and the baby grand piano in the other, the soft concealed lighting, the artistic lamps, the table with half a dozen books in bronze book-ends, the two sporting rifles and one shotgun hung on polished deer antlers over the fireplace.

"You have a mighty fancy headquarters here, Ray," said Landrum and took the chair Lanier indicated. "I heard they was pretty swell."

"You are in Lonely Valley," the host replied. "We have tried to offset some of the loneliness by doing ourselves well. It makes the place inviting to our friends. We generally have guests all summer, and quite a few come up for the hunting in the fall. Drink?"

"What have you?"

"Bourbon. My grandfather came from Kentucky and knew how to make it. He taught my father, and father cooked up a big mess of it just before the Eighteenth Amendment was passed. It's been in charred oak barrels ever since, and it's prime. Straight or highball?"

"Highball," said Landrum.

Lanier sought to be more neighborly. "We have our own soda spring on the ranch. Good as any sharp charged water you can buy. Man was up here last summer wanting to trade us out of a concession to bottle it."

He pressed a bell, and the old Chinaman slithered in from the kitchen. Lanier gave his order and added:

"Where is my father?"

"Papa go Modoc City. Tom Harmon drive him in, Ray.

"Beats the devil how familiar these heathens get with their boss," Landrum said.

"He's been thirty years on the payroll. He's earned it, dandling me on his knee." Lanier sat down and stretched his feet to the fire. "A saddle," he said, "gets a little tender after you've sat in it twelve hours. You'll stay to dinner?"

"No, thanks, I must be getting back to town. Got to get over the ridge before it is too dark." Landrum coughed and cleared his throat. "I met your father driving in to town as I was driving out. I told him I was headed for the ranch to have a little business talk with him." Landrum paused and favored his host with a meaning grin. "Of course, you know your old man an' me ain't never hit it off any too well together."

21

"Yes, I've heard that story. Suppose we permit the dead past to lie in its grave and get down to the milk in the coconut."

"The old man advised me to come out and do my talking with you."

"That's right. Father leaves everything to me now. Whatever I say or do goes for him."

"You're in luck. Most fathers want to hang on to their authority to the last. Ray, I learned recently that you folks own Lonely Valley Lake."

"My grandfather, Pierre Lanier, bought it from the state as swamp and overflowed land in 1873."

"He paid a dollar an acre for it—seventy-five thousand acres. Your grandfather must have had a dream that turned out a nightmare."

"Well, we still have a lake on our seventy-five thousand acres, and you must admit it's a beautiful lake and swarming with trout."

"Still a lake is not exactly what I'd call a profitable investment. You might make your taxes out of it if you'd rent summer cabin sites along the shore an' charge folks a nominal sum for fishing there."

"We invite our friends, and anybody can fish our lake if he comes to the house and asks permission. We do not want the shores of our lake littered with shanties; that sort of people might start a fire that would spread to our meadows in midsummer and burn our hay. We prefer our privacy."

"Of course, the taxes don't amount to much," Landrum pursued, "but you've been paying a cent an acre for fifty-six years. So you got an additional sum o' forty-two thousand dollars tied up in that lake, an' say at seven percent the interest on the whole investment runs into money."

"True."

"Want to sell the doggone lake?"

"No."

"Why?"

"We've had it in the family so long we've become attached to it."

"You'll never be able to drain it an' use the land, an' I tell you, if you could do that, you'd have the finest winter cattle under heaven. Why, that land would be worth fifty dollars an acre, my boy."

"I imagine it would feed a cow to every three acres, and one could cut enough wild hay to winter twenty thousand head. At a reasonable estimate it ought to pay ten percent on two million dollars."

"The lake," Landrum pursued, "wasn't always here. I learned that from an old Indian recently."

"The lake was not here when my grandfather first saw Lonely Valley in 1841. When he came back in '51, it was here."

"Ah," said Landrum. "The old codger saw the Promised Land before the Lord broke His promise, eh?"

"My father says his father told him it was as fine as the portion of the valley we now own."

"The lake is five miles wide, approximately, an' better than twenty miles long. There's a drop to the lake bottom of about a foot to the mile. You know how the lake come to be formed, of course?"

"Yes. Once Lonely Valley Creek flowed the length of the valley and approximately through its center. The outlet was a narrow gorge at the western end with a tall spire of lava standing on the low hill that forms one flank of the gorge. There must have been an earthquake soon after my grandfather saw the valley, for that huge lava spire toppled over into the gorge and strewed that shattered block of lava its entire width and for perhaps eighty feet of its length. Ordinarily the water could escape between the great blocks of lava, but in time of freshet the stream carried dirt and sticks and stones against and into the jam, gradually forming a natural, earth-filled dam. And so Lonely Valley became Lonely Lake."

"The trouble is," Landrum said with a knowing little grin, "that your grandfather figgered that box canyon with the obstruction in it lay in the public domain. He was so sure of it he neglected to make certain. But it wasn't. He figgered it would never be filed on for entry by any settler, because no settler would be crazy enough to file on a quarter section of black lava. He figgered on blowin' that dam out when he could afford to; but I reckon he died without gettin' together enough cash to hire engineers to do it."

"That is exactly what happened, Landrum."

"Your father inherited from him. In readin' over the old files of the *Modoc County Clarion*, I find your father figgered in a good many front-page stories."

Lanier stared at his visitor with the sort of stare one visits upon a ghoul.

"We'll not talk about that, Landrum. My father was a cowman of a day that is done. What he had he held, and frequently he had to fight to hold it."

"Oh, no offense, no offense. Everybody in the county knows he controlled the free summer range by might until the Federal government took it over and called it the Modoc National Forest. Now cowmen have to pay Uncle Sam for their summer range."

"The Laniers were there first, and it was the unwritten law of the range that he who was there first, developed the water holes, and held long and undisturbed possession, should not be disturbed save at the great bodily risk of the disturber. My father ran a man named Donald MacLean off the free range in 1888. MacLean was a fighting Scottish-Canadian—and there was a ruckus. My father shot MacLean through the leg, and MacLean's buckshot are still in father. Two of our Modocs and one of MacLean's riders were killed, and MacLean pulled out. We were too strong for him. But he had his innings. He bought some cheap land scrip and applied it to the purchase of the quarter section of worthless land that controls the outlet of Lonely Valley Lake. He bottled us and our lake up—and I respect him for it. I would have done the same if I had been in his place and had been smart enough to think of it. And my father was never so lacking in humor that he couldn't laugh at the trick MacLean had played him.

"But MacLean hasn't really hurt us. If my grandfather hadn't bought the lake, somebody else would, and it would have been drained and the land sold off in sections to nesters. Every nester would have a few cows, and they would haye wanted their share of the Lonely Valley Creek water, and that would have hurt us. And they would have banded together and crowded us off the free range in the days when it was free; and today, instead of having a permit to graze ten thousand head in the Forest Reserve, we would be cut down to perhaps a thousand, in order that the grazing privilege might be equitably distributed. Landrum, it profits us to own Lonely Valley Lake and pay seven hundred and fifty dollars a year for the privilege."

"Yes, I guess it does. Ever try to buy MacLean out?"

"Often. He would not sell—and we offered him

twenty-five thousand for it once. He prefers his revenge."

"When your father dies, MacLean—if he still lives—may conclude his grouch has been satisfied an' sell to you. Or he may die an' his heirs, preferrin' money to an inherited grouch, may sell to you. Or," he added, following a moment of silence, "to me."

"You're interested, of course."

"Naturally the sight o' two old buck goats standin' on a log, buttin' each other into a brawly stream because neither has the sense to back off an' let the other by, always interests me. I'm a business man."

"So I've heard," Ray Lanier remarked dryly. "Suppose, then, you talk business. You said you came for that purpose, and it must have been an impelling urge, for I believe my father once told you, Landrum, that if you ever set foot on his ranch you'd never drag yourself off under your own horse-power."

"Yes, an' he meant it. But the years have mellered him."

"No, they haven't. I have. He isn't anxious to leave me a heritage of hate and trouble."

"Well, when I met him on the road I asked him if I could come out to talk with him, and he said I could come out an' talk to you."

"And I'm listening."

"MacLean *might* consider selling his land to me

for a good price. I reckon he knows me an' your father have never been friendly. Now, I propose this. If I can buy him out, I'll control the situation. Then I'll pay for the expense of blowing out that natural dam, and your seventy-five thousand acres will naturally drain. Then, under the law, you can go to the surveyor-general of the state and make affidavit that you've drained your swamp an' overflowed land an' apply for the rebate by the state to you of the dollar an acre the land cost your grandfather."

"I am familiar with the provisions of that law, Landrum."

"That seventy-five-thousand-dollar windfall will put your present affairs in sweet shape. Then, because I have done somethin' for you, naturally you will be willin' to do somethin' for me. It would be worth deedin' me half the lake-bed, wouldn't it?"

"No!"

"So?"

"Yes."

"Twenty years ago your father took a crew down there an' started work blowin' out that dam without askin' MacLean's permission."

"Quite so. The old fox suspected Father might, so he had the place watched, and got an injunction from the superior court of this county forever restraining my father from trespassing on his property or attempting to blow out that dam."

28

"So you will not sell the lake in its entirety for a good price or make the other deal and deed me half?"

"No."

"Why not?"

"Permit me to inform you, Landrum, that that is my business."

Landrum lost his temper. "You're a fool. You'll sing a different song when you're broke flatter than soup on a plate."

"Perhaps you're right on both counts, Landrum. I would offer you another drink, but since you are going now and the road over the ridge is narrow and winding, that other drink might not be in order. The first one appears to have excited you into calling me a fool in my own house. I gather that you have already planned the ruin of the House of Lanier and arrogated to your unpleasant self the task of picking the bones of our ruin."

He went to the broad front portal and threw it open. Landrum, taking the hint, strode through it and out to his car parked farther up the drive. As he sat in the car, warming up his motor preparatory for the long pull up out of the valley, he glowered at Raynor Lanier.

"I tell you, young man, that one of these bright days you'll suddenly make up your mind to sell me that lake, and when you do I'll not be in a tradin' mood. Sabe? Better make a deal with me now."

"No, thanks. I can not see you in the picture at all."

"Well, I've declared in, Lanier." After a brief silence he said threateningly, "When I set out to get something I get it."

"My father is, I realize, something of a prejudiced and opinionated man, but he was always right about you, Landrum. He has always maintained that you'd cheat playing solitaire. Now, you listen to me, mister. I'm the lord of Lonely Valley, now that my father has abdicated, but the old decree still stands. If you ever come on this ranch again, you'll stay here. You're getting modern, aren't you? Muscling in on a proposition in which you haven't a dollar invested and thinking to tarry your point by running a blazer on a Lanier. Well, when our last head of stock and our last acre have been sold to satisfy our creditors, we'll still have our courage left. Good night!"

CHAPTER THREE

ON SEPTEMBER TWENTIETH RAYNOR LANIER completed his irrigating. Meanwhile, Tom Harmon, his superintendent, had, with his riders, caught up the caballada, the majority of which had been on pasture all summer, and begun to accustom them to the saddle again. The chuck wagon was overhauled and greased; the men looked to their equipment, making ready for the round-up of the cattle on the summer range. Old Felix, who had to have something to do despite the fact that his days of usefulness had passed, superintended the erection of the barbed-wire fences around some twenty-odd stacks of hay down in the meadows, against the day when the stacks should be fed.

Raynor and his men were to start for the Forest Reserve on the twenty-fifth, and the day before, Felix drove over to Modoc City to see if he could not pick up around town half a dozen extra riders who might be in the position of having spent their summer's wages and wishful for a temporary riding job with the Lanier outfit.

When he returned to Lonely Valley that night, Raynor saw that something had occurred to worry him, but forebore asking questions. He knew that Felix would, in his own time, tell him all about it. He was certain something was wrong when, immediately after dinner, Felix showed not the slightest interest in Amos and Andy; instead he settled down comfortably in front of the fire and stared into it for a long time. Finally he said:

"Son, I want you should give me back my six-shooter. An' you get a gun for yourself an' start practicin'. You can have my weapon back again when I'm gone."

"Thinking of leaving me, Felix?"

"I'm an old man, son. Not so fast as I used to be. Got to use strategy now in place o' direct action."

"It must be ten years since you've walked armed, Felix." Like his father, Raynor was approaching the crisis in a casual, somewhat roundabout manner.

Felix nodded. "All my enemies were dead then or had moved away."

"You've retired," Raynor reminded him. "When I took over the management of this outfit, I took it over root and branch—which includes your enemies. You had a run-in with Landrum, I suppose."

"No, with a stranger—middle-aged man. I had to eat crow today, an' it hurt, but I reckon crow's the proper diet for a man who ain't fully dressed. But the next time—"

"There'll be no next time for you, old-timer. The job's mine."

"No, it ain't. The outfit's yours. That bars you." And old Felix grinned slyly. "Hobbled you today, boy. After my run-in with this stranger I went down to Jim Bullen's office an' had Jim draw up a deed o' gift for this ranch an' all the livestock on it or in the Forest Reserve—every four-footed critter wearin' the Tomahawk brand, together with all an' singular the reversion an' reversions an' hereditaments thereunto belongin' or in any wise pertainin'. An' that document will be recorded at the county seat tomorrow mornin' at ten o'clock."

"Then Landrum's sent a killer after you?"

"I think so. He said he'd bust you, didn't he? Well, a good way to start, seems to me, would be to take me out o' the picture quick. I reckon it would cost fifty thousand dollars to probate my estate an' settle for the state an' Federal inheritance taxes. Takes cash to settle an estate; I never did have no life insurance, an' we're land an' cattle poor. I reckoned it would be best if I died without any estate to embarrass you."

Felix laughed—a dry, mirthless, little laugh. "Jim Bullen said most likely the Government sues for the inheritance taxes anyhow, allegin' I made the transfer to you in view o' my impendin' death an' with intent to defraud Uncle Sam out of his just due. So I had Doc Ambrose give me a thorough physical examination. Doc says I'm in grand shape for a man o' my years—no reason why I shouldn't live ten years, barrin' accidents. I had Doc make an affidavit to that effect, so if the Government sues you, spring that record on 'em. Jim says the Government is always suspicious in cases like this, if the grantor dies within two years o' makin' the grant. If somebody dry-gulches me, of course, that's a horse of another color. Nobody can prove I was anticipating that kind of a death."

"Tell me about this stranger," Raynor commanded.

"I'm settin' on the porch o' the Mountain House, gassin' with Tom, Dick, an' Harry, whilst waitin' for some unemployed cow waddy to happen along an' dare me to hire him as an extra rider for the round-up. We got talkin' about hard times in Europe an' from that to who won the Great War, an' I give my opinion to the effect that we won it, an' if France had a drop o' sportin' blood she'd pay her debt to us without waitin' until bankrupt Germany paid her. An' this stranger puts in with the suggestion that I'm talkin' through my hat. You know me. I ain't strong on verbal arguments, so I says:

" 'Time was, my friend, when for a remark like that I'd make you eat my hat. However, with the years has come wisdom an' caution, so I guess I'll keep my hat on my head.'

" 'Oh, will you?' he says—an' knocks my hat off. 'I've heard about you,' he says. 'You're known as the ol' gray wolf of Lonely Valley. You git tough with me an' I'll make *you* eat your own hat.'

"I see right off he's bent on fastenin' a quarrel on me, and as I can't defend myself I eat crow. Yes, son, I pick up my hat an' smile on. I say:

" 'Neighbor, I don't care enough about who won the war to quarrel about it. All I know is that I've won every war I was ever in except this here present one, which it's a declaration o' war to knock my hat off an' call me the ol' gray wolf o'

Lonely Valley. I ain't heeled, neighbor, but I got a wolf cub to home that'll make the Lanier honor clean again. I reckon it's time for me to get back to my den,' an' I call to Big Foot, who's settin' in the car across the street an' had seen everything that happened. He'd drove me to town this morning.

"I says to Big Foot in Modoc:

"'Come over here quiet with the car an' pick me up. Climb out to help me in just as if you ain't interested, but if you get a chance, put a knife to this man's throat an' I'll search him for weapons.'

"Which Big Foot played his part noble. This stranger has a contempt for Indians, especially Indians past their prime, like Big Foot, so he helps me into the car with a shove—an' Big Foot is on top of him like a cougar as the feller turns to go back on the porch. He takes the feller by the skelp from the rear an' tilts his head back; his knife is on this throat.

"'If you want your throat cut, my friend', says I, 'just reach for your gun.'

"So I go over him an' find a little short automatic under his left armpit an' a little sawed-off bull-dog pistol in his side pocket. I relieve him of these, an' then I says:

"'Mister, my hat cost too much money for you to eat it, but take a good bite out of your own headgear,' an' I pick his hat up an' shove it into his mouth. 'Eat,' I says, 'or die.'

"An' he et. By God, son, he bit a piece out an' chewed it up fine, an' Big Foot held him till he swallowed it, with everybody laughin' at him. Then I took my knife out an' ear-marked him so's I'd always know him again, an' told him to git out o' the country. An', son, I didn't want to do that. Me, I like peace."

Raynor Lanier looked at his side pridefully and then burst into laughter, in which presently old Felix joined.

"I was pretty rough," Felix agreed. "Come to think of it, he can have the law on me for ear-markin' him—although I didn't do more than notch it. That's mayhem, ain't it?"

"Any jury in this county would turn you loose. Middle-aged men who pick on old men needlessly, to provoke them into drawing so they can be beaten to the draw, have no standing in court. Not in this county. That killer will leave. You've exposed him. A good doctor, Felix, old pal, doesn't treat the symptoms of a disease. He treats the cause. My diagnosis of the cause of this disease is Milo Landrum, so I'm going to treat Milo. Don't worry about it any more, Felix. But while I'm away on the round-up, you stay close to home. I'll leave Big Foot and his son to guard you. I do not have to tell you how to protect yourself. You know."

"An' you have your trusted men ride armed," Felix warned. "With both of us out of the way—

by the way, who would you leave this outfit to if you got dry-gulched?"

"Tom Harmon. He's faithful. There are no more Laniers."

Felix nodded. "Well, Tom could sell the lake to Landrum if he got crowded. That would be all right. Me an' you, son, we wouldn't know it, so our pride wouldn't be hurt."

Raynor got up and started turning the dials on the radio. Well, Milo Landrum was working for a prize worth having—a little empire that would be worth better than two millions of dollars. . . . He knew that men actuated by hate and greed are capable of monstrous things. . . . He said to himself:

"If anything happens to Felix, I'll kill Milo Landrum. I'll tell him so, and he'll know I'll keep my promise."

At dawn next day he took the road with his men, driving the caballada before them, the chuck wagon following. They camped in a fenced field outside Modoc City that night. Raynor Lanier was rolled up in his bedding roll when, about ten o'clock, Tom Harmon, his superintendent, came and awakened him.

"Skunk Tallow has just ridden in from the ranch in your father's car. There's hell to pay. He says a man came to the front door of the headquarters house about dusk this evening. Ah Fong opened the door, and the stranger asked to see your father. When Felix heard a stranger was asking for him, he telephoned down to the bunk house and ordered Big Foot and Skunk Tallow to come up, stand out in front of the house in the dark, and keep the stranger covered. He made a good mark against the light from the door. Felix gave them five minutes to run the four hundred yards and get posted, then he came out to meet the man—and the fellow reached for a gun and let Felix have it."

"Killed?" Raynor asked.

"No, too low. Busted the old man's leg—but before he could finish him, Big Foot gave the stranger both barrels of buckshot."

"So Landrum had us watched. Waited until he thought there was nobody home except Felix and Ah Fong. Well, Tom, I'll take the car Skunk Tallow drove out, run over to town, and get Doc Ambrose. You pull out with the outfit tomorrow, and I'll join you up in the Reserve. You'll be camped on Rocky Creek for three days."

He rolled out, dressed himself, and departed in the car for Modoc City. Tom Harmon stared into the darkness after him.

"A chip off the old block," he reflected. "Nothing on earth can stampede that tribe. And I wouldn't give a wet cigarette paper for Milo Landrum's life!"

CHAPTER FOUR

A YOUNG MAN WITH PARENTHETICAL LEGS, and arrayed in a short, blue denim jumper and overalls turned up over high-heeled boots, came up the main street of Modoc City and mounted a horse that had been standing with drooping head at a watering trough in front of what had, once upon a time, been a saloon. He glanced at Janet Corliss shyly and lifted his hat.

"Excuse me for speakin' to you, miss, but you'd better git off'n the street. There's a herd o' cattle comin' through—feller bringin' 'em home from the Forest Reserve to his winter range. Them cow-brutes are tired an' hungry an' thirsty; they been hazed around more or less, so they ain't on speakin' terms with folks they meet afoot. They ain't used to nothin' but men on horseback, so they're liable to go on the peck. You take my advice an' climb up on that there old loadin' platform beyond the waterin' trough. It's four feet above the street level, an' you can stand there an' watch 'em come through."

"Oh, thank you so much. I'd love to see a cattle drive. I've never seen one," Janet replied eagerly.

"I sort o' figured mebbe you hadn't."

"How many cattle are there?"

"About five hundred, I reckon—cows an' calves. Reckon the beef stuff's been cut out an' shipped from Alturas. Five hundred's about as much as a feller can handle good in one drive."

Janet climbed up on the old loading platform. "Why, I can smell them," she cried, marveling that this should be so at a distance of two blocks.

"Nice smell, too," the stranger remarked solemnly. "I like it, myself. Well, I got to drift or them cow-brutes'll be hustlin' me along in front o' them." He lifted his hat and cantered away up the street.

From her safe stand Janet watched the drive come through; watched the cattle plod at a half trot through the deep dust, red eyes rolling, tongues lolling out; watched them crowd and half climb over each other when those behind pressed too closely; listened to the rap, rap, rap of horn against horn, to the low, protesting bellowing of the cows and the distressed and tired bleat of the calves. Indians riding in front of the herd scattered and stationed themselves at the cross streets; shouting and waving their riatas, they kept the cattle to the main street. At the rear of the herd more Indians rode.

Behind these last, perhaps a block, came a covered wagon drawn by four black mules driven by a half-breed Indian. Beside him on the seat sat a young white man, and beside the white man, and with a supporting arm around him, sat an oldish, full-blood Indian; in the latter's left hand was clasped a rifle. The wagon drew in beside the watering trough, and the old Indian got down; the half-breed, twining his reins around the brake, assisted the white man down into the waiting arms of the Indian, then gathered his teams together and continued the journey.

The white man walked weakly to the watering trough and drank greedily from the inflow pipe; then handed his hat to the Indian and drove his hot, sweat-begrimed face deep into the cool water, while the Indian dipped water in his cupped palm and poured it over the white man's head and the base of his neck. A few words passed between them in an alien tongue; then the Indian lifted the white man up to the raised sidewalk; the latter sat there a moment, then stretched out on his back; he half-sighed, half-moaned. Janet realized that he was very ill.

For the first time in her life the girl was seeing bona fide cow persons, so she appraised them critically. It being November and the sharp bite of winter already in the air, they wore Angora goatskin chaps over blue denim overalls, leathern jerkins over woolen shirts. Their hats were of the type always favored by their kind and in no manner resembled the monstrous headgear of the hero of a western motion picture. The Indian wore cheap boots, and his spurs were of rusty steel; the young white man's boots were hand-stitched in fancy designs, yet were stout and serviceable; his spurs were overlaid with silver. He wore in a battered old open holster a large, ivory-butted pistol snugged close to his body; his belt carried extra ammunition.

"Big Foot," said the white man, "I can't stick it. I've got to go home ahead of the drive and go to bed. Go up to the Excelsior Garage and tell Bogan to send over his sedan with a driver. I must lie down on the rear seat. I'm having a chill."

Across the street and perhaps a hundred feet further up the block Janet saw the Excelsior Garage. Indeed her own car reposed there. This cow man must be very ill indeed, when he declined to walk that far.

The Indian glanced up and down the street, as if debating the wisdom of obeying this command; then his beady glance settled on the interested Janet.

"Miss Lady," he said, coming close to her, "you like do nice thing for my boss?"

"Certainly, I'll do anything I can."

"You stand by him side; then nobody hurt him."

"Does somebody wish to hurt him?"

"Maybe so."

Janet nodded understanding of her mission, and Big Foot ran across the street diagonally up to the garage. The instant he disappeared through its door, she saw a tall, oldish man step out of the Mountain House a hundred feet down the street.

He had a pistol in his right hand, and he brought it up to the level of his hip and fired at the sick man. The bullet struck the planking about two inches from his head. Before he could fire again, Janet had made a sudden dive that was almost a tackle and hurled herself headlong on the prostrate cowboy.

"Big Foot!" she screamed. *"Big Foot!"*

Big Foot's reply was a shot from his rifle, fired from the open door of the garage—and the man under her spoke, so unexpectedly humorously that it struck the girl with the impact of a blow.

"Where did you learn to play football, Little Stranger?"

"That wretch is trying to kill you."

"Not any more, thank you. He's afraid now, on two counts. First, of hitting you and having my outfit come back to town and lynch him for doing it, and second, because Big Foot requires all his attention."

He reached an arm around and patted her on the back in comradely fashion.

"What? No more shooting? Oh, Lord, if Big Foot has downed him, I don't know what I'll do to Big Foot."

"Aren't you grateful to him for driving that murderous man away? For he's gone."

"Big Foot should know enough not to interfere in my business. Milo Landrum belongs to me. I've told him I'd kill him or be killed. It's a private war—better get off me, young lady. I ache all over. Yes, you were sufficient protection."

As Janet withdrew the protection of her body from the stricken man, Big Foot returned, picked his employer up off the platform, draped him over his shoulder as one would a child, and ran back to the garage with him.

Janet, trembling with excitement, returned to the Mountain House, packed her bags, paid her bill, brought her car from the garage, loaded the baggage, and drove out of Modoc City on the heels of the cattle drive. She had been *en route* to the office of Milo Landrum to discuss with him the purchase of her land when the shooting had occurred; now she knew she did not care to call upon Milo Landrum. She had something more important to do now, and—she was a trained nurse. Brief as had been her contact with that strange and somewhat whimsical cowboy, she had noted on his wrists and throat a suspicious-looking rash. It might be measles or typhoid fever or smallpox. And if the man didn't have a fever of a hundred and three, then Janet Corliss had never laid her cool hand upon a fevered brow.

A mile beyond Modoc City she overhauled the cattle drive, and a white man riding drag turned his horse and held up his hand.

"I'll haze 'em off the side of the road and let you pass, miss, but it will take time."

"In which direction has your boss vanished?" she queried.

"Straight ahead four miles, then bear to the left and keep right on over the hills. He's headed home for Lonely Valley, an' he's a durned sick man."

"I know it," said Janet. "I'm a trained nurse, and he needs me. What you had better do is to ride back to Modoc City and get a doctor."

"The best doctor there isn't good enough for my boss. I don't think the old fool has read three medical books since some jerk-water medical school gave him his sheepskin shortly after the Civil War. You beat it on to headquarters and telephone to the Mercy Hospital in Reno to send a doctor over in an airplane. Good landing field just below the house."

He shouted orders to his men.

"How shall I find the house?"

"Keep on until you descend into a valley with a lake in it. Big log house on a timbered knoll. Only house there. When you reach the crest of the hill above the valley, you'll see a big sign. It says, 'Halt.' Honk your horn until a man comes out of the timber, and tell him Tom Harmon said to let you pass. Don't think he'd be suspicious of a woman, anyhow; but you never can tell about an Indian."

"Thank you. What is your employer's name?"

"Raynor Lanier."

Tom Harmon rode his horse close to Janet's car and looked the girl over.

"You're mighty nice," he said, and lifted his sombrero. "I reckon you'll be useful. Thank you. And don't worry about your pay."

"I'm not seeking a professional call. That Raynor Lanier might have smallpox, and if he has, it's my duty to know it and report it."

"Thanks again. Well, crowd through on the right now, and the cattle will move away from you. Don't be afraid. My men will ride in front of your car."

Through the dust and shouting and turmoil of the drive Janet Corliss drove her car forward to her destiny.

CHAPTER FIVE

IT OCCURRED TO JANET CORLISS, AS SHE drove her car toward Lonely Valley, that, although the world moves fast in this age, there are certain areas of the civilized earth in which changes come slowly. Her grandfather had been one of the pioneers in this land through which she now drove; he had told her tales of Indian fights and massacres, of the lynching of cattle thieves and stage-coach robbers, of shooting scrapes, of strong men who rated their reputations for indomitable courage far above the value they placed upon their lives. Janet had thought all that sort of thing had gone into history, like the battle of Gettysburg—and yet, on her first day in this country, she had been witness to a drama that might have evolved in the hectic brain of a motion-picture scenario writer. She recalled, almost verbatim, what Dan Magruder had said to her before she left New York:

"That country may be settled now, but if the tales your grandfather used to tell me about it were fifty percent true, the passage of forty years may not have worn all the hair off it. Men were men in his day, and women stood for them."

Janet thought: "Well, that cool invalid I saved this morning is certainly of the old school. If he's a sample of the masculinity of this country, I'm glad I came. He was dirty and sweaty, and he wore a two weeks' growth of beard, and he might be as ugly as a warthog for all I know to the contrary, but he did exhibit a beautiful spirit. 'What!' says he. 'No more shooting? If Big Foot has downed him, I don't know what I'll do to Big Foot.'"

The memory of that remark gave her now an inkling of the young man's ferocity, his caste system. An Indian had no right to kill his white man's enemy, even in the protection of his white man, provided the latter had previously marked the enemy for slaughter. Unwarranted interference in a private war! The fact that he had been shot at mattered not at all to Raynor Lanier. The fact that he had not been hit was all that mattered. He had not been in the least perturbed. Well, it was plain to Janet that here was a man who would not bother to lock the stable door after the horse had been stolen. No, indeed. He would be much more likely to be hiding in the stable, waiting for the thief to come to unlock the door!

"And he spoke pure English," Janet mused. "Not the remotest hint of a nasal twang. His voice was cultured. That man must have a great deal of good in him. The driver of the wagon handled him so gently. Big Foot stood over him at the watering trough, and trouble and concern showed on that swarthy poker face; he washed his master's neck with cool water; he carried a rifle to protect him, and he made good by engaging his master's enemy. And that foreman, Tom Harmon—so cool and calm—who said, 'The best doctor isn't good enough for my boss.'"

"My boss!" No servility in the way Tom Harmon had said that; no servility in the way Big Foot had employed the same term. They might have meant "my child." Indian and white man loved him, were proud to serve him. Janet had observed a pistol at Tom Harmon's hip, so it seemed reasonable to presume that Harmon, like Big Foot, carried the weapon, not for his own protection, but for that of his boss. Plainly this Raynor Lanier must be a personage in this country.

As for the country itself, it completely satisfied Janet. The dreary prairies of western Nebraska and Wyoming had depressed her; so had the sage-covered, rolling desert lands of Utah and Nevada. Not until approaching Reno and observing the dim blue range of the Sierra, its higher peaks already snow-crowned, had she felt a mounting interest in her journey westward. From Reno she had branched off northwest on narrow, dirt roads until she crossed the line and came into Modoc County, California. The eastern portion of that county had not impressed her; it was too barren, too lonely; but as she pressed westward the country changed rapidly, giving way to irrigated farms, to prosperous-looking farmhouses, to herds of cattle and sheep and horses, to fresh-looking country youths driving much newer and higher-priced automobiles than the farmers of the Middle West.

She did not know that these were mountain people, as different from the men of the lowlands as an Englishman is from a German. When she accosted such a man to ask for travel information, he lifted his hat to her; he was polite; he answered her questions directly and succinctly and drove on.

She sensed that life was a little freer out here, a

little kindlier, a little less hard to live. And ever before her the mountains to the west, blue or black with timber (depending on the light) beckoned to her; the verdant little valleys between warmed her heart, and even Modoc City, when at last she came to it at nightfall, seemed neither run-down at the heel, antiquated, nor provincial, despite the fact that it was essentially a cow town.

Janet thought its broken wooden sidewalks, its jigsaw and scroll-work residences, its old-fashioned galleries in front of every store, faintly reminiscent of New England. She forgot that the pioneers in this country had walked across the plains and brought with them an Eastern concept of architecture. Here and there along the street stood great sugar pines and firs, saved from the forest, that had been cut to provide the town-site. And, although the Mountain House, where Janet had put up that first night, was a typical cow-town hotel, where all the guests ate at a long table in the dining room and passed each other great platters of plain food, Janet had enjoyed it immensely. It was part of her great adventure. She would have amusing tales to relate of it when she returned to New York.

Her dinner, room, and breakfast had cost her a dollar and a half, and the proprietor's wife, who had the only bath in the hotel, had thoughtfully permitted her to use it, and, following considerable reflection, had decided that the lone girl traveler was one accustomed to better things; whereupon she had prepared the bath and dumped a quart of bath salts in it!

"The people in this country are kind and thoughtful," Janet decided. "I'm going to like them. No inferiority complexes here—and no superior ones, either. Just folks."

The road left the desert plain, turned into a canyon, and commenced a long, winding climb. She saw deer; down in a creek bed she saw a black bear and two half-grown cubs splashing around in a pool, seeking fish. The pungent odor of the pines exhilarated her, the faint soughing of the breeze through their crowns evoked in her a sense of the mysterious.

Presently she came out on the crest of the hills—they were much higher than the Adirondack mountains, but in this country they were merely hills—and pulled up on a little grassy plateau. Before her and on the right of the road she saw a large, white sign and on it, in black letters that obviously were not the product of a sign-painter, she read:

HALT, STRANGER!
YOU ENTER LONELY VALLEY AT YOUR RISK.
HONK YOUR HORN OR YELL;
THEN WAIT FOR A PERMIT.
BY ORDER OF RAYNOR LANIER.

Janet looked around her. Save for a blue-jay in an adjacent tree and a raven flapping high above the timber, no living thing was in sight, so the girl decided that whoever issued permits to enter Lonely Valley had taken the day off. She threw in her gears and had proceeded about thirty feet when a rifle cracked off on her left and a bullet whined high over her head. Instantly she stopped and honked her horn long and loudly. Presently a tall young halfbreed came out of the timber, approached the car, and surveyed her without malice or curiosity.

"What do you mean by shooting at me?" Janet demanded angrily.

"I didn't shoot at you. If I had, I'd have hit you," the man answered soberly. "I just warned you—after you had been warned once by that sign. I guess you can read, lady."

"I beg your pardon," said Janet.

"Who are you and what do you want in Lonely Valley?"

"I'm Janet Corliss. I'm a trained nurse, and I'm headed for Lonely Valley to take care of Mr. Raynor Lanier, who is very sick. Tom Harmon told me to tell you I was to be permitted to pass."

"Where did you meet Tom Harmon?"

"About two miles this side of Modoc City, with the cattle drive."

"How do you know Ray Lanier is in Lonely Valley?"

"Because he passed this sign a little while ago, riding in a hired closed car belonging to the Excelsior Garage. He had a driver from the garage, and Big Foot was with him. Big Foot was carrying a rifle."

"You know my boss? You a friend of his?"

"No. I only know that he is a very sick man and has a great need of my services."

"All right, lady, pass on. You don't look like a killer, but if you are, you'll never get out of Lonely Valley alive. Remember that. I'd search you, but if I did my boss wouldn't like it. So I'll take a chance. Drive on, please."

"What is your name?"

"I am Hugo Lanier."

"Any relation to Mr. Ray Lanier?"

"No," he replied sharply. "I just take the name to make honor for myself. I am half-white."

"You are a faithful servant, Hugo. Milo Landrum shot at your boss this morning in Modoc City, but didn't hit him."

"Ah," murmured Hugo, "that boss of mine is a strange boy. He will not always let those who love him do his dirty work. I would kill Milo Landrum, and nobody would know I did it, but that boy says:

" 'No, Hugo. You will mind your own business. The Laniers kill their own snakes.' "

He lifted his hat and walked back to his place of concealment in the timber.

Janet dropped down over the grade into Lonely Valley, pausing as the full sweep of it spread out before her, to revel in its beauty. "And strangers enter this paradise at their risk," she soliloquized. "This feudal young lord of Lonely Valley, with his vassals, seeks privacy and gets it. I wonder why."

The road dropped swiftly to the floor of the valley. She saw a group of ranch buildings that resembled a small village. Off on a low, wooded knoll she saw a pretentious log house with a trap-rock road leading up to it from the main road, so she turned up this road and presently stopped her car under the *porte-cochère* of the Lanier headquarters. The hired sedan from Modoc City was parked there also.

Janet climbed out, walked up to the front door, and rang the bell. Ah Fong came to the door and gazed upon her inquiringly.

"Boss sick. No can see," he informed her brusquely.

"Oh, yes, can see. Must see. Me nurse, come to take care of boss."

Hearing their colloquy, Big Foot came out of a hall into the living room and stared at Janet.

"All right, Fong," he rumbled. "Me know lady."

He turned his head and, with an out-thrust of his chin, indicated that Janet might enter and follow him down the hall.

She did and was admitted to Raynor Lanier's bedroom. The lord of Lonely Valley lay on the bed, fully clothed, and the hired driver was struggling to remove his boots.

Big Foot, in order to assist, went to the other side of the bed and held him under the arms.

"We just got here five minutes ago," the driver explained. "I took it easy so's not to jar him. He's got a pain in the back of his neck."

"Undress him as soon as you have his boots off," Janet ordered. "Then bathe him in good hot water. It will not hurt him. This looks like a house that might have a real bathroom."

"It has," Ray Lanier mumbled. "I'm civilized, even if appearances are against me. Door to your left. You draw the bath, please. Can't trust Big Foot. He'd think he was going to scald a hog." His eyes were closed, but his interest was aroused, nevertheless. "Who are you?"

"I'm Janet Corliss, a trained nurse. I've come to take care of you."

"Good. I'll need you, I think. Who sent you so soon?"

"Nobody. I just happened along and knew my services would be required."

He pondered this a moment, while the driver struggled with his other boot. When that was off, he opened his eyes.

"Why, hello, Little Stranger," he said. "So you've bobbed up again—just where you're needed! Some one of my boys must have stolen Aladdin's wonderful lamp."

But Janet was *en route* to the bathroom to draw his bath. And when the bath was ready, Big Foot wrapped a sheet around his boss and carried him, as one carries an infant, to the tub, his goatskin chaps swishing and his spurs jingling at every step.

Janet began opening bureau drawers. "I wonder if he has nightshirts," she said to the driver.

"I think so," the latter answered. "I've heard he wears 'em." The information was vouchsafed in the tone of one who states a remarkable fact—information not for men, but to be divulged to a trained nurse. "Ray Lanier always has been a great hand for changin' his clothes."

Janet located a clean nightshirt and fresh sheets. She prepared the bed and handed the nightshirt into the bathroom for Big Foot to slip on his boss after getting the latter out of the tub. Janet gathered, from the strident talk going on in the bathroom, that Lanier was angry at being babied, but whatever his complaint it was lost on the girl, for both men spoke in the Modoc language. Only once did Lanier speak in English, and then to say:

"Bear down easy on me, you saddle-colored son of evil. Think you're grooming a horse?"

Big Foot's reply to that was a grunt.

Presently Lanier came weakly out of the bathroom and sank into bed. Janet opened his nightshirt, pressed his abdomen, and looked at his breast; she lifted his hands and examined his wrists; she noted a yellowish tinge to his eyes, felt his pulse, counted his respiration, and inserted a clinical thermometer, which she always carried in her hand bag, between his parched, cracked lips.

"How long have you been feeling ill, Mr. Lanier?" she asked.

"About five days. Came on me slowly, but I didn't like to quit the job until we'd rounded up the last of the cattle."

"You have pain?"

"Severe, in my head and the back of my neck. All my muscles ache, and my legs feel as if they were in a vise."

"Have you any sick-room supplies in this house?"

"No, because the Laniers are never ill. Besides, they never die natural deaths, so why invest in equipment that will not be needed?"

"Have you ice and whiskey?"

"Lots of both. But whiskey and ice are not sick-room supplies. They're a social necessity."

She smiled at his effort to be cheerful. "Have you a telephone?"

"In the kitchen. Ah Fong will show you. One long ring for central at Modoc City. How is it that you're on this job?"

"When I sprawled on you in Modoc City this morning to protect you from the man who tried to kill you, I noticed something. I suspected you of very serious illness. I had an idea trained nurses were as scarce in this country as the dodo, so I volunteered."

"You're the shadow of a rock in a weary land, Miss Volunteer. But I'll fool you. I'll not die. I wouldn't let you down after all the trouble you've taken to keep me alive. You tell Ah Fong to let you into my office. You'll find my check book there. Please bring me a fountain pen, and I'll sign some checks in blank while I'm able. Illness, like war, requires money."

"Never mind about that. I have money. I wish I had a rubber ice-bag—I'd put an ice-pack on your head first thing."

"Tell Ah Fong to cut the sleeve out of my slicker. Fill it with ice and tuck up the ends somehow."

How resourceful he was! Here, she thought, was a patient who would help her to help him. In five minutes she had the pack on his head and had given him a long drink of ice-water; then she went to the telephone and called up Mercy Hospital in Reno and asked for the house physician on duty.

Presently a tired, harsh voice said: "Dr. Weeks speaking. Who the devil is this?"

"This is Miss Corliss, a trained nurse, speaking from a ranch in Lonely Valley, Modoc County, California."

"I know the place. They kill people over there. Toughest spot on the map. Well?"

58

"I have a patient here—a young man—who is very ill. He has a rash, but I suspect it is neither measles nor typhoid."

"If you're a capable trained nurse you know perfectly well whether it is or not. Now then, where is this rash?"

"On his wrists and breast. Little brownish spots that disappear on pressure. They resemble the specks on a turkey egg."

"We're beginning to get somewhere. Is this patient of yours a cow-man?"

"Yes, he is."

"Has he been out in the Modoc National Forest recently?"

"He came in from there this morning. He's been feeling ill for about five days—"

"Any signs of jaundice?"

"Yes, in the conjunctivae."

"Tympanites?"

"Not marked. No tenderness, apparently, in the iliac fossa."

"Pains?"

"Acute in the head and neck and back. Muscles very sore and ache. He says his legs feel as if they were in a vise. Temperature 102, pulse 120."

"That will do, that will do. I don't have to get burned to know I'm near a fire, do I? Your man has Rocky Mountain spotted fever. Caused from the bite of a wood-tick. We've had three cases in this hospital this fall. Lost 'em all. The mortality is from seventy to ninety percent."

"I wish you'd get an airplane and a nurse to help me and fly over immediately."

"What about your local doctor?"

"Not wanted. I want you."

"Airplanes and nurses cost money. No cowboy can afford both at the same time. Who foots the bill?"

"I do. Cash on the barrel-head."

Dr. Weeks indulged himself in a little chuckle. It was apparent to Janet that he was not nearly so fierce as he would have himself appear.

"What is the name of your patient?"

"Raynor Lanier."

"Is that so! Never mind about the expense. I'm for that boy a million—and I've never met him. Forget what I said about the expense. I'll pay it myself and collect from the Lanier's estate if he dies or from him if he lives. His credit's good."

"Thank you. I know nothing of his credit rating myself, but—"

"But you know he's a good egg, and you're willing to take a chance? Bully for you, Miss Corliss. What have you got there in the way of sick-room supplies?"

"Whiskey, ice, and the patient."

Dr. Weeks laughed again. "I'll bring over everything and be there about three o'clock. Place to land?"

"A meadow just below the house. Hundreds of acres of it. It's about twenty-five miles west of Modoc City, and you can't miss it. There's an enormous lake in the valley, and the Lanier ranch appears to be the only one in the valley. On the east side."

"The pilot will find it. Give your patient a jolt of whiskey and feed him some milk, some soft-boiled eggs, and moistened toast." And he hung up.

The driver from the Excelsior Garage came out. "Need me any more?" he asked.

"No, thank you."

He got in his car and drove back to Modoc City, and Janet went out into the kitchen to give Ah Fong the order for the patient's luncheon. When he had eaten, she drew the curtains, told him to try to go to sleep, and left him alone. Nothing further could be done for him until the doctor arrived by plane.

Ah Fong had brought in her bags from the car. When he found her at a loose end, as it were, he said, "I give you room, missy," and led her into a large, sunny room with a southern exposure.

It was a room that had been furnished for a woman. The furniture was Spanish, also the rug; the bathroom had been done in yellow tile with dark blue borders; the closets were spacious and had been designed for feminine use. The note of good taste without extravagance prevailed here as in the living room and in Lanier's bedroom.

CHAPTER SIX

JANET UNPACKED HER BAGS AND, FILLED WITH feminine curiosity, made a tour of the remainder of the house. There was another bedroom similar to the one she was to occupy, and four more designed and furnished for male guests. There were a number of etchings, good but not distinguished. In the living room she found a large canvas of Lonely Valley at sunset. It was a splendid thing and inscribed by the artist to Raynor Lanier.

There were a few other oils and some enlarged photographs. One in particular challenged her attention. It was that of an old man, sitting erect on a splendid big horse. The man's left hand, held a bit high, clasped the reins; in his right a riata was being whirled. This old man's face was lean and proud and fierce, but Janet thought it was also handsome. A characterful face. She studied it for several minutes, then passed on to another enlarged photograph of a young man standing beside a black and white pinto horse, his left foot in the stirrup and about to mount; his face was turned toward the camera, and he was smiling gaily.

On the living-room table there were book-ends

that were wood carvings of Big Foot squatted tailor fashion. Janet looked at the books. They were inscribed by the authors to Raynor Lanier. There was a large photograph of a beautiful young girl inscribed, "To dear Ray from Leila." There was, in a deep, oval wood frame, a daguerreotype of a young woman of the fifties and a large nocturne bearing a brass plate inscribed "Moonlight in Lonely Valley." Evidently it had been painted from the veranda of the Lanier house and depicted the valley below, with the cluster of ranch buildings and a few lonely lights showing from them. It had also been inscribed by the artist to Ray Lanier and was one of the most creditable nocturnes Janet had ever seen.

The furniture in the living room was modern American of the very best design and beautifully upholstered; a grand piano stood in one corner, and covering it was an exquisite old Mandarin coat. The sole note of the countryman or the pioneer was to be found in the rifles and shotguns hung on polished deer horns over the huge fireplace. In another corner Janet saw an expensive combination radio and phonograph of the latest model.

"This," thought Janet, "is a place to live. The Lanier man has done himself well. He numbers among his intimates artists and authors, and I suspect that the beautiful lady, Leila, is an actress.

And yet his is a practical, workaday ranch, and he is a practical, workaday man. There are two rooms furnished to conform to a masculine idea of feminine taste, yet there seem to be no women in Lonely Valley. He must have guests here from time to time."

Janet now descended into an old-fashioned garden, flowerless due to the lateness of the season, walked through it and up a little stone-lined path to the timber higher up on the knoll. And here, in an amphitheater of pines, she found the family cemetery, each grave with a plain cement slab about four feet high and bearing the name, date of birth, and date of death. She began on the right and read in succession:

John Annersley—Born October 7, 1827. Died November 4th, 1852.

Mary Annersley Lanier—Born May 15, 1832. Died January 17, 1871.

Mary Edna Lanier—Born April 10, 1854. Died April 12, 1854.

Pierre Vincent Lanier, Born March 6, 1855. Died June 4, 1864.

Pierre Lanier, Husband of Mary Annersley Lanier, Born November 3, 1831. Murdered October 4, 1891.

Sarah Moody Lanier, Wife of Felix Lanier, Born February 31, 1880. Died December 25, 1906.

Felix Lanier, Born November 4, 1857. Murdered October 23, 1930.

When she had scanned those headstones, Janet knew that Pierre Lanier must have been Raynor Lanier's grandfather; that he had married the widow of John Annersley, a neighbor who had, doubtless, departed his life in Lonely Valley. Of the three children born to that union one had died two days after birth, one at the age of nine, and the third child and survivor, Felix Lanier, had, at the age of seventy-three, been murdered by an enemy.

Grandfather Pierre had been murdered too, at the age of sixty. Raynor Lanier evidently was the son of Felix and Sarah Moody Lanier, and—

Felix Lanier! Her attorney, Daniel P. Magruder, had told her of a man named Felix—a man whose last name he could not remember. And this man Felix had been the wild and woolly westerner who had run her grandfather, Donald MacLean, out of this country; the man who had wounded her grandfather, the man whom her grandfather had filled with buckshot. Yes, this must be the same Felix, for had he not died with his boots on? And he was the father of Raynor Lanier, gentleman rancher, friend and intimate of artists, authors, and possibly actresses, and enemy of Milo Landrum; the man who maintained an armed guard at the entrance to Lonely Valley; the man who would have been incensed had his retainer, Big Foot, relieved him of what he, Lanier, regarded as a holy duty—to wit, the killing of Milo Landrum!

"Three generations," Janet mused, "and the first and second died with their boots on, while the third has only this morning missed a similar fate. But the third generation is a gentleman. Still he must be a Lanier, with the code of his father and grandfather. What a strange human anomaly! And now, if he dies of spotted fever, will that mark the end of the House of Lanier? And when his men carry him up here and lay him beside his father in the little graveyard, will that mean the triumph of his enemy? Will it mean that Lonely Valley finally passes into alien hands—after three generations of Laniers have lived and loved and fought and died in it?"

She felt herself encompassed by stark tragedy; a wave of pity for Raynor Lanier swept over her. If he lived, it would be due to three things—his tremendous vitality and courage and her good nursing. She remembered he had said he would not die; that he would not let her down after all the trouble she had gone to over him. The gay devil, jesting in the face of death! It occurred to Janet that the young man with the smiling face, about to mount his horse, was Raynor Lanier; that the fierce, handsome old man whirling his riata had been old Felix, the fire-eater. But Felix was dead now, and Raynor's task in life was to take vengeance on his father's murderer.

"I'll have to argue him out of that idea," she thought. "He appears much too fine to have his life spoiled in the pursuit of vengeance. I had no idea he could be so primitive."

She did not know the school in which he had been raised, or she would not have marveled at his concept of honor, of living the full life!

She returned to the house and found the telephone ringing. Dr. Weeks was calling.

"Can't get an airplane today," he barked at her. "And there's been a railroad wreck, and I'm a railroad surgeon on this division, and I can't get over to your man. Need every nurse we can scrape up in this city. So you'll have to go it alone and take your chances. Now then, get pencil and paper and take these directions. . . . Ready? Go. Take the customary measures to make him comfortable. Put an ice-pack on his head and pack him if the fever gets too high. The medical profession hasn't had much experience with this rare disease, so it's a toss-up what to give him. Quinine bimuriate, in fifteen-grain doses every six hours and preferably hypodermically, has been known to yield good results. Personally, I recommend fifteen grains of quinine sulphate given by mouth every four hours and persisted in with decreasing doses as convalescence begins. Give him the customary doses of whiskey and strychnine to keep up his heart action, and give him Dover's powder or morphine sulphate for the pain in his head and back. Lots of water to drink—all he will take. Keep him in a dark room and free from noise. The diet should be milk, buttermilk, soft-boiled eggs, and moistened toast. If he doesn't improve within the next five days, the chances are he'll go over the river. Keep me informed of the progress of the case."

Janet read her notes back to him, and he hung up. A minute later she had the drug store in Modoc City on the wire, but that cow-town dispensary hadn't in stock half the things she required, so she called up the county seat, Alturas, where a much more up-to-date druggist agreed to fill her order and send it out within half an hour by special messenger in a motor car.

"It's only eighty-odd miles," the druggist declared. "The man will be there some time this afternoon."

CHAPTER SEVEN

THERE WAS NOTHING TO DO BUT WAIT, GIVE her patient ice-water, and renew the ice-pack on his aching head. About four o'clock she gave him a cold sponge bath and an alcohol rub, to all of which he submitted in silence and without opening his eyes, merely murmuring "Thank you" when she had finished.

At five o'clock he said: "Miss Corliss, please

switch on the radio and turn the dial to sixty-four. The market reports will be coming in a few minutes from now, and I want to know what the beef market was today."

She made penciled notes and read them to him. "Shipments today were light and quality distinctly off, with a sluggish demand. Four car-loads of smooth thousand-pound Nevadas sold for 5½c. Fat cows sold from 3¼ to 3c, canners at—"

"Never mind the canners and cutters or bulls," he interrupted. "I'm not interested in the bologna or hot-dog market, but in fat steers. I did pretty well on the fat two-year-old steers I shipped two weeks ago. Got six and a quarter. Broke a little better than even. . . . We'll have four-cent beef before we're back to seven and eight again. Thank you."

He was silent a long time. Then, "Why did you come, Miss Corliss?"

"I told you that I saw in Modoc City, this morning, that you were a very ill man, and I guessed you were the sort who had to be dying before admitting illness. I saw you had a high fever, and I—well, you interested me, Mr. Lanier. I knew you were going to require some expert nursing, and I am conceited enough to think I'm a first-class nurse."

He reached out gropingly and found her hand and squeezed it. "Lots of people in this world can think fast but—haven't the courage to—follow up their—thoughts. I am your debtor—and happy to know I can never quite pay—the debt."

Again a long silence, but he continued to hold her hand. Then, "Why did you block Landrum's work this morning?"

"One's sympathy always goes out to the underdog. You were helpless to defend yourself. You didn't have a chance until Big Foot commenced shooting."

"Good old Big Foot. He's the chief of the pitiful remnant of the Modocs, you know, and he loves me. I'm his son; adopted me into the tribe, you know. His squaw was my nurse. Good old Minnie, but what a horrible cook she was! And we had her for years. What does the Reno doctor say about me?"

"He says you have spotted fever, contracted from the bite of a tick. You'll be very ill for about ten or twelve days."

"You can't fool me, Miss Corliss. I'll fight hard not to die, but the chances are my days are numbered. I know about that disease. It's generally fatal. We've lost half a dozen riders from it in the past ten years. Please go into my office and get—paper and pen—and write what I dictate. Please! Important."

She obeyed him. "Ready, Mr. Lanier."

And slowly and laboriously, for his respiration was short and rapid, he dictated:

"I, Raynor Lanier, of Lonely Valley, Modoc County, California, being, as I am informed, dangerously ill but still of sound and disposing mind, do make, publish, and declare the following as my last will and testament.

"First: To my faithful and loyal ranch superintendent, Thomas Harmon, I give, devise and bequeath all property, of whatsoever nature and wheresoever situate, of which I may die seized or possessed, with this single exception:

"Second: To Janet Corliss, spinster, of New York City, New York, and at present my nurse, I give, devise, and bequeath all of the real property as particularly described in the deed given to my grandfather, Pierre Lanier, in 1873, by the Surveyor-General of the State of California, under the Federal Act known as the Swamp and Overflowed Lands Act.

"I direct that all of my just bills be paid by my executors, and I appoint as my executors, to serve without bonds or undertakings of any sort whatsoever, my heirs, the said Thomas Harmon and Janet Corliss. And I further direct that, in the event of my death, I am to be buried in the Lanier family cemetery beside my father.

"I bequeath to the said Thomas Harmon and Janet Corliss all of my Indians, and direct that they shall continue to employ them and care for them in the same manner as I would or could if alive to do it.

"In witness whereof I have set my hand this—day of November, A.D. 1930."

He lay for several minutes panting after this extended effort. Then: "Telephone down to the barn from the little private telephone in the kitchen. Ring two bells. Phone bells will ring all over the ranch buildings. Get Andy Martin on the phone. Andy's not quite recovered from a broken leg, but he can walk a little and drive a car. Tell him he is to get into Tom Harmon's car and drive over to meet the herd in Simmons' Meadows and bring back Carmody and Yates to me. I want them as witnesses to my will, and I want them tonight. I'll probably be delirious by morning."

Janet obeyed him instantly and waited on the veranda until she saw a man she assumed to be Andy Martin leave the cluster of ranch buildings and go swiftly up the grade leading out of the valley. She then returned to the sick room and reported to Lanier that his order had been delivered and was in process of execution.

"Thank you for sparing me guess-work. I love intelligent people."

She refilled the ice-pack and adjusted it on his head. "And now, before I order you to conserve your strength by ceasing to talk, will you tell me, please, why you have seen fit to make me one of your heirs and co-administrator of your estate?"

"Because you risked your life to save mine, a stranger. If you can be careless and generous with your life, I can afford to try to match you, and be careless and generous with my land, can I not? Besides, you're all woman. Yes, a man's woman. You protected me with your body when I was helpless. You're brave, and the Laniers admire guts. So that clause in my will is merely a token of my gratitude and admiration."

"What a strange man you are! You set much too much store by a trifling service. I knew the man wouldn't shoot if I got in his way, and, of course, he didn't. Mr. Harmon, I take it, is an old, competent, faithful employee. Why not leave him this land?"

"I have a reason. Not an unselfish one."

"How many acres in this tract of land am I to acquire if you die?"

"Seventy-five thousand, more or less."

Janet was horrified. "But you mustn't embarrass me with such a bequest. Why, I couldn't pay the taxes on it."

"I've thought of that. Please get my check book, as I requested a little while ago. I'm going to give you a check now for enough to pay the taxes for five years, and by that time you will have found a customer for the land. If you sell it for one-tenth of what it's worth you'll have the wolf of want on the run."

"Keep your money, Mr. Lanier. If I get the land—but I hope I never do—I can pay the taxes myself. While I am deeply appreciative of your action, I must tell you that I already own a few thousand acres of land in this county—cheap land, like yours, and really, I do not care for any more. Real estate appears to be impossible to move out here."

"Has anybody been trying to kill you for your land?"

"No."

"Well, I'm not so fortunate."

"Oh," Janet laughed, "does a sentence of death go with your land?"

"It would—to Tom Harmon, but not to you."

CHAPTER EIGHT

IT OCCURRED TO JANET THAT RAYNOR LANIER wasn't so magnificent after all. He seemed to realize this, too, for he went on.

"Please believe I'm not using you as a mere convenience to get rid of the bear I have by the tail and because I love Tom Harmon enough to refuse to hand the bear over to him. I could bequeath this land to my university or to another girl whose portrait you will see in the living-room, or to any one of half a dozen friends. And they would be perfectly safe in accepting it."

"But I'm not a friend of yours, Mr. Lanier."

"Don't argue with me. You head the list. You're

a girl who works for her living, you're my principal creditor, and it's my fancy to secure my debt to you. To quote an ancient Chinese philosopher, 'Good words shall gain you honor in the market place, but good deeds shall gain you friends among men.' However, I am not so generous as you seem to think. At present that land isn't worth the taxes. It may never be worth more. But your death would not help Milo Landrum acquire it cheaply, so some day he'll buy you out at a price that will put you on the sunny side of Easy Street, where you deserve to be. And I do want to do that much for you. You've saved my life once, and you're now busy trying to save it again—only this time I think you'll lose."

"Do you not realize that you may, by that last statement, have tempted me to permit you to die?"

"Don't jest with me now. I do not feel at all humorous. But you'll find that, even if I die, Milo Landrum will not be killed until after you have sold out to him. I wouldn't double-cross my own heir."

"But I thought you planned not to leave a heritage of blood to Tom Harmon."

"I do. Tom will be out of it. I'll hobble him so with my ranch and cattle he can't afford a trial on a charge of murder. And when I euchre him out of the land I leave to you, Milo Landrum will not regard Tom's life as worth taking. I love Tom. I want to be nice to him. Big Foot knows what I

75

want done. I've just explained it all to him. If I die he'll see that Landrum departs this life—after he has bought your land. Of course, if I live, I'll kill him myself."

Janet felt a choking sensation in her throat. "Mr. Lanier, you're the finest man I have ever met. You're gentle, thoughtful and kind, and you're the first man I have ever met who could make a magnificent gesture for the sake of gratitude magnified out of all proportion. It would be a shame to have you spoil all your fineness by killing that man Landrum."

"He hired my father killed."

In that phrase there spoke the primitive man. A plain statement of a fact and a condition that no amount of argument could alter or destroy.

"It's a case of kill or be killed, too," he added.

"Then, if you die, take your feud into the grave with you," she flung out at him passionately. "Go to your God with your soul unsullied by murder."

"Impossible. I promised my father. We Laniers have always kept our promises; we've played square; we've always paid our debts—and we haven't tried to be men because we yearned for a front seat in heaven or took any stock in rumors of hell-fire for sinners."

Behind that statement Janet sensed an unfaltering loyalty to a code of honor that was to Raynor Lanier a religion. She sensed, too, the sad futility of further argument.

"You loved your father, didn't you?" she said.

"I did. He was father and mother to me. He was all I had. He was a man. He was so good to me. He lived only for me. He built and furnished this house—for me. He would have been content with the old log shack his father built—He's—he's up—yonder with our people—and the man that killed him is dead. But the—skunk that hired the killer—lives—and I have spotted fever, and—the old man will know why I couldn't make good on my promise. . . . Dear old Felix . . . he died in my arms. I hadn't kissed him since I was a little boy . . . but when he was leaving me . . . and I kissed him and held him to me—he—he didn't mind—going out. . . . Women can't understand . . . they preach. . . ."

The tears came through between his tightly closed lids, and Janet bent and wiped them away—aye, and her own tears, too, that fell on the upturned face. He felt them, reached up a hand and patted her cheek, and she thought that for the first time since he could remember he was experiencing a woman's sympathy and care.

After a while he murmured, "Don't you think my valley is beautiful, Miss Corliss?"

"Yes, it is." She knew he would talk no more of his father. "And for that reason you are not going to leave it."

He shook his head slowly. He had his doubts about that. Nevertheless he managed a small

77

smile. "A wretched little wood-tick got me where Landrum failed. Comedy triumphing over tragedy. Ho-hum!"

She elected to reflect his sudden mood for humor. "Well, thank you ever so much for making me the heir to your *casus belli* with Landrum."

"He can't fight you or hurt you. It would avail him nothing to try. Now, listen while I tell you something important. There's a lawyer in New York named Daniel P. Magruder. His office is in the Metropolitan Trust Building, and he represents an old man named Donald MacLean. MacLean owns a quarter section of land the Laniers have always wanted, but he hated my father and would never sell. If I die and you inherit that seventy-five thousand acres, see Magruder and try to buy out MacLean. His grudge will die when I die. It should have died when my father died. He is an old man and he holds the key to a fortune. Get that key. Landrum's trying to get it also. Beat him to it— and he'll pay you half a million dollars for your holdings. When you get that half million, pay off the embarrassing debts Tom Harmon will inherit from me with the ranch and the cattle. You'll have enough left to be happy on. You'll do that, won't you? You're bound to wind up with half a million—just for being kind to a stranger."

"I promise—on my honor."

"Shake hands on that."

After the fashion of the West of an elder day—a day when notary publics to witness agreements were non-existent—he would bind their understanding with a hand-shake. Janet gave him her hand.

"And you're going to stay right here and fight for me and with me?" he pleaded.

"To a finish, Raynor Lanier."

"I wonder why."

"Perhaps it's because you appear to be such a worthwhile bad boy."

"You're mighty sweet. Now, what is the name of that lawyer in New York?"

"Daniel P. Magruder, Metropolitan Trust Company Building. He represents Donald MacLean."

"Write it down so you'll remember it. Then a glass of ice-water, please."

At five o'clock the man arrived from Alturas with the medicine and sick-room equipment Janet had ordered. She paid him. Before leaving New York she had, without in the least suspecting she would find use for them, packed in her baggage four uniforms and a couple of caps. She donned her uniform now and returned to Lanier's room to give him his first dose of quinine sulphate. He stared at her dully.

"Lord," he muttered, "how beautiful you are! Too bad Felix isn't here to see you."

As the sun sank over the hills to the west, the two cowboys Lanier had sent for came in.

"I want you two boys to witness my will," Lanier explained. "No need reading it to you, I reckon. I ask you to sign as witnesses on the spot my nurse will indicate. Fong will give you your supper, and you will remain at the bunkhouse tonight and have Andy motor you back to join the drive in the morning."

When the two men had signed, he shook hands with them, and they clumped out. They had not uttered one word throughout the entire scene.

"Pair of chatterboxes, aren't they?" Lanier remarked. "Lonely Valley wasn't really lonely until those two got on our payroll. They rarely speak to each other, although they are pals. If one should quit me, the other would ask for his time, too. Mighty handy to have close-mouthed men like those two, especially when they'll do what they're told to do. After two of my Indians had bumped off the man that killed my father, I told that pair of sphinxes to take the body into Modoc City and dump it on Milo Landrum's front porch. They did—in the dark—and nobody saw them do it. But they went further. They tied a shipping tag to the dead man's wrist and wrote on it,

" 'Dear Milo. You next.'

"Scared Milo to death. He figured he had to get me before I got him—and that's why he tried this morning. When Landrum hired that killer, he paid him in advance and never expected to see him again. Nobody else knows who returned his property to him, and nobody ever will, but Landrum knows. You see, Miss Corliss, it proves him guilty. His conscience made a fool of him."

"Did you find the blood money on that man?"

"I did—a thousand dollars in new bills. I helped myself to it and applied it to my Fund For Distressed Modoc Indians. Why not? Two of my Modocs had bagged the bird."

"You are absolutely at once the softest and the hardest human being I have ever met," Janet declared. "Now, pipe down and stay piped down, and speak when you're spoken to."

"Yes'm," he answered meekly.

Tom Harmon got in with the drive late the following afternoon. Janet heard the bellowing of the cattle long before they came over the hills and down through the timber into Lonely Valley. The drive passed along the lake front, and from the veranda Janet watched the thirsty brutes wade out into the lake and drink. When it had been started again for the winter pastures, she saw a horseman detach himself from the drive and ride up to the house. The man was Tom Harmon. As he came under the *porte-cochère*, he lifted his hat and stared at her inquiringly.

"He's terribly sick, Mr. Harmon. Just now he's delirious. I haven't had any sleep since you saw me last, and Ah Fong is holding him down now. I must have intelligent help. Please go to your quarters and, after you've bathed and changed your clothes, come back here for dinner. You're to live in this house, and somebody else must take over your job."

"Somebody shall. I don't know nothin' about carin' for a sick man, Miss Corliss, but I'm a hell-bender at obeyin' orders, an' Ray's often said I'm 'most as intelligent as a pack-mule."

"You'll watch him while I get some sleep. I'll need four hours. Then you will waken me, and I'll give him his medicine and take his temperature and sponge him and pack him, while you get four hours. I think that between the two of us he'll get the best of care. And I'll teach you a lot about nursing."

"I'll do anything on earth for that boy," said Tom Harmon with such simple abnegation that a lump rose in Janet's throat.

She understood now why Raynor Lanier had made him the heir to his ranch and cattle.

"Hurry, Tom," she warned. "And be sure you don't bring any wood-ticks up with you."

"Spotted fever!" Horror showed in Tom Harmon's eyes.

Janet nodded.

"I'm the only man in this country that ever got over that sickness," he said. "Miss Corliss, you ain't got any idea how sick that boy is." And he rode down to the corral with his chin sunk low on his breast.

CHAPTER NINE

FOR A WEEK THEY FOUGHT TOGETHER FOR Raynor Lanier's life—fought without hope. Twice a day Janet conferred over the long-distance telephone with Dr. Weeks in Reno.

"Stick to your treatment," he ordered her. "He has a fighting chance, and he must be a hardy citizen to be alive now."

Tom Harmon proved to be intelligent and possessed of a sort of rough tenderness. He did the heavy work, such as lifting the patient; he bathed him, he watched him and held him in bed during moments of delirium; he kept the temperature chart and noted pulse and respiration while Janet slept; and she slept only when exhausted nature demanded it.

Suddenly the rash that has given to this fever its name began to disappear, the pains abated, and Lanier's temperature dropped slowly but steadily for three days; then came a relapse. For four days it did not seem possible that he would survive; then suddenly his temperature dropped again. Slowly, like a fish that swims up from great depths, Raynor Lanier swam up to consciousness. On the fourteenth day Janet decided he was out of danger. A week later he was eating heartily and wondering how soon he would be permitted to sit up for a while.

"As soon," Janet assured him, "as Tom Harmon and I can have twenty-four hours of uninterrupted sleep. And I'm starting now. Tom isn't done in yet, so he can stick it until I get back on duty."

"You look," he told her, "like the tail end of a long, cold spring. And you and Tom have worked yourselves out of your place in the sun. If you'd neglected me for four hours at a stretch, if you hadn't worked quite so hard and faithfully, you'd both be away ahead of the game by now. And I thought I was going to escape all my worries about interest and principal and how to pay both on five-cent beef, which isn't possible; and I've got Milo Landrum back on my hands again." He cocked a humorous eye at his saviors. "You two haven't done right by our Nell."

"You know doggone well," Mr. Harmon protested loudly, "that I'd have gone gunnin' for Milo right after your funeral."

"Oh, no, you wouldn't, Thomas. I had your clock stopped. If you have any sense of shame left, you'll shave me."

"It's sure enough been tough on him to have to let his whiskers grow," Tom Harmon explained to Janet. "He's one of these la-de-da fellers that shaves every mornin' the minute he gets out of bed. Well, I shave myself, so I reckon I can shave him."

"I suppose," said Lanier to Janet, "you'll be leaving us as soon as you see me back in my clothes again. I don't know how I'm going to stand that, but I suppose it must be. Still, you might stay all winter if I provided you with a chaperon. In fact, I think you had better do that, because I'm apt to drag myself home some day leaking pretty badly, and needing you worse than ever."

"So you've got that old complex about Milo Landrum fixed firmly in your mind again, have you?"

"It's a case of kill or be killed, Miss Corliss."

"Hugo, the half-breed, would be glad to do the job for you," she flung out at him. "If Landrum does his killing by proxy, aren't you justified in doing the same?"

"Certainly not. I'm a gentleman, and Landrum's an animal. A gentleman kills his own rats."

"Do you mind," said Janet, "telling me what all the shooting's been about? I've been up in your cemetery, and I observe that the practise of dying with boots on started with your grandfather."

"Generosity—his own good kind heart—killed Pierre Lanier. In his sixtieth year he developed a fatal weakness—sentiment." Lanier grinned at Janet with the anticipatory grin of one who knows he is about to relate an entertaining tale. "There was a man over in Lassen County," he went on. "His name was Henry Bundy, and he was an egg

85

that the cook forgot. Lassen County had a dry year in 1888, and Henry Bundy with a drive of three thousand headed for our range. My father heard about it and remarked at breakfast that he was going to ride over, meet Bundy, and warn him off.

" 'Which you'll never see the day you can draw faster'n shoot straighter than your pap,' said Pierre to his son. 'An' I doubt if your fool head works as fast as mine. So you stay to home an' I'll go argue with this Henry Bundy. I'll explain to him that we only got just about enough grass on our range for ourselves an' neighbors, an' p'int out to him that 'tain't right a stranger from the next county should want in on our range just because it's free. I think I can induce him to head north into Oregon with his herd.'

"You must understand, Miss Janet, that my grandfather was as fond of my father as my father was of me. We Laniers are a clannish lot. And Pierre knew Henry Bundy. Being the head of the house, Pierre had his way, so he rode over and met with Henry Bundy's outfit at Lookout. Henry was in the only saloon there, having a drink, when Pierre came in and asked to talk things over calmly with him. Pierre was so peaceable Henry Bundy got an erroneous impression of the old boy—he didn't know that some men can be firm without talking big—so Henry Bundy said all hell and the Laniers and their Indians and white men couldn't keep him from driving his cattle up on to our range if he wanted to."

"Was it your range?" Janet asked, fascinated at the matter-of-fact manner in which Lanier told his simple tale.

"No, it was government range—unsurveyed public land—but we grazed our cattle there during the summer and had been doing that for twenty-five years. So we had a priority right. The courts would not admit that, of course, but then we never bothered the court with such trifling details. We didn't have to put up a sign that read 'Keep Off the Grass.' Everybody knew enough to keep off, because it was bad luck to forget it. My grandfather and father realized they had to be firm with all buttinskies, or they'd be regarded as weak, and presently hardier men would be running *them* off the range. So when Henry Bundy, who had a couple of notches on his gun, made his bluff, old Pierre had to call it.

"'Tell you what we'll do, Henry Bundy,' he said. 'We'll shoot it out across that there billiard table, an' the survivor wins.'

"That proposition didn't sound so alluring to Bundy, but he couldn't do much about it, because Pierre told him he might as well give himself the breaks because they were going to pull off a shooting scrape anyway. So each drew a chair up to an end of the billiard table and laid his gun on the table in front of him. This at one minute to one o'clock P.M., it being agreed that when the clock over the bar struck one each contestant was free to pick up his gun and blaze away.

"Well, the clock struck one, and Henry Bundy reached for his gun and raised it. He never fired it. Pierre reached for his a fifth of a second faster, but didn't bother to waste another fifth of a second raising it. He just tipped the barrel up as his hand closed over the butt and fired before Henry Bundy's finger closed on the trigger. He fired only one shot. That was enough. He ruined Mr. Bundy's shooting arm, and the war was over.

" 'I'll drive up to Oregon,' says Bundy.

" 'Much obliged to you,' says Pierre. 'Just for that I'll not finish you.'

"And right there his number went up, as they say in Chicago. Henry Bundy was a poor sport. He would hold grudges, and he rather felt that my grandfather had smudged his art by playing a new trick on him. So he gave some low white man a few dollars to lay for Pierre on the road to Modoc City, and the next thing my father knew, the old gentleman's horse came home without him, and there was blood on the saddle. My father decided Henry Bundy had been at the bottom of it, so he rode down to Henry's ranch in Lassen County, and when Henry saw him ride into the yard, he lost his head and commenced shooting. He never was a good left-handed shooter, and his right arm was still stiff, so Felix wafted him home. Felix was hit once—not seriously—and it provided a claim of justifiable homicide, which the jury believed. It never occurred to that jury to wonder what my father was doing down in Lassen County. They might have known it wasn't a social call."

"And now," said Janet, "your father has been murdered, even as his father before him, and you're going to avenge him, as he avenged his father?"

Raynor Lanier nodded brightly. "The Laniers get the breaks," he told her. "Like Henry Bundy, Milo Landrum commenced, shooting too soon. If he downs me, he can never supply a motive that will wash with a jury, for he's not popular in this county, and I am. On the other hand he has supplied me with a motive for killing him—self-defense. I have every reason to believe that my life is in danger, and I am justified in snuffing him out at the earliest opportunity."

"And you're going to do that little thing?"

"As sure," said Raynor Lanier, "as there's a God in heaven, I'm going to try."

"But he may forestall you."

"Quite possibly. He's smart. When he missed me that morning in Modoc City he knew his days were numbered. He knew he'd have to face a day of reckoning with me, and if he survived there was Tom Harmon and Big Foot and Hugo Lanier and the Sphinx twins."

Suddenly Raynor Lanier laughed like a jovial fiend. "All of Landrum's assets lie in this county. He can't run away from his assets. He's got to face the music, and he hasn't the courage to do that. So he's suffering. God, how he's suffering! 'The coward dies a thousand deaths, the brave man dies but one.' I'll kill him a thousand times before I give him the mercy shot."

"You'll do nothing of the sort, Raynor Lanier," Janet said quietly. "You're civilized."

"Not altogether. Never will be. Out here in Lonely Valley we're still a bit old-fashioned."

"But you're a cultured, educated gentleman."

"I've been to a university, if that's what you mean, but no university could ever supply the sort of culture I have inherited."

"You'll not kill Milo Landrum," Janet declared with an air of finality. "I'll not permit it. I'll just make it not worth your while."

"Why?"

"I suppose you'd like to know. Well, I can't tell you because I don't know exactly why myself. But I'll tell you something, Mr. Man. I'm sitting in on this game, and I'm holding cards and spades, the four aces, big and little casino, and I expect to win."

Tom Harmon was loyal. "Lady," he said ironically, "Ray Lanier will beat you to death on the sweeps."

CHAPTER TEN

SINCE THE DAY SHE HAD COME TO LONELY Valley Janet Corliss had been too busy, too worried, or too fatigued to devote time or thought to any subject except her patient. Twelve hours of continuous slumber refreshed her, however, to the point where, upon awakening at ten o'clock the following day, her thoughts automatically grappled with her own affairs.

Lanier's condition was improving so fast, and there was so little danger of a relapse, that she knew he could dispense with her services in about a week, for he would be up and walking around the house by that time. In fact, he could dispense with her services immediately, if necessary. Janet found certain satisfaction in this knowledge, for while she was sensible of more than a twinge of regret at the prospect of leaving, she knew it would be best to go. He had a way of following her around his room with those large, dark, intelligent eyes of his, and this was faintly disturbing. She knew the *penchant* of men for falling in love with their nurses—particularly men who have never been accustomed to the gentle ministrations of a woman.

Lying comfortably in bed, with the pale winter

sunlight filtering through the curtains, Janet thought the situation over calmly and with a certain amount of hard-headedness that was part of her heritage from Grandfather MacLean. She did not wish to fall in love with Raynor Lanier any more than she wished him to fall in love with her. Obviously she could not afford that. She possessed a quarter section of land that was necessary to his financial well-being and mental tranquility; she knew he would pay her for it a price based on the very limit of his ability to pay, while on the other hand Milo Landrum stood ready and willing (she felt assured) to double or treble any figure Raynor Lanier might name.

Decidedly, Janet reflected, she could not afford for business reasons to risk having Raynor Lanier fall in love with her, any more than she could risk falling in love with him. She was sensible enough to realize that, had she met him under different circumstances, and were he a dweller in the world to which she belonged, and if he paid court to her, she might find him rather hard to resist. But Raynor Lanier did not belong in this vague picture. He was a man, courageous, decent; when he should have regained the weight he had lost and his face was no longer drawn and white, Janet had a feeling that he would be more than a little handsome. Moreover, the fact that he was not a "ladies' man" would lend to him a quality of unattainableness that would make him all the more attractive. But, unfortunately, his life had not been cast in fortuitous channels. He was going to kill a man or be killed trying, and the fact that survival might mean a lifetime of woe to him was not a deterrent. Decidedly there could be no happiness in becoming interested in such a man, and Janet had a normal human desire to be happy. Happiness was something one had to stalk and capture and hold, and it was, to a considerable extent, dependent upon money. She had never been rich, but on the contrary she had never known the pinch of real poverty or hardship. Raynor Lanier's great need of her quarter section of land spelled for Janet an additional guaranty of safety and such measure of happiness as may come from financial independence, but if she remained in Lonely Valley she might have to sacrifice that.

She gave herself up to a consideration of Milo Landrum and his desire to acquire her land. Would she be justified, for mere money, in trading with her host's enemy—a scoundrel and a killer? The idea was revolting to her. She had a feeling that if she did this she must forever regard herself as a co-conspirator of Landrum's, a party to the ruin of Raynor Lanier. And whatever Lanier's faults might be, he was potentially too fine for that. Still, ruined men had a habit of recovering from the blows that Fate dealt them . . . by selling to Landrum she might make it unnecessary for him to kill Lanier . . . she had saved Raynor Lanier's life twice . . . her heart leaped at the thought that she might be able to save it again.

And then she remembered. No matter what she did, the acquisition of her land by either Raynor Lanier or Milo Landrum was now a minor issue. Landrum, the fool, had changed a war of conquest into one of vengeance and blood. Janet might stop Landrum, but no power on earth could stop Lanier, for the blood of his father was in him, and that blood cried for vengeance.

Suddenly she knew she could not play business poker with human lives for chips. In one revealing moment she knew she could not sell her land to either of them until the issue between them had been decided. She knew that the day he should find himself physically able to attend to this neglected business, Ray Lanier would drive into Modoc City and attend to it. Well, he was young; possibly he could shoot more quickly and accurately than Landrum, who was no longer young. He might survive; if he did, she could then sell to him if he desired to buy. The deal would be clean, then; there would be no taint of blood on the price he paid her, and thereafter she could go back to New York and forget him. But before that happened she would make one desperate effort to spare him the ordeal of facing Milo Landrum in the smoke; she would strive to make it possible for him to live out his life in this country where he had been born and raised, without being known, as had been his father and his grandfather, as a killer. There was just a chance that, if she acted discreetly, she might be able to do this. She resolved to call upon Milo Landrum and suggest to him that he start immediately upon a long and indefinite vacation. She felt certain he did not realize he had been marked for slaughter and that the death of Raynor Lanier would not solve his difficulty by guaranteeing him immunity. There still remained Tom Harmon, the Sphinx twins, Big Foot, and his people! Her advice to Landrum would be so sound he simply would have to accept it and act upon it. From what Ray Lanier had said, Landrum's attack upon him had been the result of panic. Well, was it possible Landrum was any less panicky now than the day he had attempted to shoot Lanier? Janet did not think so. Time cures panics, but silence and uncertainty keep them alive.

Her course decided upon, she bathed, dressed, and went in to see her patient. She found Ah Fong sitting on the edge of his bed, gazing with bland approval upon his employer, who was drinking from a bowl some dark brown liquid which the Chinaman had undoubtedly prepared for him. And that it was something unpleasant Janet felt assured, for Lanier's face was puckered with distress; he appeared on the point of becoming nauseated.

"What's that you're drinking?" Janet demanded sharply from the doorway. "I'm sure it isn't anything I have ordered for you."

A good trained nurse is always a tyrant. She has to be, since convalescent patients are always mutinous in matters of diet and obedience to the orders of those who know more about their physical condition than they do themselves. She removed the bowl forcibly from his grasp and smelled it. Then she tasted it.

"What devil's-brew is this?" she demanded angrily.

"Just a little old-fashioned medicine Ah Fong has brewed for me from Chinese herbs," he defended weakly. "It's good for the kidneys, the liver, the lungs, and the nervous system. It promotes metabolism and induces perspiration, which cleans out the system—"

"Ah Fong is a fool, and you're an imbecile, Ray Lanier. How dare you do this? Have you been taking these dreadful Chinese brews right along?"

He nodded weakly. "Ever since childhood, Janet. There are lots of efficacious medicines in the Chinese pharmacopœia."

"Why not have the Modoc Indian medicine man in?" Janet raged.

"He's been in. The day before the crisis of my illness, you went out for a walk and a breath of fresh air, and he sneaked in and did his stuff. Pulled the bed out from the wall and did a dance around it. He had a little pot of fire and burned things in it and chanted and the very next day I started on the upgrade. You can't beat proof like that."

"And what does this Chinese medicine man think of your treachery?"

"He knows the red man didn't help me a bit. Fong knows it's the devil papers *he* burned, plus some broth brewed from the heart of a wildcat, that saved me."

"You drank broth brewed from the heart of a wildcat?"

"Certainly. A quaint old Chinese custom. Everybody knows that when a hatchet man for a warring Chinese tong goes after an enemy he makes himself strong and brave by eating the heart of a wildcat."

Janet turned on Ah Fong. "Get out of this room," she ordered angrily, "and do not come in until I permit you. You—you devil-doctor."

Ah Fong glared at her with a smile that was also a sneer. "He get well. Eatum wildcat Tuesday, Wednesday he no talkee klazy. Wildcat heap good, cougar velly much better, but no can catch cougar. Ketchum tiger—o-o-o-o-o! No can beat tiger."

"Take your old brew and get out, or I'll use something hard on your head. It's a wonder you haven't killed him. Beat it."

Ah Fong and Lanier exchanged glances.

"Who boss around here?" the Celestial demanded. Here was a situation which, to his mind, demanded settlement instantly.

"When I'm sick—she is."

"Damn to hell," Ah Fong screeched, and flung out of the room.

"Will he leave your service now?" Janet queried.

"Oh, no, but he'll have a toothache and use that as an excuse to retire to his room and let somebody else do his job."

"I can do his job and take care of you, too. Ray, why in the name of common sense have you permitted him to dose you with his awful Chinese medicine? And you really didn't drink his wildcat-heart broth?"

"Of course, I did. Who am I to do missionary work on Ah Fong? It's easier to make the old man happy by permitting him to think he's helping me, than argue with him and hurt his feelings. And Big Foot would have felt bad if I hadn't let the tribal medicine man work on me."

CHAPTER ELEVEN

JANET SAT DOWN ON THE EDGE OF THE BED and stared at the amazing man. It occurred to her she was gazing at a changeling. Tom Harmon had shaved him and in the operation had transformed him from an apparent ruffian to a thin, pale-faced, but rather good-looking young man. And with the loss of a month's growth of thick black whiskers a strange gentleness and understanding, plus a capacity for tolerance and self-sacrifice, apparently had descended upon him.

"You appear very willing to give these volunteer doctors a break," she said presently. "Do I not rate a similar break?"

"You rate," he replied, "anything I can give you."

"How about a little peace of mind?"

He smiled and flashed his fine white teeth. "Are you worrying about me, Janet?"

"Of course. A nurse always worries about her patient."

"Oh," he retorted sadly—"that kind of worry. I'm sorry, but I can't fix that. I would if I could."

"Ray Lanier, you infuriate me."

He ignored this charge. "Of course, if you were worried over me because some fatality may overtake me *after* I am well, that would be different. And," he added, "very pleasing to me. I should, I think, burst with pride."

"Is your vengeance more important to you than anything else in this world?"

He nodded.

"Do you believe in God?"

He squirmed around in the bed. "We'll not discuss that. I know what you're driving at."

"Do you believe your father is in heaven?"

"Not if he met there the men who Judased him here on earth. St. Peter would heave him out for starting a riot in heaven."

"You're incorrigible. Do you believe your father had a soul?"

"Certainly."

"Do you believe that even now his soul realizes what you contemplate doing?"

"Of course. Didn't I promise him I'd do it, before he died? He approved of it."

"But perhaps he's seen the light and changed his mind."

"My dear, kind, sweet young lady, this matter has got beyond the argument state. The original *casus belli* doesn't amount to a hoot in a hollow. Milo Landrum hired my father killed, and he'll hire me killed next. Only a fool would argue with a tiger. I can escape a head-on collision with him, but it means playing the game with his rules. It means eating crow. If I deed him half of the land covered by Lonely Valley Lake, he will find a way to drain it. With the deed would have to go forgiveness of his crime. I'd have to pretend I didn't believe, after all, that he hired Felix killed. A man can't do things like that, Janet—not if he expects to live with himself thereafter."

"There is the law to take into consideration."

"I've considered it."

"But you may ruin your life."

"Better that than live with a hypocrite and a coward."

"Have you any religious convictions at all?"

"I'm not an orthodox Christian. I have a code of conduct. I'd rather be kind than pious. I'd rather die fighting for my rights than knuckle to a scoundrel or a bully. I fear," he added, "that you set too high a value on human life. I'm perfectly content to die if that is to be the price of making good with Felix."

"I'm through," said Janet.

"Thank you. I'm glad you are, although I do appreciate tremendously your well-meant efforts to save me. I do not understand you. I have never met a woman like you before. I wish you wouldn't leave when your professional duties are at an end. I wish you'd stay and give me an opportunity to understand you better. Perhaps, too, you'd get to understand me better. I'm not at all a difficult person to get along with. Haven't I been a good patient? Have I been peevish and fretful and ungracious?"

She stood over him and smoothed back his long, thick, black hair.

"You've been a darling patient, Ray," she admitted. "If I'd lost you, I would have wept for a week."

"You're so sweet," he murmured. "Perhaps I'll be lucky and find a clean way out of this mess. I wouldn't care to hurt you—to cause you to regard me as a bloody-handed murderer. Please try to think well of me until the day I give you reason to think otherwise, and please do not discuss this matter with me again. I'll help you all I can, but—there's a limit."

In silence she took his temperature, gave him his medicine, and then gave him a sponge bath and alcohol rub.

"I've got the heebie-jeebies," he complained, when she had finished. "Tomorrow I'm going to send Tom Harmon in to Modoc City to buy me a small radio I can plug in beside my bed."

"I must do some shopping, Ray. You know I came out here unprepared for such a long stay. I'll drive in and buy it for you."

"But I don't want you to go—no, that's selfish. You've been confined long enough in this house. You need a change. Is it a clear, sunny day?"

"Yes."

"Well, it is not likely to start snowing. A little early for snow, but sometimes we get it in November. If it starts to snow before you are ready to return, promise me you'll remain in Modoc City until I can send Tom Harmon for you. That mountain road is narrow, and you might skid and get into trouble and freeze to death out on that lonely mountain."

"I promise." A soft feeling of warmth surged through her in the knowledge that he could worry about her . . . it had been a long time since anybody had done that. "You dear, thoughtful fellow!" she added. "I can take care of myself."

"Who takes care of you when you can't take care of yourself, Janet?"

"I engage a doctor and a nurse."

"Isn't there anybody to worry over you?"

"Not a soul."

"Then," he said brightly, "that's my job."

"Thank you, Ray. And who worries over you?"

"Nobody, except my hirelings and my banker."

"Not even the girl Cecilia, whose portrait I see in the living room?"

"Cecilia," he said, "lives in another world."

"She's beautiful."

"And knows it. She's the daughter of a cattle broker in San Francisco. She used to come up here with her father. The old man liked to shoot snipe and duck here in the fall. He's handled our cattle for a long time. Dead now, so Cecilia doesn't come here any more. No chaperon."

"And yet you ask me to remain here?"

"A chaperon will be provided. You may choose your own, if you wish; if you can not find an acceptable one, I'll try. Are you impatient to leave?"

"No, I have no place in particular to go."

He gazed at her thoughtfully.

"I suppose," she charged, "you'd like to ask me what I'm doing in this country?"

"The thought did occur to me, but I never ask

people direct questions regarding their private affairs."

"I'll tell you. I have a number of scattered parcels of land in this country, bequeathed to me by a relative, and I came out here to look at them and, if possible, sell them. They're scattered in and around the Modoc National Forest."

"You will be unable to investigate your holdings until spring. There's probably a foot of snow in that country now. When you get ready to go, we'll locate your holdings on the map, and I'll take you in to look at them. We'll take a pack outfit, and I'll wrangle the stock and do the cooking. You can combine business with leisure. It's beautiful up there in the late spring. The escholtzia and the buttercups and the bluebells and Indian paint brush and dogwoods will be out. And the wood-ticks won't!"

"And you fully expect to be able to show me my heritage in the spring?"

"Yes—but if I should not, unfortunately, be alive to accompany you, Tom Harmon will prove just as useful."

"I'd like to remain here, if it's possible, Ray. I like this country. I like your house. I like you and Tom Harmon, bless his simple old heart, and I like Big Foot and Skunk Tallow and the Sphinx twins. Does the lake freeze?"

"Solid—in January and February. Thirty below, some winters. But the cattle winter well. They have shelter in the brakes, and they go into the winter fat, which is a protection against the cold. And I feed them plenty of hay. When the lake is frozen, I get out an ice yacht."

"I adore ice yachting."

"I'll teach you to shoot," he promised. "And I'll get you a nice, gentle, well-reined horse. Big Foot's squaw will make you a fur jacket and gauntlets, and Big Foot will make you a pair of chaps. I'll have your stirrups hooded and lined with lambskin to keep your feet warm."

"You're so kind, Ray, and I know I'd enjoy myself far more than you could possibly suspect, but—I work for a living."

"I realize that. Do not worry. Your labors for the past three weeks will net you six months' salary at your regular rates. Times are not so good just now, or I'd double that stipend. Even then I shall be in your debt. Money can not pay for what you have done for me. Money, in your case, is merely a token of appreciation and an inadequate one."

"But I am making no charge for my services, Ray."

"Why?"

"It's been such fun to do for you."

"Well, despite the suffering I underwent, it was fun to have you do for me. I accept the sacrifice in the spirit in which you tender it. You know I'm grateful. There will be no further talk, then, of vulgar financial matters. I take it you will permit me to repay you in kind by permitting me to have the fun of doing for you all winter."

"I'd love that, Ray, but surely you understand how terrible it would be for me to be your guest here while you went gunning for Milo Landrum. And that is a task I know you can not neglect, since he is gunning for you. Of course, as you said before, it would be well to have me here in case you returned home some day leaking badly in a few places. Still, what the eye does not see the heart does not grieve for—and I do *not* care for the job of worrying over you."

"I understand perfectly. Janet, if you will promise to remain here until spring I'll promise to do my best to avoid a head-on collison with Landrum. I'll avoid him until after I have showed you your lands and said good-bye to you at the railroad station."

"Sold!" Janet agreed happily.

She had great confidence in the efficacy of time as a cure-all for human passions. Now, if she could but induce Milo Landrum to avoid a head-on collison with Raynor Lanier . . . Decidedly this amazing Raynor Lanier was too young to die, too fine to be permitted to ruin his life through yielding to the dictates of his equally amazing code.

"That's a bet," he told her. "And now, may I have my luncheon? You have no idea how hungry I am."

Still wrapped in the fogs of her optimism, Janet departed for the kitchen to order luncheon for her patient. Ah Fong was in his room, so she knocked at his door and said,

"Time to cook luncheon for the boss, Ah Fong."

"No can do," Ah Fong retorted shrilly. "Me ketchum toothache."

"I'm sorry. You no ketchum Chinese medicine to cure toothache?"

"No ketchum proper medicine. Hurt like hell."

Janet went out into his spotless kitchen and commenced rattling pots and pans about at a prodigious rate. Her activities went unheeded by the old truant, so she threw a cheap water glass at the stove, and the crash and tinkle of the resultant ruin brought Ah Fong out on the run with murder in his eyes.

"You go away my kitchen, missy," he ordered. "Get to hell an' gone."

Like all his kind he bitterly resented the presence of volunteer cooks in his kitchen.

"No," Janet protested kindly, "you have a bad toothache. I will cook luncheon for the boss. Me velly fine cook. Alee time now I cook for boss."

"Toothache finish," Ah Fong protested humbly. "Get out."

Later, when she had served Lanier and returned to the kitchen with his empty tray, Ah Fong confronted her belligerently.

"You mally boss, hey?" he demanded.

Janet shrugged. "Perhaps—if no can get better man."

"Where the hell you ketchum better man? No can do."

"Pouff!" said Janet.

"Suppose you mally boss. Boss fire Ah Fong?"

"Why, of course not. I wouldn't let him send you away."

He was dumbfounded. "You likee Ah Fong?"

"Likee Ah Fong heap plenty, but no likee Ah Fong feed boss Chinese medicine and wildcat heart."

Ah Fong nodded slow acceptance of the inevitable. Presently Janet heard him caterwauling in the kitchen.

"He must have the toothache again," she suggested to Lanier.

"No, he's singing, not crying."

"Why does he sing? He's depressed and angry."

"Oh, no. And he sings because he's had a happy thought."

"Of what?"

"Of something," he answered, "that never can happen."

Lanier's condition was so satisfactory next morning that Janet felt no compunction in leaving him in Ah Fong's care for the day. The day previous she had definitely dismissed Tom Harmon, in order that he might attend to his neglected duties as ranch superintendent. About ten o'clock, therefore, she started for Modoc City. At the top of the grade she found Hugo and another half-breed standing by the sign.

"Your boss will soon be entirely recovered from his illness, Hugo," she told him. "In a week he'll be out of bed."

Hugo bowed gravely. "Please, I ask a favor. Keep the boss in the house long as you can."

"Why do you ask that, Hugo?"

He came to the side of her car. "This man you see with me, miss, he is my cousin. He does not work for Ray Lanier. He comes from the Chewaukan outfit over to Oregon, and he has come to Modoc to fix the clock of this fellow Landrum."

"You mean he has come from Oregon to kill Landrum?"

"Sure thing, miss. Nobody on the Lanier ranch can do it, but this cousin of mine—well, he is an outsider. Nobody knows him in this country. He will do the job and go back to the Chewaukan. But this will take some time. Landrum has got three men for bodyguard; they never leave him alone on the street. Now, when Ray Lanier is able to drive to town, there will be shooting. That will be the first job. But if you keep the boss to the house—say maybe three weeks—then, when he drives to town, there will be no shooting, because the job is finished by my cousin. Sure in three weeks he finds the opportunity."

Janet stared at the naïve fellow.

"And who hired your cousin for this job, Hugo?"

"No hire. Like me he is half-breed Modoc. Modocs have no reservation, no land. Government never gives rations to our people, but Ray Lanier's ranch is our reservation; we work for him. When a Modoc gets old and can't hunt and fish and work, he will starve to death and freeze to death if Ray Lanier don't take care of him. Ray Lanier is the friend of the Modocs. You don't suppose we can afford to lose our friend like this, eh?"

"Ah! So your cousin's interest is a matter of tribal concern. Very beautiful, Hugo, but you send your cousin back to Oregon. I do not wish Mr. Landrum killed. I have a plan to make further killing unnecessary."

The half-breed stared at her sullenly.

"This is work for men," he warned. "It is work for the friends of Ray Lanier. You—you are a nurse. He pays you while he is sick; when he is well you go away. You have no more the interest to stay. So why you tell me this?"

"I know what I know Hugo. This war will cease because I have the power to stop it. Besides, you know you do wrong in permitting your cousin to try to kill Landrum. Ray Lanier desires that privilege for himself. He will not be pleased if some one denies it to him."

"You don't tell him about what I just tell you?" Hugo pleaded. "If you do I lose my face. I will have to go from Lonely Valley and never come back."

"I'll not tell him—if you'll promise to call this cousin of yours off the job and give me a chance to try my hand at peacemaking."

"A man is a big fool to tell things to a woman. I am a big fool. You tie our hands—well, I will give you one week and then—no matter what happens to Hugo Lanier—not even if he take his name from me—I will go through with this job. I am here always—like the sheriff—to watch that somebody we do not know comes into Lonely Valley. I do not like this work. If Landrum is dead, I do not have to be like sheriff."

"One week is time enough, Hugo—and please do not be so angry."

But Hugo turned away and, accompanied by his relative, stalked back into the timber.

CHAPTER TWELVE

IN MODOC CITY JANET COMPLETED HER shopping, lunched at the Mountain House, and about one o'clock walked around to Milo Landrum's office. She found it occupying an entire square, stone, one-story structure.

On a bench outside the office three men, who looked as if they might be recent arrivals in Modoc City if one were to judge by their clothing, sat smoking. As Janet entered the general office, one of these men rose and followed her in.

A dyspeptic-looking man slid off a high stool at a high bookkeeping desk and inquired her business.

"I wish to see Mr. Milo Landrum."

"And the nature of your business?"

"Personal and private."

"I handle all of his personal and private affairs, Miss."

"Not all of them, I'm sure. Just now Mr. Landrum has some affairs so personal and so private that he doesn't even like to think about them himself, because they are provocative of worry. Those are the affairs I wish to discuss with him, with the hope I can relieve him of some worry."

"I think, Bean," said the man who had followed Janet in, "it's O.K. to let her see him. She's not a gun moll."

"Follow me, please," said the man Bean and led her into Milo Landrum's private office.

It was a dingy, dusty, and somewhat disordered place that reeked of tobacco smoke, lack of ventilation, and the odor of drugs. Landrum was seated in a shabby old Morris chair with one leg up on another chair. Janet observed a pair of crutches in a corner, and two holstered pistols and a cartridge belt were lying on the desk.

"Excuse me for not gittin' up," he greeted her. "I've had an injury to my leg, an' it hain't healed yet."

"Bullet wound?" Janet suggested.

"That's good guessin'," he admitted. "Another inch either way an' I'd have lost my laig, I reckon. What's your name, young woman?"

"My name doesn't matter. Besides, I have a reason for not answering your request. So Raynor Lanier's Indian wasn't the bad shot his boss thinks he is?"

"He's a hundred percent perfect. He only got one shot at me, and he didn't miss. Set down. Then sing your song or tell your story."

Janet found a chair and faced him.

"Do you know, Mr. Landrum, that you have crawled into a hole and dragged the hole in after you; that there is no escape for you?"

"Maybe," he suggested without interest, "I'm one o' those fellers that can tunnel through to the other end."

"I observe you have engaged the services of three gorillas as a bodyguard. You require a larger standing army. Raynor Lanier's liable to ride into Modoc City with a truck load of good men and true, surround this office, and put your face and his on the front page of the *Modoc County Clarion*."

"The Laniers've been making the front page 'o that journal for the last fifty years, quite regular. You the bearer of a message from Ray Lanier?"

"No, Mr. Landrum. It was entirely my own idea to call upon you and talk things over. It has seemed to me that now is the time for somebody to exhibit some real intelligence—"

"Well, now that's mighty sweet of you, young woman, mighty sweet."

Landrum's unsmiling lips and eyes belied his pleasant words. Janet studied him. In point of age he might have been anywhere from forty-five to sixty; his hair was iron-gray, thick, straight, and rebellious; it came down over his brow in a bang. Janet guessed he was of medium height and would weigh well over two hundred pounds. His face was long and narrow; his ears, extraordinarily small and lobeless, grew close to his skull; his eyes were round, deep set, and of a peculiar pale shade of brown. Although outwardly he appeared calm, she guessed he was inwardly excited, for she could see a pulse beating in his temple at a rate well above normal. His face was florid, and he was some thirty pounds overweight. Janet suspected he might be the victim of high blood pressure.

"Well," he reminded her, "I reckon you'll know me the next time you see me."

"It is a matter of amazement, Mr. Landrum," the girl went on, "that you go to such trouble and risk to acquire another man's assets at bargain-counter prices."

"Go on," he ordered her.

"You've started a fight you can't win. Even if you succeed in killing Ray Lanier you'll have to carry on, for when Ray Lanier's gone there will be Tom Harmon to meet, in addition to some of Mr. Lanier's white riders and a small company of Indian riders. You can't kill the best and only friend those Indians have and survive indefinitely. Really, Mr. Landrum, you have been most unwise in that by attacking Raynor Lanier you have furnished him with an excuse to kill you on sight, plead self-defense, and be acquitted on his plea."

"He sent me a message I couldn't ignore."

"I've heard about that message. How do you know Raynor Lanier sent it? You can not prove he sent it, so your action was the result of fright. One could scarcely accuse you of having a conscience."

"Listen, young woman. A little while before Felix Lanier got killed he had a run-in with a stranger up at the Mountain House. Old Lanier got the drop on this stranger, took his guns away, an' then ear-marked him like he'd ear-mark a calf, so's he'd know him again if he met him. Naturally this stranger went out to Lonely Valley an' busted the old man—an' when some Lanier man killed this stranger, Ray Lanier had the body

115

dumped on my front porch with a message tied to its right wrist. I can read writin', an' I can read signs an' draw my own conclusions. I'm accused o' hirin' that stranger to kill old Lanier, when everybody in this county knows the old man had more enemies than some folks have hay; that the only reason he lived as long as he did was because God had him by the hand. But can I argue the matter with Ray Lanier? Not much. The Laniers only argue in the smoke. They get an idea in their heads, an' nothin' but death can get it out. So all I can do is act."

"You're due for a great deal of action, Mr. Landrum. To begin, you *have* to face Ray Lanier. That is inevitable."

Landrum commenced to fidget; his eyes grew more baleful.

"And, of course," Janet went on, "those hired gunmen of yours will not stand by you in a free-for-all fight. Their kind do not fight like that. Such a resolute person as Ray Lanier will find no difficulty in running them out of this county. And then—"

The pulse in Landrum's temple beat jerkily half a dozen times, then settled to the old rhythm. His face went white, likewise his hands. His right hand flew to his left breast suddenly, fearfully; then his fingers explored his vest pocket and came away with a cigar. Nevertheless, he had betrayed himself, for Janet Corliss was a trained nurse, and to trained nurses, as to doctors, many things are instantly visible.

"He has a touch of angina," Janet thought, and her heart beat wildly in this realization. "Ray will not have to kill him. If I can only keep them apart six months, worry and fear will settle this issue. A sudden fear, a bit of undue excitement—and this man's heart will pop like a toy balloon."

Aloud she said: "Well, Mr. Landrum, if you can burrow your way out the other end of the hole you're in you're quite a fox. Ray Lanier will not hire you killed. That is not in accordance with his code of honor. But I do know that some men who love him are even now watching you, for a chance to kill you before you kill him. They have been forbidden by Ray Lanier to do this but—they will not obey him."

Landrum sighed. "It's certainly hard on me to have to take the fall of some other feller's play," he protested. "I can't run away even if I was the runnin' kind—which I'm not."

"No, you're hobbled with golden leg-irons—a prisoner to your assets. There is an old saying that there are no pockets in a shroud."

"I think," he replied, while his curious gaze swept her slowly, "that you're just a smart female lawyer."

"What you think, you merely suspect; but what I know—I know. For instance, I know that you have angina pectoris—possibly an aneurism. So I prescribe for you a total lack of excitement and worry. And a long vacation might add years to your life. You have all the wealth you require. Why not cease piling up wealth for a year? A great many things can happen in a year. You should try the climate of Mozambique or Surabaya or Topolobampo. I'm going to do the same when I can afford it."

"This interview is ended," he told her harshly. "Get out. If you was a man, you'd go out in sections. I'm more than nine years old, and I don't scare none too easy."

"Oh, very well," she replied carelessly. "Whom the gods would destroy they first make mad. I'll send a wreath of cactus to your bier."

And with that parting shot she left him; she laid the flattering unction to her soul that, as an unofficial ambassador, she had carried the situation off very well. She had planted a little seed; given time, it might develop into a beautiful shrub.

CHAPTER THIRTEEN

UPON HER RETURN TO THE LONELY VALLEY ranch she found Hugo and his half-breed cousin just leaving the house to return to the former's post on the top of the hill. Both stared at her with blank Indian stolidity, nor did Hugo, as formerly, lift his hat in token of respect. She wondered what they were doing there.

She removed her hat and coat and went into Lanier's room, and the instant she faced him she sensed a subtle change in his attitude toward her. She reached for his wrist, as a matter of habit, and felt his pulse; she ran her hand over his brow.

"Quite satisfactory," she announced. "Did you have a good appetite for your luncheon?"

"Excellent," he replied without enthusiasm.

"I bought a little radio for you," she continued a little breathlessly. "I'll bring it in from my car and plug it in beside your bed. And I called at the post office for the mail. Here it is."

"Thank you," he said with chill politeness. "I'll read it later. I think I'll have a little nap now."

She realized she had been dismissed; that he found her presence, for some unknown reason, irksome, so she left him. In about two hours she looked in on him again. His mail, opened and scattered on the bed, indicated he had read it; he was lying on his back, staring at the ceiling, and on his face she detected distress and worry.

"Now, what's happened?" she demanded.

He looked at her a long time before answering; even the cold scrutiny she had been subjected to by Milo Landrum could not equal this. Silently he handed her a letter. It was from the Modoc Commercial Trust & Savings Bank and read:

"My dear Ray:

"With reference to your late father's note for one hundred thousand dollars ($100,000.00) to this bank, and which was endorsed by you following his death and the transfer by him to you of all his assets immediately prior to his death:

"At your father's request this note was extended six months. At a meeting of our Board of Directors held yesterday it was suggested by the chairman of the board, Mr. Landrum, that you might request a further extension when the note falls due on January 2nd. Following a discussion the Board decided that, in view of the present financial situation throughout the country, the best interests of this bank would not be served by granting such renewal.

"While the loan is secured by chattel mortage on certain cattle, I must point out to you that the security has depreciated greatly in value. At the time the loan was made the best grade of beef was selling at ten cents on your ranch. The same quality of beef now brings five cents.

"In view of our long and pleasant business relations with the Lanier family, I take the earliest opportunity to notify you of our earnest expectation that the note will be taken care of at maturity and to impress upon you very earnestly that no extension can possibly be granted.

"With kindest personal regards and regretting exceedingly the change in policy which makes this course inevitable, I am,

Sincerely,

J. G. Henning,

Cashier."

Janet looked up. "Is this blow Number Two?" she queried.

He nodded.

"You expected a renewal?"

Again he nodded. Then: "I had fully expected to pay twenty-five thousand on account of the principal, pay the interest to date, and renew, despite the depreciation of the security. And I could give additional security. You might have noticed the bank did not suggest this."

"But, for all its firm business formality, I seem to detect a note of friendliness, of sympathy, for you on the part of this cashier."

"Of course. He's our friend. But the chairman of the board is Milo Landrum. The *Modoc County Clarion*, which you brought me, carries a story of Landrum's acquisition of a controlling interest in the bank and his election to the chairmanship of the board. He has captured the last independent bank in the county, and I shall have to pay my note at maturity or lose my cattle. And if that should happen, I'd be out of business. I'd have to sell the ranch—and ranches are not salable now. But even if I pay the note, this action of my bank spells horrible embarrassment to me, because I shall be left without operating capital."

"I think," she said, "that what you should have now is something to rally your nerves," and she left him, ostensibly to get it.

In the kitchen she called up Milo Landrum in Modoc City.

"This," said Janet, "is the presumptuous young woman who called upon you this afternoon."

"What do you want now?"

"I want an extension of one year on Ray Lanier's note to his bank. You have ordered the note called at maturity. Mr. Lanier will pay the interest and twenty-five thousand on the principal, and that's a fair proposition. He might feel kindlier toward you if you did this now. On the other hand it may possibly occur to him to settle all of his business with you with remarkable celerity."

"And if the note is renewed, what do I get out of it?"

"Ray Lanier will keep out of your way, and his defenders will be called off. I know who they are, I'll tell on them, and they will be squelched. If Ray Lanier gives his word, you know he'll keep it."

"What's your interest in this matter anyhow?"

"To promote peace."

"I thought so. Well . . . you might be useful, young woman. I'll trade whenever you're ready."

"Telephone your bank that I shall be in to the county seat tomorrow with Ray Lanier's check and a new signed note. At present he is ill abed and can not attend to the matter himself. Thank you very much."

She returned to the sick room with the potion she had promised him.

"You look unusually pleased about something," he charged coldly.

"Ray, what's the matter? You're displeased with me."

He considered this charge. Then: "Yes, you're too smart for any mere man to delude. I am displeased with you. I have lost confidence in you, and while it breaks my heart to say so, I want to pay you off tomorrow morning and send you on your way."

"You're the lord of Lonely Valley. Whatever you say goes with me, Ray."

"I'm still grateful and always will be, Janet, but—you've got me running in circles. At present you are, broadly speaking, a member of my household. Why have you found it necessary to have truck with my enemy?"

"Oh! So Hugo's relative followed me and saw me call at Milo Landrum's office?"

"Exactly."

"Hugo has had the insolence to have me spied on. He has double-crossed me, so now I shall double-cross him. He told me he had imported that half-breed cousin of his to kill Landrum, in order to spare you. Ray, that must not be. Send that cousin packing. Call Hugo in and lay down the law to him. I've promised Landrum you will avoid him for one year, and I want you to make good on that promise I have made in your behalf."

"You are not authorized to make promises in my behalf. As a member of my household, supposed to be loyal to me, you have traded with the enemy."

"And to good effect. Ray, I've just talked with him over the phone, and in return for my guarantees the bank will accept payment of the interest and twenty-five thousand dollars on account and renew for one year. I told him I'd bring in the check and a new note tomorrow."

"There are two reasons why I can not do that. In the first place I have not been paid for the beef I sold just before I was taken ill, and so I haven't got the money to pay the bank tomorrow—"

"I'll loan it to you," she assured him eagerly. "I'll wire my attorney to sell some securities I hold—"

"Not at the present price of those securities. I decline to permit you to sacrifice for me. And I decline to ask a favor of the man I am going to kill; I decline to accept a favor at his hands. I can go broke, and I can die with my boots on, but Tom Harmon will bury me with my self-respect intact. Please give me my slippers and a dressing gown. I'm going to get up."

"I forbid it."

"Ah Fong," he shouted—and the old Chinaman came running in.

"My slippers and dressing gown," he commanded, and Ah Fong dutifully produced them.

Lanier slid out on the edge of the bed and donned them. "Lift me up, Ah Fong," he demanded, and the cook helped him to his feet.

Lanier threw an arm around the Chinaman's neck and started out of the room, with Janet following, terrorized. Before the wall telephone in the kitchen he paused. Ah Fong brought him a chair, and he sat down.

"Call Landrum," he commanded Janet, "and tell him I repudiate your arrangement. Don't argue with me. I run my own show."

She obeyed him.

Landrum's sole comment was, "Very well, young woman, very well."

"Now," said Lanier, "be good enough to telephone down to the ranch buildings and tell Tom Harmon to come up and carry me back to bed. My fool legs have gone back on me."

In ten minutes Tom Harmon arrived, picked his boss up as if he were a child, and deposited him back in bed. Then he disappeared, but returned presently and shook his employer's shoulder.

"All hell's to pay an' no pitch hot," he complained. "The girl's in her room, and I can hear her crying to beat four of a kind. What do you mean—makin' that girl cry? Ain't you got no gentlemanly instincts, you young fool?"

There was no answer, so Mr. Harmon bent over his youthful boss and peered down at the latter's face. It was streaked with tears; tight as he tried to close his eyes, the tears would seep through. Tom Harmon's calloused hand ruffled his dark head. He was fifteen years older than Raynor Lanier, and to the superintendent the latter was more like a son than an employer.

"I don't want to talk out o' my turn, son," he murmured, "but is it something you can't tell me?"

The head was shaken in negation, so Tom Harmon sat down on the bed and waited patiently and in silence for his youthful boss to get himself in hand again.

After a while Lanier said, "Tom, I had it all fixed up for her to stay—and now I've got to send her away."

"The hell you say!" There was distress and fervency in his simple statement.

"Tom, whether she knows it or not, that girl has

fallen in love with me. She tipped her hand—tried to do something so fine and magnificent for me I—I couldn't help but realize the situation."

"Something you couldn't accept?"

"Yes, Tom."

"Well, you always was one to roll your own hoop."

"I've quarreled with her, Tom. She went in to see Landrum—tried to make a trade with him—He'll think I sent her—think I'm bluffing—afraid—I made her call him up and repudiate the deal—"

"You," said Tom Harmon, "are stronger meat than she's been used to where she comes from. She thought you was tenderloin—and you're a piece from between the horns. Yes, sir, she certainly spoke out of her turn, but from where I sit I don't see no real reason for all this to-do. She meant right."

Lanier picked up the letter from the bank. "Read that," he ordered.

Tom Harmon dutifully read it. In silence he laid the letter down on the bed.

"She'd actually got Landrum to agree to renew that note if I paid the interest and twenty-five thousand on account of the principal; and when I told her I didn't have twenty-five thousand just now, she offered to sell some securities she has and loan me the money. Hell's fire, Tom, I can't be pitied by a woman."

"I have heard," Harmon replied drily, "that female sympathy is a mighty sweet thing to have when a feller needs it. Boy, this Janet girl is a thoroughbred, so why you're sending her away beats my time."

"Tom, I can't have her around any more. I'm under a debt of gratitude to her I can never pay. I'm going busted higher than Haman, sooner or later. I'm going to kill Landrum, and I may have to do time for it; or Landrum may kill me—and I can not afford—"

"Ah," said Tom Harmon softly, "I begin to see a light at the end of your tunnel. You in love with this girl, boy? Answer me straight!"

"Of course, you old fool. Who wouldn't be? But I—just—can't afford her. I wouldn't break her heart just to possess her a week or a month or a year—and then—"

He waved his hand to the east, and Tom Harmon knew he was referring to the little family cemetery. Tom said nothing, although he did look unhappy.

"And you run right up the hill and tell Hugo to lay off and to make all his relatives lay off. Pass the same word to Big Foot. After all, he's their chief. They obey him. Don't scold Hugo . . . Just put him in his place and tell him I will not take my name away from him if he behaves."

"I'll do that, of course. But this nice girl is brokenhearted, Ray. She was pullin' the sobs clear up out of her shoes. I stood outside her door an' listened."

"She'll get over it, Tom, but if she stays here to the finish she'll know real heartbreak. I've got to clear the record before I permit any sentimental entanglements. She didn't come here to earn money. She told me so this morning. And I—I told her I'd pay her off in the morning and she'd have to go."

Tom Harmon stood up. Thoughtfully he rolled himself a cigarette. "Well," he said presently, "I'm goin' to tell her she don't have to do no such thing."

"Tom Harmon, mind your own business."

"The Lanier business is my business."

"You dip your beak into this and you can have you time, Tom."

"You're delirious. Why, I been on the payroll so long I can be fired long enough to ride into Modoc City and tunnel Milo Landrum, but I'd come right back as soon as they let me out of the pen." He raised his arms and yawned prodigiously. "Me—at my age—gettin' mixed up in a love brawl. . . . Well, it's no comfort to me to set here an' watch you suffer."

He departed to tiptoe down the hall and pause again outside the door of Janet's room. No sound of woe reached him, so he ventured a timid knock at the door.

"Who is it?" Janet's strangled voice challenged.

"Tom Harmon. I got thinkin' maybe some fresh air would do you a whole lot o' good. You ain't never seen that thirty-foot mahogany speed boat Ray has in the boathouse down at the lake, have you?"

"No, Tom."

"Well, it's a lovely fall afternoon, an' the lake's as smooth as a pan o' dish-water, an' I'm goin' to take that boat an' voyage around a little. She does thirty-five miles an hour, an' at that rate o' speed on water I've knowed folks to have a lot o' grief blowed right out o' them. Suppose you come out with Uncle Tom Harmon an' leave this spiteful patient o' yours to simmer down an' get logical. Just now he needs a lot o' lettin' alone."

The door opened, and Janet stood facing him. And then plain, human old Tom Harmon had a marvelous inspiration.

"I shaved this mornin', Miss Janet," he whispered, "an' I'm wearin' a clean shirt. So if you feel like you'd like to cry on somebody, why I'm a candidate."

Janet went into his arms and cried on his shoulder.

"Hush up," he pleaded. "I know all about it, an' it ain't worth cryin' about. If you think you're sufferin', you'd ought to take a look at him. However, we'll let him suffer. Serves him right. He ain't got good sense. Now you put on a heavy coat an' that little round cap I like to see you wear, and we'll go for a boat ride."

"I—I—I'm—going—in the—morning," Janet sobbed pitifully. "I—I'm—heart-broken—I—I tried to save him—and I made—a mess—of it—oh, Tom, Tom, I've made a—mess of—everything."

"A mess of anything, Miss Janet, when seasoned with noble intentions, is just so doggoned sweet it's got to be throwed out to the dogs. You ain't got no idea what you done to Ray Lanier."

"I have. I—hurt him—cruelly. I—I—crucified his—pride."

"You think that, of course, an' he'd let you get away with the fool notion, but me, I know better. You didn't hurt him nohow. You just teched him on a soft spot—an' he had to do something or he'd have busted out cryin' in front of you. So he pulled a fight. Come now, get your things on an' I'll take you for a fast boat ride."

"Promise me you'll not tell—Ray—I cried."

"I promise not to tell him a word of what takes place—not since the moment I knocked at your door. But don't worry. He never asks questions."

"And promise me you'll stay here for dinner. I—it would be embarrassing to be alone with him—now."

"You win."

"I'll stay at the Mountain House a few days, Tom, and telephone you every day to learn how he's getting along. Then I'll go away and never bother him any more."

"You will like hell," said Tom Harmon.

But he said it to himself, for quite suddenly he had made up his mind that the best interests of all concerned would be conserved by keeping Janet Corliss a prisoner in Lonely Valley.

"Thanks a lot for inviting me to the boat ride, Tom. I'll go with you now."

It occurred to Tom Harmon that he would have to cut the telephone line and steal the spark plugs out of her car, but he was a resolute fellow and equal to any enterprise.

CHAPTER FOURTEEN

TOM HARMON WAS A MAN WHO OBSERVED much, thought with extreme concentration on whatever he had to think about, and was an excellent judge of conversation both as to its timeliness, its quantity, and its quality. He had got Janet's car out of the garage and was seated in it, under the *porte-cochère*, when she came out to join him. Out of the tail of his eye he saw that she had, most amazingly, by means wholly unknown to the honest fellow, quite destroyed the evidence of her recent weeping.

"You drive, Tom," she announced cheerfully, and got in beside him.

Harmon glanced at the dash clock. "In one hour

and a quarter it will be dark, Miss Janet. We'll just have enough time to run down to the end of the lake and back."

He drove her down hill and across the lower meadow to a small boathouse that floated on two huge forty-foot fir logs off the point where Lonely Valley Creek entered the lake. Extending from this boathouse far out into the lake Janet observed two parallel lines of wooden buoys about forty feet apart; these, she judged, marked the ancient course of the creek before the lake had been formed. While she waited on the float, Harmon unlocked the boathouse doors, made certain the boat contained plenty of oil and gasoline, turned over the motor, and warmed it up. With a tobacco-stained index finger he motioned her into the boat and backed out, swung in a small turning basin, and sent the boat at its maximum speed of thirty-five miles per hour down toward the open lake. The speed of their passage created a breeze that blew sharply in Janet's face and, as Harmon had foretold, had the effect of sweeping her recent emotion away.

When he had cleared the charted channel, Harmon slowed the boat down and told Janet to take the wheel. This thrilled her. Indeed, in the matter of speed, there is no thrill comparable to driving a perfect speed boat, on perfect water, on a perfect day. Tom Harmon kept a smart lookout for floating logs, and Janet pushed up the throttle and followed the compass course he gave her. Thirty-five minutes after leaving the boathouse Harmon again took the wheel, and presently the boat crept along the shore at the extreme western end of the lake; then, for the first time, he spoke to her.

"See that gorge? Out in this country we call 'em box cañons. Used to be a tall monument o' black lava on the left-hand side 'way back in the '40's, and it toppled over into the gorge an' formed that there dam. That's why we have this lake. Nature sometimes does a better job than a high-priced engineer."

"And the land on which this dam has been formed—is that the land owned by Donald MacLean?"

"Yes, and for quite a distance on each side of and below it. MacLean knew what he was about when he got some cheap land scrip together, bought this controlling quarter section, an' bottled up the Laniers. I call him the two-million-dollar grouch."

Janet gazed with vast curiosity, not unmixed with awe, upon this evidence of her grandfather's pugnacity and perspicacity.

"I want to land and look at all of it," she said, so Harmon edged the boat in alongside some broken blocks of lava protruding from the water at the face of the dam and Janet climbed out and up.

The water that formerly had escaped over the top of the dam and thus kept the lake at a constant level had, with the years, eroded a channel into the left side of the gorge, which was limestone capped with black lava. The result was an overhang about eight feet broad and with a constantly downward dip. The dam itself was about forty feet wide, and for thirty feet of its width it was now dry, the overflow tending to be diverted more and more each year into the side channel under the overhang, as the erosion carved greater egress for it. The dam extended down the gorge for about seventy feet and tapered gradually down to the level of the ancient creek channel beyond.

When she rejoined Harmon she said:

"Tom, in fifty or sixty years there will have been eroded around the left side of the dam a new channel so large that gradually Lonely Valley Lake will be drained. There will come a day when the outflow will be greater than the inflow."

"Nature's a slow engineer, but she's efficient. Give her time, an' she'll get there, Miss Janet. But fifty years is too long to wait. Barrin' accidents, Ray Lanier may have fifty years before him, but Milo Landrum ain't. Milo's got to get his while the gettin's good."

"Tom," Janet asked him earnestly, "if Ray Lanier and Milo Landrum each should survive to the day when Ray Lanier is forced to sell Lonely

Valley Lake to Landrum for get-away money, or Landrum should get him foul and take it away from him on a legal technicality, what do you suppose this quarter section would be worth to him? Until he acquired it, he'd be in the position of a person all dressed up with no place to go."

Tom Harmon thoughtfully rolled and lighted a cigarette, giving himself fully a minute to consider her query. Then he looked up at her as grave as a Buddha and said,

"Miss Janet, if that day ever arrives, don't you sell Milo Landrum this dam-site for a cent under half a million dollars."

She stared at him, very red of face. So he knew! To prove he did, Tom Harmon nodded a grave affirmative.

"How did you find out?" she demanded half angrily.

"No stranger can come into Lonely Valley, much less into Ray Lanier's house," he replied, "without the O.K. of Thomas Hallowell Enoch Harmon, Esquire. When Ray's able to, he gives the O.K., but when he's so sick he don't know whether he's in bed or in Congress the job falls to me. I hate to admit it, but I prowled through your baggage the first day I got in with the cattle drive. I found a big fat envelope an' up in the left-hand corner of it the words, 'Daniel P. Magruder, Metropolitan Trust Company Building, New York.' I'd heard o' this Magruder. The Laniers had some correspondence with him once. So I peeked inside an' found a parcel o' unrecorded deeds. I took them deeds down to my own quarters an' copied off the legal descriptions o' the land they conveyed. Then I got the map o' Modoc County that shows the townships an' sub-divisions—an' blocked off your land in red crayon. Then I knew. After I knew, I put the envelope back in your bag and tried to forget all about it. I find that ain't so easy, Miss Janet."

"Have you told Ray?"

"No. My business was just to make certain you hadn't come to poison him, or neglect him an' let him die, while pretending to nurse him. I didn't figure your private business was any o' Ray's business—after that."

"I have difficulty in understanding why my private papers constituted any of your business, Tom."

"I hated to do it, but I had to know things. I've felt like a skunk ever since."

"Tom, I wish you hadn't confessed."

"It's been on my conscience."

He looked so doleful that Janet was forced, against her will, to smile.

"I'd like to be forgiven. If you can't be forgivin' now, I think maybe you will later on. Me knowin' who you are an' why you're in this country may prove lucky for you in the long run."

"I will forgive you now, Tom, on the

assumption that desperate circumstances demand desperate measures—that the end justified the means."

"You're a true-blue sport, an' a true-blue sport never knows a regret, Miss Janet. You take my advice an' don't record them deeds; an' if Landrum starts projectin' around this lawyer o' yours, warn your lawyer not to tell him your grandfather's dead an' you own the property. Have your lawyer tell him the land ain't for sale at no price."

"But it is for sale, Tom. I came out here to sell it—if not to Ray Lanier then to Landrum. I planned to play one against the other. Mr. Magruder told me to do that."

"Which was sound advice—from where he sits. But you can count Ray Lanier out. He can't compete with Landrum, an' I guess you know that now, don't you?"

"I realize it, yes."

Harmon flipped his cigarette butt overboard and prepared another, while he considered his next speech. "You can get a lot o' money from Landrum for your land—at the right time. That'll be when he knows he has Ray Lanier on his knees. Landrum's smart. He don't never start nothin' he don't aim to finish, an' you can bet a small five-cent bag o' tobacco he's got big medicine up his sleeve. For one thing he won't kill Ray, because we'll watch Ray too close, an' don't you worry none about Ray killin' him—not just yet."

"That is very comforting information, Tom."

Harmon twiddled his thumbs and gazed pensively off toward the darkening horizon. "Half a loaf is better'n none," he resumed. "If Landrum gets Ray down with his shoulders touchin', Ray'll sell him Lonely Valley Lake—cheap. He'll need the money to finance his business. He needs money now, an' if he gets a couple o' more pokes, what's he goin' to do? He talks fierce, but if it comes to a show-down—whether it's worth losin' his ranch an' cattle or killin' Milo Landrum, he'll give up the thing he hates an' cling to the thing he loves. He's right human, Ray is."

Janet decided that Harmon was developing into a sage.

"We just got to play a waitin' game," he resumed, "an' it would be money in your pocket to stick around here an' play the game with us. When Landrum's ripe for an offer, I'll let you know. I'll tell you how to handle him. He's right human, too."

"It's selling Ray Lanier out, of course, Tom, but then—"

"Don't feel sorry for him. Don't show him you pity him. It's dog-eat-dog in this world, you're a lone woman, an' you got to look out for yourself."

"I fully intend to."

Tom Harmon heaved a sigh. "This situation

sure is bindin'," he declared. "Well, let's get back home. We'll run up the south shore. It's deeper there, an' maybe I can show you a deer or a bear comin' down to drink about this time of the evenin'."

The sun sank lower and lower as they cruised at half speed in the deep shadow of the tall firs along shore. The silence and the mystery of this primeval wilderness were as balm to the distress resulting from Janet's recent stormy interview with Lanier.

Suddenly she said, "Tom, Ray told me once that no outsiders' boats were permitted on this lake because it is so shallow for most of its area that the wind kicks up a very bad chop, making it dangerous for small boats."

"That's right. Folks in this country got a habit, too—or they used to have—o' rowin' out in the lake, settin' off a stick o' dynamite, an' then gatherin' up hundreds o' dead trout that come to the surface. They'd take 'em home an' salt 'em down for the winter."

"There's another boat on the lake this evening, Tom. I can make out indistinctly the sound of an outboard motor."

He stopped his boat, shut off the motor, and listened. "Somebody crossin' from the north side," he decided. "The last o' the sunset light's shinin' on that side. We ought to see them in a little while."

Harmon started his motor and crept along the wooded shore. Thanks to a muffler on the exhaust, they proceeded silently, until they came to a little rocky islet standing out some thirty feet from the shore. Harmon slowed down, ran the boat around in back of this islet, and tied it up. Then he and Janet climbed to the top of the islet, lay down behind a screen of scrubby bushes, and gazed out across the lake.

Coming diagonally toward them from the middle of the lake, and entirely visible in the waning light which still flooded that area, a boat was approaching slowly. It contained two men, and as it came closer the roar of the outboard motor sent crashing echoes reverberating along the lonely shore. When it was almost abreast of the islet, it turned and chugged up the lake in the deep shadow of the south shore, rounded a promontory, and disappeared.

Tom Harmon deliberately, and in his customary silence, rolled and lit another cigarette. "Give 'em time to get where they're goin'," he suggested presently. "I figger they're goin' to follow this shore until they run aground about a mile from the upper limit o' the lake. Reckon they'll wade ashore then, drag their boat in under the bushes along shore, an' make camp. Just as well we don't let 'em know we saw 'em. They'd feel embarrassed."

"How do you know?" Janet challenged.

"Because they crossed the lake at about its middle. That made sure they couldn't be seen by anybody ten miles away—anybody at the Big House or around the ranch buildings, of course. And ain't they makin' their approach up the south shore in the deep shadow? Besides, their skiff is painted light green with a dash of aluminum paint in it. Camouflage—like the water. An' they've come over pretty late."

"Do you know them, Tom?"

"Total strangers to me."

"Well, I've seen them before. They were sitting on a bench in front of Milo Landrum's office in Modoc City this afternoon when I called on Landrum. They're part of his bodyguard, I imagine."

Tom Harmon's plain features puckered in vast amusement. "Poor ol' Milo," he murmured sympathetically, "he can't cash a bet, can he?"

"Is he trying to cash one—tonight?"

"I think so. Anyhow, we know them two boys ain't landin' on the Lanier ranch after dark for the purpose o' holdin' a prayer meetin'. Maybe they're figgerin' Ray Lanier's fool enough to pass between a lighted lamp an' a window."

"But how did they get here, Tom?"

"There's three ways folks can come by. One, over the road from Modoc City, is closed. They'd have to argue with Hugo an' his men. The other is over the Forest Service trail from Lookout.

That's out of the question, because there's a gate leadin' from the Forest Reserve out into the Lanier ranch. That gate is kept locked, an' they'd have to get the forest ranger or his guard to open it. Rangers ask questions of strangers in Lonely Valley. The third way is by boat—and they took it."

Tom smoked his cigarette to a finish; then they got back into the boat, and headed diagonally down the lake again to within a half-mile of the north shore, where they turned and headed for home at top speed. It was quite dark, and Janet feared they would be unable to find the marked entrance to the old channel of Lonely Valley Creek. She suggested to Harmon that he switch on the searchlight.

"An' have them two across the lake see it?" he demanded. "I'll just have to smell my way home by steering for the lights o' the Big House on the hill. We got to creep."

When they reached the landing, Tom Harmon did not wait to close the boathouse doors, in such a hurry was he. He leaped into Janet's car, and they drove straight across the meadows to the ranch buildings, bumping recklessly. When they got there, he leaped out.

"Good night. Thanks for your company, Miss Janet. Don't tell Ray what's doin', an' don't answer the doorbell tonight, an' don't let a light burn in Ray's bedroom. Can you obey orders without questionin' them?" he added almost fiercely.

"Always have. Trained that way, Tom. Good night and take care of yourself." And she turned the car and rolled away up the road toward the Big House.

CHAPTER FIFTEEN

JANET PUT HER CAR IN THE GARAGE AND went into the house *via* the kitchen, to be met with an accusing glare from Ah Fong.

"Boss klazy," he informed her. "Boss thinkee maybe something happen out on lake, you no come back. Wha' for you so late? You no gottee business makee boss klazy."

Janet was sensible of a distinct thrill at the Chinaman's announcement. Ray Lanier did not want her to stay in Lonely Valley, yet the strange fellow still could worry about her! She gave Ah Fong a smile of commendation and went on into Lanier's room.

"Ah Fong informs me you've been crazy with worry because Tom and I stayed out on the lake so late," she greeted him.

"I've been half-crazy, at any rate," he replied irritably. "Here it is almost an hour after dark— and you should have been in before dark. I'll

144

roast Tom Harmon for that. I worried, thinking Tom might not have been able to find the channel and you'd be out all night and freeze to death."

"You have a poor opinion of Tom's intelligence. Wouldn't he be apt, in that event, to land somewhere, build a fire, and save my life and his own? Besides, the moon will be up in an hour."

He growled something unintelligible.

"Moreover," Janet continued spitefully, "why should you start worrying over me so soon? You do not like me any more, and you're sending me away from here bright and early in the morning."

"I have a reason for that, and it isn't dislike," he protested.

Instead of continuing the conversation, she felt his pulse and thrust the thermometer into his mouth.

"You have half a degree of temperature," she announced.

"It's a wonder I haven't burned up."

"Nonsense! Have you had your dinner?"

"No, I was waiting for you. What the devil kept you and Tom out so late?"

"Oh, we lost track of time and had to search for the channel!" she replied with a smile.

He did not question her further, and she went out to the kitchen and returned with the tray bearing his dinner. Then she went out into the dining room and was served by Ah Fong, who glowered at her malevolently. After dinner, in absolute silence, she bathed her patient, gave him an alcohol rub, changed his bed linen, and bade him go to sleep.

"Thank you, but I shall not sleep."

"The effect," she retorted, "of a ferocious temper."

"If you're not too tired, I wish you'd play rummy with me."

"I have to pack my bags. Sorry."

The wistful pleading of a collie dog was in his eyes, but he did not answer. Instead he turned his face away and sighed. She got him a bowl of water, toothbrush, and paste, and he brushed his teeth.

"Tomorrow," she informed him, "you may get out of bed and sit in a chair; you might walk around the bed twice. The day after tomorrow you may, if you wish, and with the aid of Ah Fong, walk out into the living room and sit there for a few hours. Thereafter you will gain strength at an amazing rate, but you should not venture outdoors for at least a week after you find yourself able to walk about the house. And now, as I am leaving very early in the morning, I shall say goodby to you."

He reached over to the commode, found his check book, detached a check, and gave it to her. She saw that it was for a thousand dollars.

"If I could afford it," he said huskily, "I'd have written that check for ten thousand."

"You might just as well have done that, because I'll never cash this check anyhow."

He reached for her hand and drew it up to his lips. "Goodby, my dear," he half choked. "Goodby, good luck, and pleasant green fields for you always."

"Thank you, Ray. I haven't the faintest idea what this is all about, but whatever it is, it's your business. Just tell me you really don't dislike me."

He shook his head slowly; it was obvious that he could not speak. She bent over him.

"And goodby, good luck, and pleasant green fields for you, old Funny Face," she said softly.

She drew the curtains down and turned out the light.

"Don't draw the curtains, please," he protested. "They'll flap and keep me awake."

"Not when the windows are shut."

"But I want lots of fresh air. And I don't want the light turned out right away. I'm going to read myself to sleep."

"Will you please permit me to manage you this last night?"

There was excited pleading in her tones, and it was not lost on him. He reached up, turned on the reading light over his bed, and looked at her sharply. She knew he wanted her to explain, but it was contrary to his raising, contrary to his mountain code, to insist on explanations from one who did not care to give them voluntarily.

"Please telephone down to Tom's quarters and tell him to come up immediately," he ordered. "I want to talk to him."

"Very well, but put that light out while I do."

He reached up and pulled the switch chain. "You needn't bother telephoning Tom," he said. "He isn't there."

"How do you know?"

He laughed softly in the darkness. "There's danger abroad tonight. Somebody must have got past Hugo and his men, so Tom told you to keep my room in darkness. Well, he's right. A man could creep up on the veranda and pot me through the window yonder. Tom told you, too, not to tell me what he knows—what you both know—because if you didn't know it, he wouldn't have bothered to warn you not to tell me. He'd have guards around the house. Told you to keep the lights off and not answer the doorbell, didn't he?"

"Yes, he did. Now don't ask me anything more."

"What did you see out on the lake? Tell me," he commanded.

"Tom told me not to."

"I can't be trifled with, and it takes a smarter woman than you to deceive me. Usually our kind of people do not have to be told things. We deduce them. Come clean, Janet."

She decided she had no alternative save to

break her promise to Harmon and tell him. He groaned in his helplessness.

"They've come to burn my hay," he told her, "because that's the most terrible thing that could happen to me. If we have a hard winter and no hay, my cattle will die. They're fat now, and I have to keep them fat, because fat keeps out the cold. A thin cow can't survive a hard winter in this country. It's been a dry year in this state to the south, and I couldn't find pasture to ship them to if I wanted to. Hay is high and scarce. It would cost me fifty thousand dollars to save the herd if they burn my hay. Landrum wants to destroy my security to the bank he controls; then he'll get a deficiency judgment against me and grab all my cattle for a song he'll sing himself. A few thousand thin cattle will not pay my note with Landrum, the only buyer, when they're sold at public auction by the sheriff, so he'll attach Lonely Valley Lake. By Judas, that man's smart! And he sent them over in a boat because water leaves no trail."

"I wouldn't worry, Ray, if I were you. Tom Harmon's on the job."

"I'm not worrying. I'm just wild because I can't do the job myself Tom is certain to do—and that is kill those two arsonists."

He lay there in the dark without speaking for another minute, then, "There are stacks scattered all over a seven-thousand-acre meadow. That means a lot of territory to cover, make a getaway, and be back in Modoc City by daylight to prove an alibi. They couldn't cover the ground afoot. Janet, go to the telephone and ring three long bells. I have an outpost down in that corner of the ranch—a cabin occupied by Hugo's brother, Theodore, and his half-breed squaw. Try to get him on the telephone. If he answers, tell him all you have just told me, and he'll know what to do."

She returned in five minutes to report no answer to her call.

"I thought so. Now step out on the veranda, look southwest, and see if a long way from here you see a faint light."

Janet obeyed, but could see no light.

"From this height I can always see the light in Theodore's cabin," he told her. "No answer to our telephone and no lights means they've got Theodore and his wife. I thought they'd do that. A job of this sort has to be planned in advance.

"Those two men discovered Theodore has a light motor truck at the outpost. He uses it to carry salt out to the cattle and to travel between his outpost and the ranch commissary for supplies. Yes, they'd need his truck to cover that big meadow, because they'll have to be across the lake again before the first stack flares up. And they'll have another use for the truck—to carry their cans of kerosene and a box of candles.

"This is how they'll do the job, Janet. They'll scoop out a little cave in the lee of a stack, so the wind won't blow out the lighted candle they'll set there in a base of kerosene-soaked hay. In two hours the candle will burn down to its base—and bingo! the stack's afire. I hope Tom will figure that out. If he gets the men but lets the hay go up in smoke, I'm afraid he'll be out the best job he's ever going to have. I hope he'll get there in time."

"He will," Janet assured Lanier. "He was moving fast the last I saw of him, and I'm sure he'll have time to get there and intercept them. They can not work in the dark very well, so they'll wait until the moon comes up. We have a full moon tonight."

"I never thought of that. Janet, you're the shadow of a rock in a weary land."

"That's the second time you've told me that. And still you're resolved to banish me."

She stood beside him a moment, wondering how she was going to say goodby to him in his extremity.

"I'll not be seeing you again," she said finally. "So goodby again, old Funny Face. Goodby and good luck. I'll be gone early in the morning."

He did not answer her.

She went out into the living room, selected a book from his small but distinguished library, and sat down before the log fire to read until Tom Harmon telephoned a report of his night's work. She had a feeling, amounting to a conviction, that he would report in.

CHAPTER SIXTEEN

UPON LEAVING JANET, TOM HARMON RAN over to the ranch mess hall, where the men were sitting smoking their after-dinner cigarettes. He went straight to the wall telephone and rang three long bells repeatedly. Receiving no answer, he turned to face the company.

"Two of Landrum's killers are in the valley tonight," he announced. "Big Foot, you take Skunk Tallow and Little Coyote and Felix, and guard the Big House until morning. If you see anybody prowling around there, shoot first and investigate afterward."

Before he could give them their orders the Sphinx twins were hurrying from the mess hall.

"Saddle my horse, too," Harmon called after them.

He permitted himself a small smile. Smart pair, the twins. Not having been assigned to duty at the Big House, they knew there was work afoot elsewhere and that Tom Harmon would lead them to it.

Harmon ate his supper hastily and went to his own cottage for his leather jerkin, his six-shooter, rifle, and ammunition. When he emerged, the twins were waiting for him, mounted and leading his horse. He swung into the saddle and cantered out of the quadrangle formed by the cluster of ranch buildings, the twins at his heels, taking the road that ran parallel to the high-line irrigation ditch. The faint sheen of starlight on the water enabled them to keep to the road in the darkness. An hour's riding at the little, easy cat-lope of the trained cow horses, and they passed through a gate into the great meadow. Here one of the twins spoke.

"They got Theodore, Tom."

"Sure. His light's out, an' he didn't answer the telephone."

"Moon's comin' up," the other twin announced.

"Don't be such chatterboxes," Tom Harmon warned, and cantered across the meadow until he reached a grove of firs about fifty yards from one of the stacks. They backed their horses into the deep shadow and dismounted.

"Tie their tongues down," Harmon commanded. "Can't have 'em nickerin' an' givin' us away. Then lead 'em off on a flank. Don't figger on gettin' any horses killed, either."

The horses' tongues were tied down with buckskin thongs.

"I think they're out to burn the hay," Harmon explained then. "Naturally they'll start with the stacks farthest from the lake an' work toward the lake. They came in a boat. They'll follow the old road from Theodore's shack up to this first line o' hay stacks, an' I'm figgerin' they'll start with the stack yonder, on the sheltered side of it. The feller that plants the lighted candle will have to crawl in under the barbed wire fence around the stack. [The stacks were all fenced to keep the cattle from them until the season for hay feeding should commence.] It'll be bright moonlight, but they won't see us in the shadow o' these firs, so we ought to get them from here. If we don't get 'em—an' I don't claim to be no dead shot in the moonlight—they may hide behind the stack an' fight it out. So we won't take chances. We don't any of us want to get killed, an' we can afford to lose one stack o' hay to save our skins."

He chuckled malevolently and from his inner breast pocket drew a small cardboard carton. From his side coat pocket he produced a candle and a six-ounce bottle; then he strolled over to the windward side of the stack, lighted the candle, dropped some grease on the bottom of the carton and in its center, pinched out the light, stuck his candle in the grease, tucked short wisps of hay around the base of the candle, and poured on this inflammable material the contents of the bottle. Then he relit the candle, gouged out a little orifice in the base of the stack, tucked the carton into it, and piled some hay in front of it. Satisfied that the burning candle would not be seen, he rejoined his men.

The moon rose above the mountains to the east

and shed its light over Lonely Valley. The brilliance increased as the moon mounted into the heavens. Sleeping cattle could be discerned faintly for a distance of three hundred yards.

Suddenly the watchers in the little grove heard the distant sound of a heavy blow, followed by a metallic crashing. Nobody made any comment on this, for all three men knew the sound had been made by Theodore's truck striking a loose plank in a rough bridge over one of the smaller irrigation ditches. The truck, running without headlights, had struck the bridge at too high a rate of speed. As it approached, the rattle of its progress became more and more audible. Presently they saw its dark bulk leave the road along the western fringe of the meadow and come straight across the field toward the stack they watched. It pulled up in the lee of the stack, and two men got down off the seat. One walked around the truck and stood at the left front wheel with the truck between him and the group beside the fir tree, while the other lifted a five-gallon can from the truck and carried it to the fence. He shoved it under the lowest wire and crawled in after it.

He was busy at the side of the stack for about a minute, then Tom Harmon saw him strike a light and stand up.

"Let him have it," he ordered in a low voice.

The volley crashed out, but the man at the stack

did not fall. Instead, he ran around to the other end of the stack. An instant later a steady spray of fire came from the truck; a stream of bullets whispered over the heads of Harmon and his men, and with one accord they bent low, separated and got behind trees, where they cast themselves flat on the ground.

"Machine gun," Tom Harmon yelled during a momentary pause in the firing. "Those skunks are smarter'n I thought. Kept one man on guard! Don't shoot, or you'll be a target. He can't see us."

Evidently the same strategy occurred to the man crouching behind the truck. As his legs were not visible, Harmon concluded he had crawled up on the running board, where he would be protected by the body of the automobile. For the nonce, therefore, the affair was a stalemate.

"Are you O.K., Twins?" Harmon called.

"O.K.," they replied in unison.

"It'll be too bad for you, when daylight comes," taunted the man behind the truck.

"That's what I'm waitin' for—better shootin' light," Harmon shouted back.

The tittering laugh of the Sphinx twins was audible.

Thus an hour passed. Then, from the truck, the taunting voice reached them.

"The stack ain't goin' to burn. One of your bullets must have snuffed the candle—if that's what you're waitin' for."

"You must be kinder cramped over there, mister," Harmon called back cheerfully. "But don't worry. We'll move you right pronto now."

As he spoke, a tongue of flame licked up from the windward side of the haystack. When a half-minute had passed it was roaring up the stack and spreading along the sides and top. The men in the clump of firs waited patiently, for they knew the heat of the conflagration would drive the man from the far end of the truck into the open, and force the man behind the stack to evacuate or roast.

The scene was now illuminated brilliantly. The moment for final action had come, and the man behind the truck knew it. He rolled from his cramped position and stood up. Over in the clump of firs he saw about half a man's body behind a tree and fired at it instantly.

A second later the twins fired, and the man's head and shoulders disappeared behind the truck, but they could see his body outstretched on the ground. They charged toward the truck.

A glance showed their work in that quarter had been completed, so they circled the blazing stack. Far out in the field they saw the other man running. They emptied their magazines at him, and he fell; whereupon they risked a scorching to run the truck out into the field to save it from being burned. Then they went back to their old haven in the fir grove.

"Get 'em?" Tom Harmon demanded.

"You bet!"

"Well, anyhow—it was a—small stack. I'm tunneled. Put me—in the truck—an' carry me up to—the Big House—after you've called at—Theodore's cabin."

A quarter of an hour later Theodore and his squaw, lying bound and gagged on the floor of their cabin, heard somebody walk in. Then that somebody struck a match and lighted the kerosene lamp on the kitchen table, glanced around him—and grunted after the fashion of one who has discovered no more than he has expected to discover. He removed the gags from the mouths of Theodore and his squaw and untwisted from their wrists, knees, and ankles the pieces of copper telegraph wire with which they had been trussed up. Having completed his office, he went outside without once having spoken, and climbed up on the driver's seat of Theodore's truck.

Theodore and his squaw stiffly followed him out. Well up in the bed of the truck and under the driver's seat they saw Tom Harmon lying on a bed of hay. In the rear of the truck body two other men lay, sprawled on each other, but there was no hay under them. The other twin rode his horse, leading the other two.

Theodore leaned in and touched Tom Harmon on the brow, whereupon that individual opened his eyes and said cheerfully:

"Hello, Theodore. Next time you—have visitors—don't answer the knock—at the front door. Get your gun—sneak out the back door—and surprise 'em."

The white blood in Theodore made him articulate. "Tom, Tom," he pleaded, "what happened?"

"They tunneled me."

"But we got the skunks right here," the twin who was riding announced, and they drove away.

CHAPTER SEVENTEEN

AS THE NIGHT PASSED, JANET LAID ASIDE HER book and surrendered her mind to contemplation of her private affairs. Her conversation with Tom Harmon that afternoon was recalled. Until Lanier had so suddenly dismissed her, she had thought vaguely of telling him that she was now the owner of that quarter section of worthless land that for more than forty years had been as a pistol pointed at the Lanier heads. Because of her sympathy for him she had considered assuring him of safety in that quarter. She was glad now that she had not done so, for it would have constituted a deplorable weakness, a ruling of herself by her emotions rather than by her head. Of course, she felt desperately sorry for him.

What woman wouldn't? He was the sort of man any woman would yearn to help, to protect. But—after all—he was practically a stranger to her, so why should she even remotely contemplate sacrificing her own financial interests to aid his? Five hundred thousand dollars Tom Harmon thought she could get from Milo Landrum for her land if and when he was satisfied that Raynor Lanier was helpless, headed for bankruptcy. Of course, this was merely Tom Harmon's opinion, yet Janet knew it had merit.

Five hundred thousand dollars! Well, suppose she sold it for half that. An income of a thousand dollars a month—a cute little four-room apartment in New York—trips to Bermuda and Florida—a summer in Europe—all the good shows in town—a jewel of a Swiss maid she knew of—her frocks without months of saving, of figuring, of miles walked and days spent searching for bargains. . . .

She strove to convince herself that she felt for Raynor Lanier a just resentment due to his shabby treatment of her. He had given her a check for a thousand dollars—a sum he could not remotely afford. He wanted to be magnificent; his prideful spirit would not brook the thought of financial obligation to her, although she had thrust other and more valuable obligations upon him. Well, he couldn't help that. She found herself making a sorry failure of her attempt to dislike him, or even feel a fair element of annoyance toward him. Whatever had caused him to wish to dispense with her services immediately was his own business. After all, she was a trained nurse, and trained nurses come and go. They live for a while in other people's houses, stumble over other people's secrets, pocket their checks, and go, leaving behind them ruthlessly the beginnings of what might have been fine and wholesome friendships; they do not come back unless invited.

The ancient clock over the mantel struck eleven. How long she had sat there pondering all this! And then the knocker on the front door struck loudly—once, twice, thrice—and Raynor Lanier called from his room:

"Janet! Janet! Come here—quickly!"

She ran down the hall to his room.

"My pistol is in the lower drawer of the bureau," he said eagerly. "Get it for me—and leave the door open. Somebody is at the front door. Remember, somebody called to see my father—by God, if they've called to see me, let them in! Lift me up in bed. Straight up, please . . . It's late—and nobody comes visiting in Lonely Valley after dark."

She got out pistol and belt. He threw open the cylinder and spun it, snapped it closed again.

"Now open the door and let them in," he commanded. "Do not be frightened. They won't

161

harm you. I'm the prize they're after—but they've got to fight for it."

Janet was trembling violently as she threw open the front door. On the porch without stood the Sphinx twins, each with an arm hooked under the arm of Tom Harmon, whose body hung limp in their grasp, his feet buckling oddly under him. They half-dragged, half-carried him in, and a tiny trickle of blood made a trail behind him across the floor.

Janet stepped to the entrance to the hall and called to Raynor Lanier:

"It's all right, Ray. It's only Tom Harmon."

Then she closed the door to the hall, procured a blanket, spread it on the divan, and motioned the Sphinx twins to lay Tom Harmon on it. Having done this, the two stood by, staring apathetically at the superintendent, vouchsafing no information.

She bent over Harmon.

"What happened, Tom? Where did they hit you?"

"Right hip an' breast . . . Lung, I guess. They had a—machine gun—Twins got—both."

He opened his eyes and smiled up at her. "Guess you're not—goin' in the mornin'—after all, Miss Janet. You wouldn't leave—a brand-new patient—in the lurch—would you?"

His lips and his mustache were fringed with a bloody froth, so she ran, got a towel, and wiped it away. Then she gave him a drink of whiskey and left to prepare a bed for him.

The Sphinx twins carried him in and assisted Janet to undress him; then one of the twins went outside and returned with a large, metallic first-aid case.

"Brought this up from Tom's house," he explained. "Always have it on hand in case o' accidents—fix a man up till the doctor comes. Thought you'd need it." He sighed deeply as if this long speech had wearied him.

Said Tom Harmon, "You two boys ain't no more use tonight, so get on with your job."

The twins clumped out, and Janet examined Harmon's wounds. The one through the hip was a flesh wound, and the bullet had missed the bone. There was a small shred of his trousers imbedded in the wound, and this she removed. The bullet through his right breast had passed between the ribs and emerged two inches from his spine; an examination of his clothing convinced her that no particle of his leather jerkin or shirt had been carried into his body, nor was he bleeding profusely.

"Well, there's nothing to do, Tom, except wash your wounds with a sterile solution and put an antiseptic dressing on them," she announced.

She found the necessary materials for the operation in the portable medicine cabinet, and when the dressing had been completed she tucked him under the bedclothes, washed his face and hands, and gave him another drink of whiskey. There was nothing else she could do. If he lived—he lived. If he died—he died.

He declared his wounds did not hurt half so much as a toothache he had once had. "Only burned one stack," he started to tell her, but she forbade further speech.

"We'll learn all about that tomorrow," she warned. "The effort of talking might bring on a real hemorrhage."

But Tom Harmon was undisciplined. "Good thing—Ray's on the mend—an' able to take—my place—while I'm laid up. Ain't you glad—they shot—me, Miss Janet?"

"I'm not, Tom, you poor thing. Why should I be?"

There was a leer of infinite cunning in Harmon's plain features as he replied: "Because it—gives me—legitimate—personal grudge agin Landrum—from tonight on. Ray can't—deny me my—innings now—can he? If he does—won't obey him. Case now o' which—one of us—gets Landrum first—an' if you play your cards—right—an' keep Ray in Lonely Valley—I'll get well—an' beat him to Landrum—an' then you won't never be—unhappy about—blood on Ray's—hands. Then folks—can't say he's—a killer—like his—father an'—grandfather."

Her emotion almost choked her. She stood, humble and abashed, in the presence of his nobility. And he didn't even know how noble he was—or that he was noble at all, in fact. He strove merely to be practical.

She turned out the light and went to Ray Lanier's room. He still held his pistol.

"I heard a car come up the hill," he said. "Who was it? Where from? Where's Tom Harmon?"

She explained the situation to him fully.

"Is Tom going to die?" He exhibited neither sorrow nor surprise.

"Perhaps not. People frequently recover from lung punctures, provided there are no complications. I should say he stands better than an even chance, for he has the physique of a grizzly bear."

"Before you go tomorrow," he begged her, "telephone to Reno and have a doctor and two nurses sent over in a plane. Got to have the best for old Tom."

"And after that I can go?"

"Yes."

"Well, I'll not," she burst out on him furiously. "You're not the only person to be considered here. Tom Harmon is just about the finest man I've ever met, and I'd die if some other nurse took care of him. I'll stick until Tom is out of danger, and then I'll go, and in the meantime, Mr. Raynor Lanier, all I want from you is civility and not too much of that. And I've burned your check."

"Very well, Miss Pepperpot. Please put my gun back in the bureau. You must think I'm a timid person to have asked you to get me my gun, but I never take undue chances. Then will you please be good enough to leave me alone. . . . You can drive me crazy without quarreling with me, you know."

"I hate you," Janet flung at him.

"That's good. I have a break in my bad luck— at last. Good night. Please do not neglect Tom."

She knew he was deliberately taunting her now, and it enraged her to realize that he had the power to do this. He tried to meet her fiery glance bravely, but eventually quailed before it, and instantly, as she beheld his hang-dog look, her heart softened toward him once more.

"You're not much of a success as a snarly-yow, are you, Ray?" she taunted him in turn.

He did not answer, but turned his back upon her and hid with his hand the exposed side of his face, like a sulky litle boy.

Janet turned on another light. "The back of your neck is rosy red, too," she said gently. "Why don't you draw the blankets over your head and hide that blush also?"

He drew them over his head with a savage jerk, and Janet thought she had never seen anything so ludicrous. She had a mad desire to hug him for it.

"He's just an overgrown little boy," she went on aloud, "and he talks about killing people. And he sulks, too. Gets all snarled up in his thoughts and sulks, and what a sight is that, my countrymen?"

He heaved himself out on the edge of the bed, stooped, found his slippers, put them on, and donned his dressing gown which lay across the back of a chair. Janet went quickly to him to steady him.

"Get back into bed," she commanded.

Instead of obeying her he threw an arm around her shoulders.

"Help me into Tom's room," he ordered in a choking voice. "I've got to see the old boy. Got to show some interest in him—dying, perhaps—in my service."

She saw that he was suffering far more than she had suspected in view of the almost stolid manner in which he had received the news of Harmon's mishap.

She supported his trembling body down the hall to the room where Tom Harmon lay gazing calmly up at the ceiling. A lump came in her throat when she saw him reach for Harmon's hand and hold it in silence, and when Harmon, to hide his embarrassment at this touch of affection and concern, growled like a broody hen:

"Get to hell out of here, Ray. The way you act—folks would think—I was hurt—more or less."

Lanier sat down on the edge of the bed, but he did not let go his man's hand. Janet saw his chin tremble ever so little, and the thought came to her that between some men there can exist a fraternal affection so profound it can be understood but not expressed. She left the room, feeling that her presence was an inexcusable intrusion.

She went out on the veranda to be alone with her thoughts. The full moon was directly overhead, its effulgence casting a broad streak of silver light down the length of Lonely Valley Lake. A breeze had come up, and the soft swish of the waves upon the shore came up to her like a continuous sigh, as if the lake grieved for the men who had died because of it. The ranch buildings loomed lonely and mysterious; she heard the distant lowing of a cow. From the grass along the creek came the quack of ducks feeding, and afar a tiny pinprick of light gleamed, proof that Theodore and his wife were safe again in their cabin at the outpost.

Big Foot came around the corner of the house with a bucket, a mop, and a rake. He raked the fine trap rock on the drive in front of the house, then with his mop obliterated thoroughly the gory trail made by Tom Harmon when the twins had carried him into the house. She opened the door and pointed to the same trail on the floor of the living room, and Big Foot grunted and carefully mopped that clean. Then he looked up inquiringly at her.

"Tom die?"

"No. I think he will get well."

"Mebbe so you let Big Foot see Tom?"

She took him down to Harmon's room. Tom was smoking a cigarette. He waved a careless hand at Big Foot.

"Big Foot makem all things clean," the old Indian announced. "Sheriff come no looksee blood."

"It's agin the law," Tom Harmon said to Janet, "but there—ain't no law—in Lonely Valley but—the Lanier law. Please give that old—*colorado maduro*—horsethief—a big drink—o' whiskey. He's shakin'—an' I know—why."

Janet forcibly removed the cigarette from Harmon's lips.

"Take him, Big Foot," she ordered, indicating Raynor Lanier, and Big Foot picked his youthful boss up and carried him back to his room.

"I have two children to care for now, instead of one," the girl complained.

"Please bring the bottle and two glasses in here," Lanier begged gently. "Big Foot and Big Boss are going to pin one on together."

"Lonely Valley," Janet cried out at him, "is the habitat of lunatics. I have never before met such crazy men as you and Tom Harmon."

"You'd be surprised at the things you can scare up out of the tall timber, Janet."

"You're a pair of antiques in a modern setting."

"I hope you like antiques, Janet."

To her own amazement and disgust she choked

back her tears. She thought: "Lonely men in Lonely Valley! And this one drinks with his Indian! The prideful democrat!"

To Raynor Lanier she said,

"Where I come from a man would not drink with his servant."

"Big Foot," he replied, "is not a servant. He is my Indian father. I am blood brother of the tribe, duly initiated, and my Indian name is White Pelican. Even as a child my beak was fairly prominent."

Impulsively she reached over and tweaked his beak.

He grasped her hand and held it a moment, and there was that in his eyes which Janet knew no woman had ever seen before. Her heart was singing as she left him, but she did not wonder why. She knew. She loved him; she knew he loved her. But he would not tell her so. . . .

Why? Well, that was a bridge they would cross when they came to it.

CHAPTER EIGHTEEN

JANET WATCHED TOM HARMON CAREFULLY throughout the night, but he developed no alarming symptoms and she was satisfied that he was bleeding very little internally, for only occasionally would he cough and raise a little blood. She had anticipated that he would exhibit more signs of shock, but he declared that being shot wasn't half the hardship of having to drink milk—and he a cowman!

When she brought Lanier's breakfast tray in to him she reported on Harmon's condition. "Unless pneumonia sets in, or a piece of his clothing has been carried by the bullet into the lung, I think he will make a quick recovery," she said. "You will understand, Ray, that a bullet passing through tissue cauterizes it with the friction and hence sterilizes it. If no foreign and unsterilized substance has been carried into the wound, I shall not worry about him."

"We can't take a chance," he replied. "Telephone that doctor in Reno and tell him to fly over here with another trained nurse, and never mind the expense."

"There is really nothing that the doctor can do, although I'll telephone him the first sign of disturbing complications. Lung wounds can't be probed for foreign substances, such as a fragment of cloth. If Tom has anything like that in him, he'll die. The care of his wounds is simple enough."

"I dare say you are entirely capable of caring for him, Janet, but—"

"Do you wish to have the news of this shooting affray known, Ray?"

"No, no, of course not."

"Then don't send for the doctor unless an emergency presents itself."

"Doctors can be trusted with a patient's secret."

"Not this kind of patient. When a doctor is called to treat a gunshot wound or a stab wound, it is his duty to report the case to the nearest peace officer. If he refuses or neglects to do this, and the news leaks out, he may lose his license to practise. Only disreputable practitioners risk that."

He grimaced in disgust. "The sheriff and the district attorney came around after my father was shot. They tried to make me admit that I had killed the man who shot him and dumped his body on Landrum's porch, but I proved I had been camped with my men near Modoc City when it happened, and swore the deed had been done by a party unknown. And that was true. I didn't know the killer—both Big Foot and Skunk Tallow got a shot at him. I did not know which one had hit him. The district attorney or the sheriff will be around again today—probably late this afternoon. They have to motor over from the county seat."

"How are they going to know?"

"I'm not certain, but I have a suspicion Tom sent the Sphinx twins in with those two incendiaries last night, and Landrum's cook probably found them on his porch when she went out to get the milk. Tom didn't tell me this, but then he never discusses or reports the obvious. I know how he works." And Ray chuckled pleasurably. "Guess I'll get up and have a look at Thomas myself. If he's bearing up to my satisfaction, I'll risk a total lack of publicity."

Tom Harmon was not only bearing up to Lanier's satisfaction, but he was absolutely cheerful, except on one subject. Janet had removed his tobacco and cigarettes and was adamant in her determination not to give him even one little whiff. He had a degree of fever, but that was no more than was to be expected, and he was resigned to doing without a doctor for the present.

Janet bathed him, dressed his wounds again, changed the bed linen, and, leaving him in charge of Lanier, who sat in a comfortable chair opposite him, retired to her own room and slept until luncheon time. When she returned to him she found that his temperature and pulse had not altered, and he had slept some. He was in more pain, however, so she gave him some morphia to ease the pain and put him to sleep.

About two o'clock, as she and Lanier were chatting together in the living room, where Lanier was lying on the divan, the knocker on the front door was given three sharp bangs.

"Ah," Lanier murmured. "The peremptory challenge of the law. Sam Gorton is like that. He never leaves you in doubt for an instant that he is the sheriff. Ah Fong will answer."

Ah Fong did—and a short, broad man of about forty stepped briskly in. He sported the traditional headgear of a cow county sheriff, as well as handle-bar mustachios. The sight of Lanier appeared to surprise him, for he stood in the middle of the room and stared at him.

"Hello, Sam," Lanier greeted him cheerfully. "Have a seat. Miss Corliss, permit me to present Sheriff Gorton."

"Howdy, Ray. Pleased to make your acquaintance, Miss Corliss. If you don't mind, young lady, I'd like to have a word or two with Mr. Lanier in private."

"Oh, never mind her, Sam. She's my nurse, and you haven't got anything to discuss with me that I wouldn't care to have her hear. Sit down and tell me what's on your mind."

Sheriff Gorton sat down without troubling to remove his hat. He fixed Lanier with an accusative glare and said,

"Well, Ray, I see you been up to your old tricks."

"You'll have to be more explicit, Sam."

"How about them two dead men that was dumped on Milo Landrum's front porch last night?"

"Sam, I give you my word of honor this is the first news I have had of any such commendable enterprise on the part of persons who are

174

unknown to me but who, I feel assured, must be friends of mine with my interest very much at heart. Two of them, you say?"

"Two," said Gorton.

"Last time there was only one," Lanier resumed in a musing tone, "and he wasn't identified. Who were the two most recent arrivals?"

"You know mighty well who they were. Two o' Landrum's bodyguard."

"I have never seen his bodyguard. I have been dangerously ill with spotted fever for a month. This young lady is my nurse. I haven't been out of the house. In fact, this is the first day I have been up, and as you may have noticed, I'm not dressed. Just lazying around, trying to get back my strength."

"You have employees."

"Yes—and if those two men bumped into my employees on this ranch and were recognized, you can bet your sweet life they never got out of Lonely Valley the way they came in. Have you any idea, Sam, where they were killed—and how?"

"One was hit through the head once from in front, and the other got it three times through the body from in back."

"Why, he must have been running, Sam."

"Plain case o' murder, Ray."

"Well, what do you expect me to do about it—sit down and cry?"

"I expect you to come clean with me."

"You're an optimist."

"Ray Lanier, I'm goin' to land the parties that done this."

"Why such an active interest in Landrum's bodyguard? A bodyguard is well paid to take undue risks. Those two men must have gone out looking for trouble and bumped into more than they could handle. Of course, I realize you have to make some sort of official investigation, but why didn't you start in with Landrum?"

"He don't know a thing about it."

"You mean he wouldn't tell. Well, why do you expect me to help you make a success of your investigation? I'm not seeking publicity. I tell you I had nothing to do with that killing, but if you want to scout over the ranch and interview my employees I have no objection. You might find blood-stains and empty cartridge shells, although I doubt that any of my men would be so stupid as not to clean up after their job."

"Look here, Lanier, I ain't goin' to waste my time foolin' with you. You tell me you been sick, but you're all over it now an' busy gettin' back your strength. Well, you can spend a few days in my jail gettin' it back, because I'm here to arrest you for murder or subornin' murder. Get dressed an' come with me."

But Raynor Lanier only smiled and shook his head. "No use, Sam. You'd never get by my outpost on top of the hill. My men would be instantly suspicious if they saw me riding in your car."

"I got a posse outside."

"And have you a warrant for my arrest?"

"No, I can arrest you on suspicion."

"And while you're driving me into the county seat somebody will take a shot at me from the timber, eh? Really, I couldn't allow that. I'll go peaceably with you, however, provided my men, mounted, are permitted to ride ahead and on each side of the road through the timber."

"You'll be safe with me. I'm runnin' this show."

"It was Landrum's idea that you come out here and arrest me on suspicion, was it not?"

"He seemed to think you was the only one he could, in fairness, suspicion."

"Well, I suspect him of being far from philanthropic where I am concerned, so unless my riders can be part of the procession I really don't see how I can go with you."

"Get up an' dress," Gorton commanded.

Raynor Lanier sat up, reached under the pillow on which he had been reclining, and produced a pistol of a size and caliber popular with the Lanier clan for half a century. "Now, then, Sam, what about it? Are you going peaceably, or must I create a scene in the presence of the lady? Confound you, Sam, you force me to be impolite to a guest in my own house. Get going. Ah Fong!" he shouted.

Ah Fong appeared from the kitchen, took in the situation at a glance, and opened the door leading to the veranda.

"You wouldn't dare shoot," Gorton sneered—and Lanier fired.

The sheriff's hat flew off his head.

"You shouldn't keep your hat on your head in the house and in the presence of a lady," he reproved Gorton mildly. "On your way, or I'll kill you where you sit."

Gorton shot out through the door like a frightened rabbit, and Ah Fong closed and locked it.

Lanier stared at the bullet hole in the oak wainscoting. "Got to put a new piece in there," he told Janet. "Sorry I had to frighten you, but Sam needed persuading. He bluffed—and I bluffed just a little harder."

"Oh, Ray, you'll be in such trouble!" Janet was deathly pale and trembling.

He shrugged. From the front of the house came the sound of an automobile starting, and Lanier walked unsteadily to the window and looked out. "Six of them in a seven-passenger car, Janet. They're going. And Sam Gorton forgot to pick up his hat. They must have cut the telephone line from the outpost, or Hugo would have telephoned me they were coming." He yawned. "Life is full of trouble, isn't it? How soundly old Tom sleeps! He didn't hear that shot."

"But Gorton will return with a warrant."

"No," he told her decisively. "He'll confer with Landrum, who will forbid the banns, now that the first plan didn't work. Gorton will not be anxious to return. He's a fool, but not such a fool as to beard the Lanier in his den—put over a raid without a shred of evidence to justify it. What I know I know, but what Gorton knows he imagines. And one of the things he imagines strongly is that he can't get me out of Lonely Valley without a pitched battle. Janet, how about a game of dominoes?"

But Janet retreated to the haven of Tom Harmon's room to reorganize her shattered nerves. When she returned two hours later, Raynor Lanier was asleep, with a stock magazine spread over his face. In a corner of the room she saw Big Foot and, close to his hand, a rifle. In the kitchen Skunk Tallow sat, with a rifle close to his hand also. And about eight o'clock that night the Sphinx twins came up and relieved the Indians.

CHAPTER NINETEEN

THE FOLLOWING DAY TOM HARMON'S temperature was down half a degree; he was a healthy fellow, and his wounds started to heal by first intention. When three days had passed, Janet felt assured that pneumonia would not develop and ceased to worry over him. And then they had another visitor. This time it was Lee Elkins, the district attorney, a well-dressed young man of pleasant address. Janet realized, by the very inflection of his voice as Lanier had greeted Elkins, that Elkins was a welcome visitor. She was certain of this when Lanier summoned Ah Fong and ordered drinks.

"Well, Ray, I see you've been having adventures again," Elkins announced in the casual tone of one who states a fact and anticipates no denial of it.

"Yes, Lee, we had a little ruckus here a few nights ago. Have you seen Gorton?"

Elkins nodded and grinned. "He didn't get far, did he?"

"No. I haven't a great deal of confidence in Sam. He's too windy. And he's too close to Landrum. Landrum made a great fight for him the last time Sam ran for office. Spent quite a little money on his campaign. I suppose, Lee, you came over to get the straight of it from me?"

"If you care to tell me. I don't know anything, and neither does Sam Gorton, and I know you and your people well enough to realize that if we're going to ascertain anything you'll have to tell us."

"I'll tell you, but not Sam Gorton."

"Sam has been picking on me to issue a warrant for your arrest, together with a dozen John Doe warrants, so he can arrest your entire crew. I thought I should consult you before issuing them. Gorton has no objection to making an official fool of himself, but I have."

"I knew you'd do that, Lee." And without the slightest hesitation—without even exacting a pledge of silence from the district attorney— Lanier told him the story of the fight at the haystack, concealing only the identity of the men who had participated in it. He even exhibited the machine guns which the twins had captured.

"And there's a skiff down at Theodore's cabin and a new outboard motor. I imagine we could trace the owner of that motor by the number on it; perhaps we could even trace the builder of the boat, for it is of recent origin and home-made. But why bother? I know who's back of it all, and when the final accounting is due, justice will be done."

"Well," Lee Elkins decided, "we'll hold an inquest tomorrow and decide that the deceased came to their deaths at the hands of a party or parties unknown. That will end it, as far as my office is concerned. Your people are plainly in the clear, and I doubt if I could convict Landrum of anything. He's smart. He covers up rather well. By the way, he's sick abed. Almost had a stroke when he found his men had been sent back to him that way."

"You knew, of course, Lee, that he took a shot

at me in Modoc City not much more than a month ago?"

"Yes, I heard about that. Going to prosecute him?"

"No. I have a sound legal reason now for believing my life is in danger from Landrum."

"You're a Lanier through and through. Landrum, of course, thought his life in danger from you."

"It was—although I never threatened him, Lee. Well, when I pay my debt to that buzzard—as I shall—do you think I'll go to the pen for it?"

"I do not. You have no enemies in this county, and Landrum has a great number. No jury would convict you. I'd have to prosecute you, of course, but in all honesty I'd move dismissal of the charge on the grounds that it was justifiable homicide and that a conviction would be impossible—a trial merely a waste of the taxpayers' money."

Lanier cast a slow sideways glance at Janet, followed by the ghost of a triumphant smile. He turned to the district attorney.

"Better stay all night, Lee. I'll fix you up with some shooting clothes and a shotgun. My duck pond has been baited for a month, and the blind is dry. Better go down and enjoy yourself this afternoon. A high wind is blowing, and the birds will be pitching into that pond by the hundreds. They don't like to stay out on the lake when there are whitecaps on it. Geese should be in shortly."

"Thanks, Ray, I will."

He turned to Janet.

"I suppose you haven't had a very pleasant time in Lonely Valley, have you, Miss Corliss?"

"You," she replied, "constitute the first pleasant note in my life for a month."

"She thinks I'm a bloodthirsty savage, Lee."

"Man, she's right! Don't worry about him killing Milo Landrum, Miss Corliss. The minute Landrum gets back on his feet, he'll have urgent business elsewhere. Right now he's a badly frightened man. You see," he went on, "Ray and I have been friends since childhood. So I called on Landrum and had a little confidential chat with him. Told him he needn't expect me to work myself ill trying to convict Ray Lanier after Ray killed him. I urged him to go away from this country. And on my way back through Modoc City I'll tell him that if he declines to make himself scarce I'll send the Grand Jury after him. He'll go."

Tom Harmon improved steadily, but for reasons of his own he claimed he felt poorly. He said there was a mysterious pain in his chest and declared it would be months before he could sit a horse again. Janet had a suspicion he was shamming merely to keep her on in Lonely Valley, for with the first healing of the holes in him she knew he would no longer require her services.

A week after Lee Elkins' visit Raynor Lanier left the house for the first time. He had gained in flesh and strength at an amazing rate. Janet found him one morning mounting a horse in front of the house. He was booted and spurred and wore black Angora goatskin chaps and a leather coat with a high fur collar that came up around his ears; he carried a pistol on his hip, and she saw the stock of a rifle protruding from the scabbard on his saddle. To Janet he appeared quite a romantic figure. The Sphinx twins were in attendance and rode off behind him. When he returned for luncheon, the pallor of his recent illness and confinement to the house was gone; he was ruddy, clear-eyed, and as happy as a child.

"Rode down to the big meadow as far as Theodore's outpost. Prowled around and looked at the cattle," he announced. "They look well, and there's grass enough for another month; after that we'll have to start feeding some hay. But ten miles in the saddle was enough for me. I came home in Theodore's truck."

He kicked off his chaps in the living room and went whistling through the house as if he hadn't a care in the world. The following day he asked Janet to go to Modoc City with him in her car. He spent an hour there in the general store, purchasing cheap heavy underwear, overalls and shirts, bolts of cloth goods, shoes and stockings for women, a ten-pound tub of the sort of candy known as "grocers' mixed," a half-dozen bright plaid shawls, and several sacks of beans, onions, and potatoes.

"Christmas presents for my Indians, male and female," he confided to Janet. "Now you help me pick things for the kids."

The bill amounted to over five hundred dollars and he wrote a check for it. Janet wanted to reprove him for his prodigality, and he seemed to sense this, for he said:

"Usually I give the tribe only half a dozen old cows to slaughter, but I'm providing an extra big Christmas this year, because it's liable to be the last."

They had left the general store and were walking across the sidewalk to Janet's car when she saw Milo Landrum coming up the street. He still limped and walked with a cane. Raynor Lanier saw him and stood watching his enemy approach; apparently Landrum did not observe him until a distance of but sixty feet separated them, and then his right hand went up, palm out, in the ancient Indian sign of peace. Instantly Raynor Lanier's arm went up in the same sign— and Landrum came on. They did not remove their glances from each other; as Landrum was about to pass he said in a low mumble,

"I'm not heeled, Lanier."

"I wouldn't shoot it out with an unarmed cripple, Landrum. How soon do you anticipate being able to walk without a cane?"

"Couple o' weeks."

"You'll keep that long, but see that you're wearing your weapon when next we meet."

"I'm through wearin' weapons," Landrum replied. "They only git a man into trouble."

Only the tensity of the situation deterred Janet from bursting into laughter at the look that came over Raynor Lanier's face as Milo Landrum made his remarkable pronouncement. It was the first time she had seen Lanier absolutely deprived of his mental equilibrium.

"Why—why—you cowardly sneak," he ground out. "So you figure I'll not draw on an unarmed man."

"I hear that's something your father an' grandfather never done."

Lanier's arm shot out; he grasped Landrum by the collar.

"You led from a sneak that time, but you've played the hand all wrong, Landrum. This just doesn't happen to be your day to die. I didn't come in to town today to get you. But one day I'm coming and whether you're armed or not that day, you're going to pay your debt to my father."

And he ran his hands over Landrum's person.

A voice of authority spoke just behind Lanier.

"Leggo him, Lanier.

Lanier removed his hand from Landrum's collar. "I wasn't going to hurt him, Sam. Just wanted to hold him while I talked to him and frisked him for weapons. He's in no danger. I'm going to let him have a Merry Christmas."

Lanier turned to face the sheriff but Janet, who had retreated to the door of the general store the moment she sighted Landrum, never took her glance off the latter. As Lanier turned to face Sam Gorton, she saw Landrum's hand steal slowly up to his lower right vest pocket. There was something so furtive in his action that automatically she ran toward him. She was within two feet of him when his hand came out of the pocket, and in it Janet saw a very short pistol. She launched herself at him, seized his wrist with both hands, and bent the weapon downward, at the same time screaming,

"Ray, he's armed!"

Ray Lanier whirled and drove his right fist into Landrum's side. The older man collapsed instantly, and Lanier placed his foot across Landrum's wrist, pinning it to the wooden sidewalk; then he stooped and picked up a double-barreled Derringer, of .44 caliber and with both barrels loaded.

"Gimme that," Sam Gorton ordered, and Janet saw him jab Lanier in the small of the back with his six-shooter. "You don't kill nobody with me around."

"No, but Landrum would have killed me with you around, and you would have sworn he did it in self-defense, merely because I was fool enough to lay my hands on him. He said he wasn't armed—and I wanted to make sure he told the truth—so I frisked him for a regular weapon. He held out on me. Had this Derringer in his vest pocket and tried to shoot me when I turned to speak to you."

"We'll discuss that later, Lanier. Put both hands up over your head an' close together."

Lanier obeyed, and Sam Gorton snapped handcuffs on him.

"Got you, didn't I?" he exulted. "Knew if I hung around until you left Lonely Valley you'd spend Christmas in my jail. I'm goin' to charge you with assault to commit murder . . . lemme see. Yep, you're wearin' a gun, too. So I'll also charge you with carryin' a concealed weapon."

He reached up, removed the Derringer from Lanier's hand, and put it in his own vest pocket. Then he unbuckled Lanier's belt with the holstered pistol attached and hung it over his arm. He placed his own gun back in its holster and then, deeming his prisoner safe for the moment, he bent over the prostrate Landrum and shook him gently. Landrum was not unconscious; he was suffering agony, however, from the pain of the blow, and all the wind had been knocked out of him.

And then Janet Corliss gave evidence of the pugnacity and partizanship inherited from Donald MacLean. She remembered that in her handbag she carried still the little pearl-handled .32 caliber revolver with which she had armed herself for her drive alone across the continent. She opened the bag and, unseen by Sam Gorton, passed the gun, butt first, to Ray, who grasped it eagerly, despite his manacled wrists.

Sheriff Gorton lifted Landrum to his feet and supported him about a minute; he even dusted him off and replaced his hat. Then he turned to claim his prisoner—and found himself looking down a pistol barrel.

"Up with them, Sam, my beamish boy," Lanier commanded softly, and Gorton, following a second's hesitation, obeyed. "Drop my gun and belt, Sam," Lanier continued in velvet tones. "Then drop your own. Mr. Landrum, sir, be good enough to remove your Derringer from the sheriff's person and lay it carefully on the ground. Also his keys. Now back away, both of you. That will do. Janet, please pick up that arsenal and place it in the car. Now, both of you smart Alecks will proceed to the Mountain House. I'm going home. Good morning, gents, and a Merry Christmas to you both."

As the dismal pair started down the street, Lanier backed to Janet's car parked at the curb; Janet opened the door for him and he climbed in, still facing his quarry. Then she climbed in the other door, took the wheel and started the car. In defiance of traffic regulations she turned in the middle of the street and started for Lonely Valley at fifty miles an hour. A mile outside Modoc City she pulled up, unlocked the handcuffs; then sped on again. Lanier had not spoken, and she found herself incapable of speaking to him. She could not have found words to express her thoughts; she could not even look at him, for all her attention was required for the road.

Suddenly he said, "Stop, Janet, please."

She obeyed mechanically, and he got out, lifted up the rumble seat, and abstracted a rifle and two boxes of ammunition.

"Sam and one or two of his deputies will be almost certain to get a car and follow, Janet. They'll have rifles—and they can drive this road much faster than you can and with more safety. So I'll wait here and stop them on this sharp curve, when they slow up. You wait a few hundred yards up the road and I'll rejoin you presently."

He stepped off the road into the timber and disappeared. Janet drove on, and in a wide space in the road around the next curve, she pulled up to wait. About twenty minutes later he rejoined her. He was carrying three rifles now and another six-shooter. He stowed this armament in the rumble seat, took the wheel from her, and proceeded back to Lonely Valley at a leisurely pace.

After a while he said, "I love people who never ask foolish questions."

"Why should I?" she managed to say. "I can see the picture."

"I'll never see a picture half so beautiful as yourself handing me that shiny little pistol of yours, Janet. By Judas, you're taking on the protective coloration and habits of your environment."

"Was Landrum's meeting with you intentional?"

"Of course it was. Somehow he and Gorton got word that I was in town with a lady, and, of course, they knew I would avoid a brawl in your presence. So Landrum appeared on the scene to make his little play about not going armed any more. And he pretended lameness. Did you observe he left his cane where I knocked him down and didn't limp at all as he walked away with Gorton? Scheme to delude me. Sam Gorton was standing in the door of the drugstore just across the street. He's one of the best wing shots in this country and if I had reached for my gun to get Landrum, Gorton would have got me. Then Landrum saw a chance to kill me. Both he and Gorton would have sworn I was manhandling him at the time. Grand opportunity for a legal killing. If Gorton had had to plug me his excuse would have been that I had a Derringer in my hand and was resisting arrest. Undoubtedly they would have made their story stick. You would have been the only witness to contradict them— and two to one always wins." He chuckled softly.

"You didn't want to see your patient spend Christmas in jail, did you?"

"I smelled a crooked deal—and you were just too gorgeous throughout it all. Ray, I just couldn't let them triumph over you."

"You're a brick. If you hadn't acted as you did they'd have me up in court at the county seat tomorrow morning and I'd be put under very heavy bonds to keep the peace with Landrum. I might have got a jail sentence, too. The Laniers are regarded—and justly so—as bad medicine."

"What will happen now?"

"Nothing will happen while I remain in Lonely Valley. Sam Gorton will not dare come after me there. He's afraid he'd never get out alive, and I'm inclined to agree with him. Sam's as crooked as a bucket of worms—when he thinks he can get away with it—and my father and I both worked hard to defeat him for his office of sheriff. He holds grudges."

"Do you think he'll try to arrest me for handing you that gun?"

"Oh, no. He didn't see you hand it to me, and he's cussing himself for not frisking me more thoroughly. He thinks it's a little extra gun I had thrust down the band of my trousers. One he overlooked."

When they reached the outpost on top of the hill, Lanier handed over to Hugo the two rifles, the two pistols, the handcuffs and the sheriff's keys.

"Sam Gorton will be along in a little while, Hugo," he told the sentry. "I told him I'd leave these here for him. Give them to him."

"I let him go into the valley, Ray?"

"No."

"All right," Hugo replied. "Then he won't go."

Arrived at the Big House Lanier ran Janet's car into the garage, while she entered the house by the front door. When he came in through the kitchen a little later he walked straight up to her and took both of her hands in his.

"You know what I think, don't you, Janet?" he said, and then, with a bright smile, dropped her hands and turned to Tom Harmon, who had taken advantage of Janet's absence to don his employer's slippers, dressing gown, and pajamas, and take a little walk around the house.

To Harmon he related their adventure of the morning. Strangely enough, Harmon made no comment; he merely looked at Janet and smiled; his eyes were eloquent of admiration. Then, as if he had been listening to a report of the commonplace, he got out a harmonica and commenced playing softly "The Cowboy's Lament."

CHAPTER TWENTY

AFTER LUNCHEON LANIER TOOK HIS GUN AND went down to his baited duck pond near the lake. The moment Harmon and Janet were alone the former said, apropos of nothing,

"So you've made up your mind to throw in with him, eh?"

"I do not understand you, Tom."

"Goin' to let the tail go with the hide?"

"Come again, Thomas."

"You've fixed it all up with Ray, eh? Goin' to stay with us till spring?"

"Oh, no."

"I was thinkin' some," he replied mournfully, "of gettin' my sister Mollie Keyston over here for a chaperone. Mollie lost her husband six months back an' she's out of a job. You'd like Mollie, even if she is my sister."

"I'm leaving here within a week, Tom. After what happened today I know what will happen a few days from now, and I'm not going to remain and see it happen. It would be too painful. It would have happened today had I not been present. Ray was magnificent—and just because he was so magnificent—because I have become firmly convinced that he has no alternative save

194

to shoot it out with Landrum, I'm not going to remain here and embarrass him. The day after I leave Lonely Valley he'll go to Modoc City for Milo Landrum and all the fat sheriffs and deputy sheriffs in town will not stop him."

"That's why I wanted you to stay—so you'd stop him."

"I've given a great deal of thought to his situation, Tom, and have made up my mind that I haven't the most remote right to interfere, directly or indirectly. This is Ray Lanier's game, and he has to play it under his own rules. It's a terrible game to have to play, but no woman can do it for him. His fate lies on the knees of the gods."

Harmon abandoned his argument. "Better leave me your New York address, Miss Janet. You may be needed as one of Ray's witnesses. But don't you fret about him goin' to the pen. You heard what the district attorney said, didn't you?"

"I am very unhappy here," she cried desolately. "Why should I remain here and suffer? Ray Lanier's wonderful but—well, when he kills Milo Landrum he kills my only prospect for selling my land for a very great deal of money, and that destroys the sole reason for my presence in California. But I would not advance that argument in order to bend him to my desire. It is a circumstance not of Ray's making—none of his business. He must protect himself, and I think he ought to kill Landrum and do it immediately. I would—if I were in his position. Good heavens, Tom, it's the only thing to do! But I shall not be here when it's done. I—I—just couldn't bear it. Some day, when it's all over and if it has ended happily, I'd like to come back to Lonely Valley— properly chaperoned, of course. I hope that will be next spring. Ray said he would take me out into the country to look at some scattered parcels of land I own."

"You can forget about that scattered land. I've located it all on the map and I know every piece and so does Ray. Gettin' title to those patches o' range was just some more o' your granddaddy's foresightedness—just another one of his plans to ruin Felix Lanier. Those parcels o' land surround water-holes an' creeks up in the Modoc National Forest. In the days when that country was free range an' before it was all included in the Forest Reserve, anybody could file a homestead on any part of it. Your smart relative didn't file homesteads, however. He bought up a lot o' cheap land scrip an' applied it to the outright purchase o' those lands so's he could control the water on the free range. Cows got to have water, but with the water-holes fenced an' guarded Felix Lanier would have been out o' luck. He run Donald MacLean off the free range by force, but Donald MacLean wasn't licked, even if he did run away. He jes' set about plannin' to run Felix Lanier off later—by force—the force o' the law. If there was any fightin' to be done then the sheriff would have to do it. Donald MacLean had been shot up once by Felix Lanier but he didn't figure to have it happen again. He aimed to have that free summer range all to himself."

"I wonder why he didn't?"

"Maybe he didn't have enough money to buy cows to stock it. Maybe he couldn't locate the right sort o' winter range. He had to be set in a big way before declarin' war on Felix Lanier again—an' while he was gettin' set Uncle Sam came along, withdrew all that free range from entry an' included it in a Forest Reserve. So MacLean decided to forget his plan. He couldn't fight the United States Government, could he?"

With a woman's illogical viewpoint Janet said: "Why couldn't he? The land was his. He paid taxes on it. He could have fenced those water-holes had he cared to."

"If he had, the Government would have sued to have 'em condemned for public use. You try keepin' the Government out o' its grazin' fees an' see how far you get. Miss Janet, all that land ain't worth the taxes to you—an' the taxes don't amount to nothin'. Some day I'll look around for a lot o' fair government land in one solid block an' the Government'll trade you that for your water-holes, an' glad to do it."

"So then," Janet replied sadly, "I'll not come back in the spring."

"Early summer," Harmon opined, "would be better. You could come back to put flowers on his grave on Decoration Day—if you had to."

"Don't jest so, Tom, please. You'll make me cry."

"But you'll have to stay in California until after the funeral."

"Whose funeral?"

"Ray's or Landrum's. You'd come to Ray's, of course—"

"I would not. I couldn't bear it."

"If it was Landrum's you'd come up, wouldn't you—just to see Ray an' sell him your dam-site at a price he could afford to pay? Something's better'n nothin'. He'll be as liberal as he can be. In fact, when he realizes what a whalin' lot o' money he did you out o' by killin' Landrum, I got a notion he'll deed you enough land in reclaimed Lonely Valley to make up for your loss. That'd make a sizeable ranch an' you could sell it."

"No, I wouldn't permit that. I'd hold Landrum up, but not Ray Lanier. He doesn't want strangers in Lonely Valley. It's all his. After I've gone, Tom, and if and when he emerges safely from his argument with Landrum, you may tell him I own that dam-site and that he can have it for whatever he can afford to pay for it. No strings attached. I'm not an Indian giver. I'll leave a deed to it with my attorney and he can send my attorney his check. He can make the terms of payment anything he wishes."

"Come over here an' set alongside o' me," Harmon commanded in a husky voice. "Come, Miss Janet!"

She obeyed, and he put his great arm around her shoulders and drew her head down on his shoulder.

"The Lord only made one woman like you an' then He destroyed the mold," he told her. "Now, you have your little cry out an' you'll feel better. Lordy, girl, I only want you to keep Ray here until I can walk again. Haven't I told you Landrum's my meat?"

"He isn't. He's Ray Lanier's meat. And I wouldn't have Ray hide behind any man. I—I love him, Tom—and I wouldn't love—any man —who wasn't a man—clear through—and worth loving."

Said Mr. Harmon hastily: "I'm through. You win. Pack your straw suitcase an' your old carpet bag an' leave day after tomorrow. Just stay to have Christmas dinner with us." He patted her paternally. "Spunky gal, that's what you are."

"Can't stay around a man you love—when he —doesn't love you," she sobbed. "You do understand, don't you, Tom?"

"Sure, sure. I'm a smart feller, that-a-way." He sighed deeply. "Yes, I'm more or less weary o'

199

bein' a doggoned old he-chaperon. Goin' to git out o' this house when you leave an' go down to my own private shack."

"You mustn't. You've got to remain here and guard him."

"Oh, all right, all right, only I don't belong here—all weighted down with secrets an' private confidences like I am. That's the trouble with me. I got a full innercent face like a grandfather's clock, an' folks confide in me, whether I like it or not."

"Tom, you're the dearest man in the world. Will you write to me when I'm gone and tell me all about everything?"

"Yes, if you can read it. I ain't had much schoolin', Janet. Just enough to read brands an' ear-marks, but I'll do my best." And, perhaps because this was a tender subject, he hastened to change it. "I suppose you know we're going to have a Christmas tree down to the help's mess hall tonight?"

"Yes, Ray told me. He bought a lot of presents for the Indians today and the twins were to bring them out in a truck. Do you have a Christmas tree every year?"

"No. Last time was the year before Ray's mother died. Reckon it would have hurt Felix to keep up the practise. On account you're here Ray thought he'd revive the custom. Reckon the Indian kids'll like it."

After dinner that night Janet and Lanier drove down to the mess hall. They were anxious to have Tom come, but he declared the exertion would prove too great for him. Some twenty adult Indians with perhaps ten children were gathered in the yard in front of the mess hall awaiting their arrival.

Ray and Janet were received with the customary Indian silence, although Big Foot, being the chief, said:

"Hello, Ray. Hello, Miss Lady. Pretty nice you give Modocs big time. Everybody happy and say thank you."

He then turned to his people and made a brief speech.

"He's telling them about you and what a different sort of white woman you are," Lanier explained.

"It takes him a long time to say it, Ray."

"Oh, he's telling them other things, but they're merely an assumption on his part and more or less private, so I think I had better not tell you what they are. Now I have to make a speech. I'm the boss, but I'm also a tribal brother, initiated with due ceremony when I was born."

A chorus of grunts and a brief nodding of heads followed his three-minute speech in the Modoc language; then everybody trooped into the mess hall and the distribution of presents began. The toys and clothing for the women and children Lanier distributed personally, but the rations he turned over to Big Foot, for distribution by him according to tribal needs. For the hired men of the ranch there was an envelope containing for each a month's pay in cash. Janet had given a pop-gun and a cap pistol to each of the Sphinx twins, whose saturnine faces melted at this sly tribute to their ferocity; she had a carved leather belt with a silver buckle for Lanier and a necktie for Tom Harmon. And when all these gifts had been distributed there still remained two.

"For you, Janet," said Lanier, and handed her a great, square, heavy package.

Even before she removed the covering she knew it was a picture. It was—the oil painting of Lonely Valley she had noticed on his living-room wall. Pinned to it by a tiny thumb tack was a card and on it she read:

"For Janet.
Something to remember me by for I dread the thought of being forgotten by one I shall never, never forget or cease to reverence and feel grateful to.
                                                    R.L."

"Oh, thank you, Ray," she whispered, "but what I really wanted is the kodak photograph of you—the one where you have your foot in the stirrup about to mount your horse. A distinguished artist painted this. You prize it. You—"

"I want you to have it. And you shall have the kodak picture, too."

"It will leave a bare spot on your wall."

"No, it won't. I want to photograph you before you leave and make an enlargement. I want something more than a memory of you, my dear."

She looked at him, and the thought came to her that if all those Indians weren't present she could have kissed him—an appreciative and sisterly kiss. However, she knew he would not have relished that.

"I'll accept this painting in the spirit in which you give it, Ray," she said instead. "I'll never forget you. I couldn't. Some day I may have a home where I can hang this—and think of you whenever I look at it."

"Here is another present for you, Janet."

He handed her a little cardboard box. Within it, on a bed of absorbent cotton all too evidently torn from the roll in Tom Harmon's room, lay a heart-shaped coarse gold nugget worth perhaps fifty dollars. In a scrawling, uncertain hand had been written on a card:

"Deer Mis Jannit:
"You laber for love so I give you my hart. Have wore it 20 yrs. for luck. I hope it brings you luck. Merry Chrismess from
    yore true frend,
    T. H. E. Harmon."

Silently she handed the gift and the card to Lanier. He smiled at her sadly, put his arm through hers, and led her out of the mess hall to their waiting car. She could not speak. Her heart was too full. Nor did Lanier speak until, having run the car into the garage, they walked around to the front of the house to enter by the main portal. In the darkness of the veranda he took her hand in both of his.

"It's not such a very merry Christmas, is it?" he murmured, and kissed her hand. "You know how much it hurts me to see you leave, do you not, Janet?"

"I didn't know," she choked, "until tonight."

"If, in the future, I find it possible to ask you to come back, will you come?"

"Yes." The word was a whisper.

Christmas day was the longest day Janet had ever known. In common with Lanier and Harmon she sought to throw off the restraint that was the outgrowth of the tragedy that hung over Lonely Valley. There was nothing to do, nothing she could say that she wanted to say. Harmon and Lanier indulged in some humorous repartee, but there was no life in it and it died a natural death. Late in the afternoon she went for a walk down along the shore of Lonely Valley Lake and watched the myriads of waterfowl flying overhead; she counted the snipe that rose from the soggy meadows in front of her and zigzagged away, croaking raucously. Far out on the lake a golden bittern boomed, and a loon's mocking laughter answered it. But the effect of her walk along the lonely shore was to deepen her depression, and when she returned to the house and found Lanier at the piano playing "Traumerei," she knew, by his choice of melody that he, too, was depressed. Ah Fong had cooked an excellent Christmas dinner, but they partook of it in anything but a Yuletide spirit; immediately after dinner Tom Harmon, always discreet, hopped away to his room on his one sound leg and left Janet and Lanier alone.

The silence between them grew so oppressive that Janet had to say something. So she chose the subject foremost in her thoughts. "Well, Ray, when do you contemplate the completion of your unfinished business with Milo Landrum?"

"If Tom were able to attend to business I'd do it tomorrow, Janet. However, since I may not escape with a whole skin, it is necessary that Tom should be on the job here to look after my interests. If I should not return alive those interests would be his and yours."

"In that event you're safe for a month. Tom doesn't require my services any longer, so I am leaving in the morning."

He bowed his head, as to the inevitable, but made no comment. His silence stabbed her.

"I shall return to New York," she went on, with

difficulty. "The business that brought me out to this country turns out to be no business at all. Up until recently I had hoped to turn a profit, but after considering the matter in all its lights I realize my situation may not be capitalized except in the event of certain fortuitous circumstances. And I can not afford to wait for them to come to pass."

He nodded as if understanding her but she knew he didn't, in the least. After a while he rose, removed from the wall the photograph she had requested, retired to his office and autographed it:

"For Janet from Ray, Lonely Valley, California, Christmas, 1930."

"I'll crate the oil painting in the morning," he told her, "so you can express it back home without injury."

"Are you going to be able to pay your note to the bank on January second?"

"No. The wholesale butcher in San Francisco to whom I sold my steers has gone into the hands of a receiver. I shall probably not lose more than twenty percent of my claim, but I shall not get that for a year."

"Then the bank will foreclose the mortgage on your two thousand head of cows?"

"Of course. Landrum will buy them in at the auction that will be conducted by Sheriff Gorton within ten days after the bank has secured judgment against me. I doubt if there will be other bidders, so Landrum will get them for perhaps twenty dollars a head. They're worth fifty. Of course their sale will leave perhaps a sixty thousand deficiency judgment against me, and some of my remaining assets will be attached and sold to satisfy that. I imagine, if Landrum should be living at that time, that the asset he will have the bank attach to satisfy its deficiency judgment will be the land covered by Lonely Valley Lake."

"Does Landrum know of your debtor going into the hands of a receiver?"

"He must know it. There was a story about it in the *Modoc County Clarion*, and I was listed as one of the creditors, together with the amount owed me. This wholesale butcher was a very heavy buyer in this county, so naturally his failure makes local news in the paper."

"Can you weather the storm, Ray?"

"If I can mortgage my ranch for enough to pay my note to the bank and leave me operating capital, I can weather it. If the bank takes Lonely Valley Lake and discharges my indebtedness to it, I might be able to make a government loan on my remaining three thousand head of cows. However, whichever way the cat jumps, I'm no longer the big cattleman of this county; and three more years of low prices will finish me."

"Have you any definite plan for your salvation?"

"No, although, of course, I shall fight to the finish. In only one particular have I a definite plan. Milo Landrum shall never own Lonely Valley Lake."

"I suppose, when you do not pay your note on the second, suit will be filed on the third."

"No, no. You under-estimate Landrum. If he moved into action so soon he'd have the cows in thirty days, but what would he do with them? The southern part of the state has had one of the driest years in a decade and there is no good pasture to which he could move my cattle after getting them. Hay is scarce and very dear. So Landrum will just naturally let me keep the mortgaged cattle until just before the cows begin to drop their calves, which is about May first in this country. That action will force me to feed and care for the cattle all winter and he'll get them shortly after April first, which will insure him the possession of their calves also."

As if he regarded this as a great joke on himself he laughed a little. "Really, Janet, that man is so smart it's almost a shame to kill him."

"And what will he do with the cattle in April?"

"Why, when the local chief ranger of the National Forest learns that I shall have two thousand cattle less next year than I had this year, he will cut my grazing privilege by that number—and give it to Landrum, who will thereupon throw the cattle up into the reserve and forget all about them until next October. By that time he can sell them and he's bound to emerge with a nice profit."

"But when your remaining cows and his get all mixed up on the summer range how are you going to tell them apart?"

"Oh I'll vent my brand on all those foreclosed cattle. That is, I brand them again on the opposite side which cancels my original brand. Then Landrum will run his brand on them and probably ear-mark them again."

"How interesting," the girl remarked. "Suppose he found it impossible to graze the cattle in the Forest Reserve after acquiring them by foreclosure? What then?"

"Why, I imagine they'd be more or less of an embarrassment and expense to him. When you own cattle you've got to have a place to range them. Milo has several good ranches but they're all stocked at present. And summer range will be very scarce in this county next year, due to the accumulation of cattle which in normal times would have been sold this fall. They're being held over for a better price."

"Something tells me, Ray, that Landrum, or Landrum's bank, isn't going to foreclose on your cattle. He'd rather renew your note for a year than suffer loss and embarrassment with your cattle, and he'll not attach Lonely Valley Lake until he knows for a certainty he can drain it."

She reached over and patted his hand. "You be of good cheer, Ray. You're never out until you're counted out, and when I get back to New York I'm going to call upon a man who has money to invest. I'm going to explain your position to him, tell him about your financial situation and see if I can not induce him to make you a private loan. So you will please not despair until you hear from me."

"Thank you," he replied. "You're mighty sweet."

He went over to the piano and struck a few minor chords, then let his fingers rest tenderly on the keys. Janet followed him, and stood looking down at his lean, tanned face. She knew by his expression that she had touched him again on his soft spot. How susceptible he was to kindness and sympathy! She suspected he had not known very much of it previously, since in happier and more prosperous days, he had not required it.

"You know that I am fond enough of you to do anything I can to help you, don't you, Ray?" she asked.

He smiled sadly, but did not answer.

CHAPTER TWENTY-ONE

SHE PACKED HER BAGS THAT NIGHT AND breakfasted with Tom Harmon and Lanier the following morning. Both were exceedingly lugubrious. The meal finished, Lanier brought her car around to the front of the house and Ah Fong carried out her luggage and stowed it. Janet followed him back into the kitchen, intent upon tipping him liberally, but Ah Fong was not that sort of house servant. He declined the money graciously but firmly. What he wanted was information.

"Where you go?" he asked.

"To New York."

Ah Fong sighed gustily. "You no come back?"

"Maybe."

"You no mally boss?"

"No."

"You no likee?"

"Oh, very much, Ah Fong. He no likee me."

Ah Fong threw back his head and let loose a peal of coyote-like laughter. "Missy, you klazy. But no can help that. Bimeby you come back. I here jus' same when Missy come back. Goo'-by. Good luck."

"Ah Fong, why do you laugh?"

"Ketchee plenty big joke. Wha' for you no mally boss? I know. He no ask."

"Well, what of it?"

"Boss no got papa. Felix live then Felix ask Missy: 'How you like mally my boy,' allee same talkee China fashion. Melican boys velly funny." He transfixed her with an index finger, and lowered his voice. "You savvy why boss no ask you mally him?"

"No, I do not."

"Him in plenty big trouble. Losem plenty money and must kill Landlum for save face, because Landlum kill Felix. Makeum boss plenty sick," and Ah Fong laid his hand on his abdomen and tried to appear dolorous. "Who' for mally you now, maybe next week somebody kill him. No good. But—bimeby he talkee. You see. I know. Many time I catchum look-see when you not know. Boss look-see with eyes allee same lookin'-glass." And Ah Fong winked.

Janet's heart was beating with happiness when, after having given Tom Harmon a hug and a light kiss on his furrowed brow, she found herself alone with Raynor Lanier. She was behind the wheel of the car and he was leaning over the door, gazing at her with eyes that did, indeed resemble looking-glasses, since his soul was mirrored in them. Finally he said, with an effort:

"Be careful driving over the mountain and don't try to push east beyond the county seat. They've had snow over that way. Leave your car in the Alturas garage there, with instructions to ship it to you. Take the train from there East—or wherever you're going first, but don't try to get out of this county by motor car. Promise?"

"I promise."

"Well, then, I'll not delay the parting." He held out his hand. "Goodby, Janet. I'd like to say a number of things to you now, but it's too difficult a task. I'm going to ask you to try to imagine what you'd say if you stood in my shoes."

"Not goodby, Raynor. *Auf Wiedersehen!*"

"No. Goodby."

"But I heard you playing *'Auf Wiedersehen'* after I retired last night."

"It's a lovely little melody."

She smiled upon him as one smiles upon a child. She was not distressed at the parting now, he saw with wonder.

"I'd kiss you goodby, Ray, if you weren't so standoffish, because really you're a dear and I'm terribly fond of you. I've never met a man like you before, and something tells me I never shall again."

He reached in an arm, drew her down to him, and kissed her in a brotherly fashion. She started the motor and slipped in the gear.

"Take care of yourself, Ray."

"I shall."

Just before she rounded the first curve on the

road that led up the grade out of the valley—the curve that would cut off her view of it forever—she stopped her car and looked back. Raynor Lanier was standing on the steps of his house gazing after her. She fluttered her handkerchief at him . . . he waved back. From the door in back of Lanier something red fluttered. That, she knew, was Tom Harmon's bandanna handkerchief. From the side of the house, just outside the kitchen door, something large and white waved. That, she knew, was Ah Fong's kitchen apron . . . She wept a little then, but not with sadness.

At the top of the grade she stopped by the warning sign and honked her motor horn for Hugo. When he finally emerged from the timber she called to him gaily,

"I'm going away, Hugo."

"Good," said Hugo, and turned his back on her, for it would be long before he could find it in his half-breed heart to forgive her for having put a stop order on his cousin's plans to take up a white man's burden.

When Raynor Lanier came back into his house, Tom Harmon balanced himself on his crutches and leered at him.

"What are you feeling so funny about, you chuckle-headed baboon," Lanier demanded irritably.

"I was jus' enjoyin' the jack-pot you're in."

"I am not enjoying it." Coldly.

"Well, you got a farewell kiss you wasn't expectin'."

"And didn't want."

"You lie. You did. An' now that she's gone an' I have her permission to tell you something about her, I'm goin' to let fly. Ray, that Janet Corliss is old Donald MacLean's granddaughter."

Raynor Lanier sat down in the nearest chair and stared at his superintendent.

"An' what's more," Mr. Harmon continued with malicious enjoyment, "the old wolf's dead, and she has inherited that hell-anointed dam-site an' all the water-holes up in the Forest Reserve. Which puts the kibosh on you killin' Milo Landrum, because if you do that you'll be eucherin' that grand girl out of a bankroll a greyhound couldn't jump over. You can't buy her quarter section, an' Landrum can an' will. You got a blood feud agin Landrum, but it's in the discard now. She saved your life three times, an' it's up to you to show your gratitude. Now, do you tunnel Milo Landrum as per schedule or do you let him live?"

It was then that Raynor Lanier did the only weak thing, the only childish thing Tom Harmon had ever seen him do. He commenced to weep. It is bad enough when a strong man weeps, but it is terrible when he weeps silently and because a combination of untoward circumstances has deprived him of his vengeance and made of him an apostate; for to the Lanier clan just vengeance

215

was a religion. Tom Harmon pretended not to see him and limped away to his room.

In about an hour Lanier rose, went to the telephone in the kitchen and called up Milo Landrum's office. Mr. Bean answered the 'phone.

"I am Raynor Lanier, Bean," the young man announced, "and I wish to speak to your boss. I have something of interest to say to him."

"I don't think he wants to speak to you, Lanier," Bean quavered.

"Oh, he will not mind speaking to me over the telephone. I can't bite him from this distance. And I do not wish to call upon him if it can be avoided in any way."

He waited about two minutes, then Landrum's voice said gruffly: "Well?"

"Do you feel in a trading mood this morning, Landrum?"

"No, not with you, but I might work myself up to it."

"Well, to begin, I give you my word of honor I'm not going to kill you. That old conceit of mine is in the discard."

"Now, that's what I call right reasonable Lanier." The ice in Milo Landrum's voice appeared to thaw perceptibly. "But I won't be outdone in common sense, neither. You got my word of honor I'm not goin' to kill you."

"I have no confidence in your word of honor, but let that pass. The issue between us has arisen out of your desire to own the lands on which Lonely Valley Lake now lies. You called on me one day to ask my price on those lands but I was not prepared to sell. I am now."

Landrum chuckled pleasurably. "You bet you are. But then I told you you would be—an' I told you, too, that when you finally got ready to sell you wouldn't find me so generous in the matter o' price."

"That was before you got yourself into the jackpot. You've got a good hand now, Landrum, but still I would not advise you to over-bet it. You're playing table stakes with me and don't forget it. I said I wouldn't kill you and that goes, but if you get snooty to me, my bucko, I may conclude to permit one of my employees to tuck you away in Abraham's hirsute bosom. Now, damn you, make your choice. Do you want those lands or do you want a funeral?"

"I guess I prefer the lands," Landrum admitted with a mirthless little laugh. "What's your proposition?"

"I'll deed those lands to you in return for my note to your bank, canceled, plus two hundred and fifty thousand dollars cash."

"Nothing doing," Landrum barked harshly. "I got you where the hair is short—"

He heard a click. Raynor Lanier had hung up. The abrupt termination of the interview disturbed Landrum, because it created in his mind more strongly than ever the thought that he had a desperate man to deal with; it occurred to him presently that the lands, at the price, were a gift. Of course, if he accepted, he would be open to a hold-up by Donald MacLean, but this thought was not a deterrent. He would blow out that dam without consulting Donald MacLean. So he waited half an hour and then telephoned to Lanier.

"I'll accept that proposition," he announced, "on condition that neither, directly nor indirectly are you to present me with a funeral after the deal is closed."

"I give you my word of honor that if somebody should waft you hence after we have traded, I will have had nothing to do with it, directly or indirectly—and that's saying a lot, Landrum, because the job of renouncing my vengeance on you for the murder of my father has shaken me like an ague. But you know I'll keep my word."

"I don't know whether you will or not," Landrum taunted, "but I guess I'll have to make the experiment. I'll have the deed prepared an' the first chance you get come to my office and sign it an' I'll hand you a certified check for two hundred an' fifty thousand dollars and your note canceled."

"Thank you, Landrum. You realize, of course, that after you have drained the lake you are entitled to a rebate from the state of one dollar per acre from the Swamp & Overflow Lands Trust Fund."

"If I hadn't you and I wouldn't have traded."

When he returned to the living room Lanier found Tom Harmon standing on his crutches studying him inquiringly.

"You looked pleased," Mr. Harmon challenged.

"I am, Tom. I've been talking to Landrum and he's going to buy the lake lands for two hundred and fifty thousand and hand me back my note, canceled."

"Well," the philosophical Harmon replied, "that's better than a swift kick with a frozen boot. The deal leaves you intact in business an' with a quarter of a million dollars workin' capital. Yes, I approve o' that deal, because it leaves Miss Janet free to apply the screws to him later on. I wonder if he thought of that."

"Of course he did, but he will acquire the lands so cheaply he can afford to pay a stiff price for the dam-site. And, of course, he figures that with me out of the picture old MacLean will have no objection to selling to him, for, of course, he doesn't know the old man is dead and that he has to deal with a woman. However, I imagine he plans to blow the dam out without bothering to consult Janet."

"We can't permit that, can we?" Mr. Harmon queried softly.

Raynor Lanier laughed. "That's my ace in the hole. I'm going to buy that dam-site from Janet myself, permit Landrum to start work on it, then file my deed for record and have him enjoined forever from monkeying with my property."

"Better keep your money an' watch the dam-site for Janet," Harmon opined drily. "You'll always have to watch it anyhow. Six months in jail an' a heavy fine for contempt o' court won't bother that old hyena any. An' at that he'd mos' probably lie out of it."

"You're right, as usual, Tom. We'll have to build a snug little cabin on the property, stock it with provisions and install Hugo and his family there to watch it, and report any operations instantly."

"After which," Harmon went on quizzically, "you'll have to keep a man on the payroll to run down to that dam-site every day an' report instantly the murder of Hugo an' his squaw an' papoose. Dang you, son, if you an' your lawless ol' man hadn't been so law-abidin' you'd have had that lake drained forty year ago an' saved all this trouble. However, there's still a way out. About a month after you close your deal, there'll be a new face in hell an' it'll be the spittin' image o' Milo Landrum. We're forgettin' all about my feud with the ol' buzzard."

"I'm not. I promised I wouldn't, directly or indirectly, have anything to do with his removal. I gave my word of honor and that promise included all my employees."

"I'll respect your word of honor, Ray. When I

git ready to go to war I'll resign your employ. In fact, I'll resign a month before that just to spare your feelin's."

"Tom, I forbid it."

"Take a jump in Lonely Valley Lake," Mr. Harmon retorted cheerfully. "I'm free, white an' more than twenty-one years old an' this here is my personal affair with my personal honor involved. No man can put two holes in me an' not have two holes put in him if I survive. An' I'll be right careful where I bore my holes. I promise you they'll be less'n two inches apart."

"Tom, it will break my heart to have to fire you, but I'll do it if you persist."

"Jake with me, son. I'll pack my duds an' go to live at the Mountain House in Modoc City, if you'll confer a last favor on an old an' trusted employee an' send me to town in your car. I don't want no notice an' I don't want no month's salary in lieu o' notice."

"So be it, Tom." The words came, softly and huskily; then, for the second time that morning, Raynor Lanier lost control of himself and wept in that same terrible silence. But his woe had no effect whatsoever upon Thomas Hallowell Enoch Harmon, although the latter did have the decency to turn his back upon his employer and depart for his room, muttering something about packing his plunder and getting out of such a hellish atmosphere.

CHAPTER TWENTY-TWO

WHEN JANET DROVE INTO MODOC CITY AND saw Milo Landrum standing on the porch of the Mountain House, an impulse seized her to tell him exactly her opinion of him. So she pulled up in front of the hotel.

"Hello," she saluted him. "Aren't you afraid to be out without the sheriff to look after you?"

He bent upon her an ophidian stare and chewed at his cigar until it was tilted upward at an acute angle. "I reckon you ain't up to date on the local news, young woman," he replied drily.

"I'm post-dated on it so far as you're concerned. I'm leaving this country today, Mr. Landrum. My nursing jobs at the Lanier ranch are finished, so I'm off to greener pastures. But before I go I want to say to you that you are the most cold-blooded, murderous, scheming, cowardly scoundrel I have ever heard of. You've been pretty busy of late suborning murder and arson, and twice you have attempted murder personally; but that sort of work is all behind you now. I left Lonely Valley at nine o'clock this morning, and simultaneously the open season on you commenced."

"I don't think so," Landrum replied with the

utmost assurance. "Ray Lanier telephoned me less'n half an hour ago to propose an armistice. I got that young feller stopped because I got him licked. I'm goin' to let him survive in the cattle business an' carry on just as him an' his old man been doin' all their lives, in return for a deed to that land covered by Lonely Valley Lake. Lanier an' I have come to an understandin', so if you ain't got nothin' better to do, suppose you mosey along an' forget matters that ain't none o' your business."

"And has Raynor Lanier given you his word of honor he will not kill you after you have acquired your pound of flesh?"

"He has."

"Then he will keep his word, of course."

"I know he will."

Janet smiled triumphantly. "Yes, Mr. Landrum, you're safe from Raynor Lanier. But you're not safe from Tom Harmon. Tom has a crow of his own to pluck with you, and believe me, he'll pluck it as soon as possible."

"Harmon?" Landrum was disturbed. "Why, I ain't never had no fuss with Tom Harmon."

"Oh, yes, you have. The night your men came to burn the Lanier haystacks there was some shooting—and Tom Harmon was hit twice. One of the wounds was almost fatal. I nursed him back to health. He can't walk yet, but when he can he'll be around to see you. And if he fails of his mission two other resolute men will finish the job for him. You win—but you lose. And now, having spoiled the day for you—and the comparatively few days remaining to you, Mr. Milo Landrum—I'll accept your advice and mosey along away from matters that do not concern me. I hope you have a lovely funeral."

He appeared stunned. She gazed contemptuously upon him, enjoying the fright she had inflicted, for she had, though in small measure, a share of feminine ferocity where those she loved were concerned.

"So that's another pair of boots, eh? You monster!" she derided him.

She slipped in her gears and rolled out of Modoc City and on toward the east.

That night Milo Landrum telephoned Lanier and explained the obstacle, in the shape of Tom Harmon's vengeance, which had arisen between them and their trade. "I can't move an inch, Lanier," he declared, "until I'm assured your foreman won't declare war on me. I understand you pay him two hundred an' fifty a month, an' it seems to me you'd ought to be able to handle him. Jobs like that ain't possible to find these days an' I never knew an old cowman that wouldn't string with his boss. You threaten to fire him an' he'll come to his milk. Me, I offered him ten thousand dollars today to forget his grouch, but no, he's still on the peck."

"I know it," Lanier mourned. "Believe me, Landrum, I've done everything possible to get the notion out of his head but I can't budge him. I've pointed out to him that by his action he will work himself out of a good job, ten thousand dollars cash money and my friendship, in addition to ruining me—and still he stands pat. So I have fired him. I gave you my word of honor I would not, directly or indirectly, be a party to your funeral and I interpret the word indirectly to mean that I must be responsible for the acts of my employees in so far as your safety is concerned. I've made good so far. Tom Harmon is no longer on my payroll. I'm going to give him until after breakfast tomorrow to recant and go back on the payroll again, but if he still refuses to oblige me he'll drag his obstinate tail off this ranch ten minutes after he's swallowed his coffee."

"I believe you're on the level about this, at that," Landrum replied not without a faint note of admiration in his gruff tones. "Well, work on him." He was silent a moment, then added: "If you don't, I'll have to."

When Lanier reported the result of that interview to Tom Harmon, the foreman merely grinned. Infuriated, Lanier said harshly: "You get off this ranch tomorrow."

"I was all set to go this mornin', if you'd been thoughtful enough to provide me with transportation. But you didn't and now I'm so annoyed at you I've made up my mind not to resign. An' I won't be fired, neither. I've been a definite part o' the Lanier organization for so long I can't be amputated from it. How'd we both get along if you got rid o' me?"

"I'll manage somehow. There are as good fish in the sea as—"

"But sometimes an' for long stretches the fishin's mos' almighty poor, Mr. Lanier. You'll kindly oblige with a maximum o' silence. You keep on soundin' your horn an' pretty soon you'll tootle up somethin' you'll be ashamed of later."

"My story is soon told, Tom. I repeat it—you're fired."

But Tom Harmon only shook his head. "Can't be done, Ray. I promised Felix I'd stay with you. Before he died he knew that now was the time for all good men an' true to come to the aid of the party, which that party is you. 'Tom,' he whispers, 'you got to admit you ain't a gentleman any more'n I am. But I made a hell of a mistake. I raised my boy a gentleman. When there's plain, everyday killin' to be done a gentleman's handicapped. Any time you see my boy wrastlin' with his handicap you git back o' him.'"

"I wouldn't be wrestling with that handicap if you hadn't told me who Janet was," Lanier almost shouted. "If you'd let Nature take her course I'd be sitting comfortable and happy in the

226

county jail right now and somebody'd be shaving Landrum with cold water and a dull razor."

"I know," Harmon answered humbly, "but that situation riz up because I harkened to my original instincts, which are to be pure in word, thought an' deed. I let my own sense o' gratitude an' friendship for Miss Janet get me down for a little while before I remembered that Felix had a prior claim to them sweet sentiments. Why, that old daddy o' yours gimme my first watch. I admit he'd saved up cigar certificates to get it but it looked like gold at the time. I was ten year old then. When I was twelve he gimme a shot gun an' a real horse; at fourteen he gimme a man's rifle; at sixteen he gimme a six-shooter an' at seventeen he let me help him hang two cow thieves we caught in the act. At nineteen I was his foreman. A feller just can't forget little things like that. Why, Felix wouldn't let me smoke until I was twenty-one, which I've often thought since his thoughtfulness maybe saves me from bein' a runt."

"I think," Raynor Lanier cried passionately, "that the kindest thing I can do for you is to regard you as temporarily insane."

"Maybe so, maybe so. My father was a mite peculiar in the head. He followed Felix into that scrap with Donald MacLean an' got killed for it."

Abruptly Lanier terminated the argument by retiring to his room.

"Licked," Mr. Harmon soliloquized. "Licked to a frazzle!"

On the outskirts of the county seat a man signaled Janet to stop.

"You Miss Corliss?" he demanded.

"Yes," Janet answered, surprised.

"I'm from the Alturas Garage. Tom Harmon telephoned a little while ago, described you and your car, and asked me to come out here and stop you. He wants you to telephone him."

Janet drove the messenger back to the garage and called up Tom Harmon.

"Hello, Spit-fire," he greeted her. "What you mean by tellin' Milo Landrum all about my pious intentions regardin' him?"

"He was so cock-sure and arrogant, Tom, I had to take him down off his high horse. He told me he and Ray had come to an understanding."

"Yep. After you left I told Ray who you are. Like to knocked him over. Right off he realized that if he killed Landrum he'd be killin' the only sound prospect you got for sellin' your dam-site at a good figger—an' he ain't low enough to exhibit a lack o' gratitude. It was pretty hard on him to have to violate his promise to ol' Felix, but I reckon he come to the conclusion his father'd want him to do just as he'd agreed to do. He felt it was his duty as a man to promote the sale, even at some personal sacrifice, so he called Landrum up an' told him he'd lay off him, provided Landrum give him back his note, canceled, an' two hundred an' fifty thousand dollars. That was more'n Landrum wanted to pay but after thinkin' it over he come to the conclusion it might be safer to be a mite generous, so he accepted. On his part Ray gives his word of honor not directly or indirectly to have a hand in any killin' of Landrum, if so be somebody takes a notion he'd look becomin' in a coffin."

"But I'll not have Ray Lanier make such a sacrifice because of his exaggerated sense of obligation to me."

"Well, I knew you'd feel that way about it, but I didn't argy with him. He's figgerin' safety first for him an' you. After all, that lake ain't never done no good to the Lanier clan an' Ray can git along without it. He wants to stay in the cattle business an' to do that he's got to climb out o' debt an' acquire enough cash capital to enable him to stand up under the losses we're liable to have for a couple o' years until the world gits normal agin."

"Oh, Tom, he mustn't sell for such a ridiculous price. I'm certain I can raise the money to save his cows."

"Well, if you can, don't you let him know nothin' about it. He don't lean on no woman in a fight. However, Miss Janet, thanks to you, the deal's all off now. Landrum warned me he'd let his verbal option slide unless I agreed to settle with him for cash. He wouldn't admit he sent them two men over to burn Ray's hay, but I reckon he figgers I'm entitled to some compensation for the pain an' sufferin' I been through. Of course he didn't put it that way. Said he couldn't begin to imagine the source o' my grouch agin him, but if I'd forgit it he'd give me ten thousand dollars not to block his deal with Ray."

"And what did you reply to that?"

"I told him all the assets he's got couldn't save him from me the day I was able to set foot to ground. I had to kill that deal, didn't I? Of course, if you can't raise a hundred thousand dollars, let me know quick."

"I understand perfectly, Tom. I'll wire you at the earliest possible moment the result of my efforts. Goodby, you old dear."

CHAPTER TWENTY-THREE

DANIEL P. MAGRUDER, OF PHELPS, CHINN & Magruder, sat at his desk wondering whether he should buy a hundred thousand dollars worth of steel and hold it for a rise, or sell it short and wait for a new *débâcle* to materialize in the stock market.

While he pondered, two small, cool hands closed over his eyes and held him. Knowing he was expected to guess the identity of the owner of those hands he said promptly,

"Little Janet Corliss?"

Instantly he was released.

"How did you know?" Janet demanded, and reached over his shoulder to kiss him.

"You're my only youthful woman client, my dear. No widow or spinster would dare to get so familiar with her attorney. Sit down in that chair yonder—in the light—and let me have a look at you?"

Janet obeyed, and Daniel P. Magruder helped himself to a long and satisfactory look.

"When did you return, Janet?"

"Just came up from the Grand Central station. My bags are in your ante-room."

"When people are in such a hurry to see me I always infer that they are financially ruined or about to be. Well, I've collected a few small dividends for you during your absence. Want them?"

"No—that is, yes, but there's no hurry."

"Well then," he smiled, "tell me all about it."

"Uncle Dan, I've been having the most thrilling adventures."

"For instance?"

"Shootings and killings and burnings and intrigue and scheming; and overdue notes at a bank and mortgages on cattle and a man who knows better than to pass in front of a window after the lights are lit; a blood feud and Indians and cowboys and cows and calves and green feed and some wonderful men and some terrible men—"

"Ah," he interrupted. "And which of the wonderful men have you fallen in love with, my dear?"

"I was coming to that. His name is Raynor Lanier, and he's the son of Grandpa's old enemy, Felix Lanier."

"And what has old Mr. Felix Lanier to say about that?"

"Nothing. He was murdered last October."

"So they're still killing each other out there just as they did in your grandfather's day? And this Raynor Lanier? Is he a chip off the old block?"

"He's terrible, Uncle Dan—and I love him to death."

"And you're going to marry him?"

"Ah, there's the rub. I do not know. He hasn't asked me and, unless I do something about it, he never will."

"Bashful?"

"No, just old-fashioned. He's in a peck of trouble and too fine to invite me to share it with him. Uncle Dan, he needs a hundred thousand dollars to pay a mortgage on his cattle. If he doesn't pay it, his enemy will take the cattle at half their value, and—"

Daniel P. Magruder commenced to chuckle. "And you want me to lend him the money and take over the cows as security, eh?"

"Yes," Janet replied eagerly, "and they'll all have little calves in the spring and that will make additional security. Then he has a gorgeous fifteen-thousand-acre ranch besides, and it's not encumbered, and in a year or two he'll have seventy-five thousand acres more. And it's so beautiful, Uncle Dan, you'd just adore it. It's called Lonely Valley."

"And this lord of Lonely Valley, Raynor Lanier—did he suggest you helping him out of his dilemma by chance?"

"Of course not. He'd die before appealing to a woman for help."

"Has he ever killed anybody?"

"Not yet, but he will if I'm not careful."

"Will that make a difference to you?"

"No. It's a self-defense job, and he may not be able to avoid it."

"Calm yourself, Janet, start in at the beginning and tell me everything in an orderly manner. Cold facts only. Now, then, where did you first meet this bloodthirsty young man?"

So Janet started at the beginning and told him everything. At the end of an hour Magruder declared he had the entire picture.

"Well Janet," he added, "you left here hoping you would have some unusual adventures, and your desire has been granted. I am inclined to believe I should give my consent for you to marry your cattle king, but I never take anything for granted."

He swung his swivel chair and gazed out of the window a long time before he spoke again. Then:

"It was quite a shock to me, Janet, when your mother married Joe Corliss. Nice chap he was, too—good looks, good family, lots of charm— and no head for business. I thought I could have done a better job of taking care of your mother. However, she didn't think so. And she never really got over Joe's death. She was a one-man woman . . . well, Janey dear, I want you to be happy. You're a bit close to me, child—"

He turned from the window, but Janet was not there. She returned presently, however, carrying a suitcase, from which she took the silver-framed kodak enlargement of Raynor Lanier which Ray had given her when she left the ranch, and which he had inscribed to her.

Magruder studied the picture. "Character in that face, and character in that chirography," he decided. "I'll bet his old man was mighty proud of that boy . . . Well, I have a hundred thousand dollars crying for investment at six percent—"

"Seven, darling," Janet interrupted. "He'll pay seven because just now he's paying eight."

"I'm not greedy. I've always been satisfied with five percent net. If the security is ample I'll save your man, Janet, but only on one condition: he is not to kill Landrum. If he should ever marry you, he must not come to you with blood on his hands."

"I wouldn't put that ultimatum up to him, Uncle Dan. I want that man, but I'll not hobble him. He's holding his own hand, and there aren't any trumps in it, but he'll have to play it as best he can. However, why argue that point? He shook dice with his hired man for the privilege of killing Landrum—and the hired man won."

"Janet," Magruder replied, "you're your ferocious old grandfather's ferocious young granddaughter. But how about this quarter section of land you own and which is the key to that lake bed?"

"Well, if he asks me to marry him, Uncle Dan, I'll be so grateful I'll give him that key for a wedding present."

"Oh, well, wire him to hold on to everything until spring. I've got to go out there and look things over, but I can't do that in midwinter. I tell you frankly, however, Janet, that as a business venture it does not appeal to me. Even though the security should be more than ample, the young man may not be able to work out of debt, and in the long run I might be forced to foreclose on him. With you married to him at that time, I'd suffer if I had to foreclose."

"I'm not asking a favor, Uncle Dan. In fact, I

didn't mention the matter of a loan. You did. And I'm offering you an opportunity to rent one hundred thousand dollars at seven percent on liquid security. With his cows and his land Ray has enough to pay you—and somehow, I suppose, he could start all over again."

"And if that were necessary—would you start all over again with him? Would you be willing to darn his socks and patch his overalls and cook his meals and bear his children? Would you endure the loneliness, self-sacrifice, and lack of social intercourse attendant upon being wife to such a man?"

"I would. And like it—because I'd always know he was worth it."

Magrauder took about a minute to let that statement sink in. Then: "Well, I have the money available, and I'll loan it to your man, provided you indorse the note. We've got to be businesslike about this. I never mix sentiment with business."

"You're a sweet prevaricator, but we'll not argue that. Oh, you darling! May I send him a telegram at once?"

"No. I have known telegraph offices in country towns to leak. You will not even write him, because I have a suspicion that the Raynor Laniers of this world prefer to go to jail rather than be under financial obligation to a woman. You leave this entire matter to me. I have had considerable experience leading lost babes out of the financial woods. You are not to worry, Janet, and you are not to interfere. I'll save the young man, if he'll permit me."

"I know you will, Uncle Dan—provided you live." Janet reached over and felt his pulse. "Sixty-four. Hum-um-m! Slowing up. Stick out your tongue and say 'Ah-h-h-h'!"

Magruder shook with quiet mirth. "Many a true word is said in jest, my dear girl—and I am sixty-five years old and a sedentary ruin."

He squared around to his desk and drew a check to Janet's order for one hundred thousand dollars.

"Now, you deposit that in your bank," he instructed her. "Leave entirely to me, while I live, the job of saving your cattle king. If I should die before the crisis comes in his affairs, you will have the money on hand to do the needful for him. Now I'll ask you to sign a promissory note, so this deal will be quite regular. Not that you'll ever be called upon to pay the note. Meanwhile, no letters and no telegrams to the ruffian Lanier. Promise?"

"Oh, but I know he expects a letter from me."

"Write him all you wish to—but do not mention business. That fellow is on the spot, as they say, and I have a great curiosity to observe how he gets off it—and to know what sort of fighter he is. He shall not be saved until hope has fled."

"But he'll suffer so in the meanwhile, Uncle Dan. Please do not make him suffer."

"Suffering, my dear, is good for young men. It mellows them. If suffering makes this fellow quit, he's not the man for you. If it makes him fight all the harder, you'll be happy with him. This is my show, and you must permit me to run it. Now, scram out of here. I have other clients much more important to me financially than you, and one of them is waiting outside now."

CHAPTER TWENTY-FOUR

ON THE MORNING OF JANUARY THIRD TWO men on horseback rode down into Lonely Valley. One of them was Skunk Tallow, Big Foot's son, and the other was a cowboy from one of Milo Landrum's ranches. Skunk Tallow had vouched for the cowboy to Hugo as they passed the outpost on top of the hill, and both men rode directly to the Lanier house. Ah Fong admitted them.

"Here is the mail, boss," Skunk Tallow announced in English. "I meet this man on the road, and he say he want to see you, so I bring him along. He have no gun. Hugo search him."

Lanier advanced to meet the cowboy.

"I know what he wants," he said smilingly. "He has a fatal document to hand me."

The cowboy grinned, removed his hat, and took

from it a copy of a summons and complaint in action of Milo P. Landrum versus Raynor Lanier, in the matter of an unpaid promissory note assigned to said Landrum by the Modoc County Commercial Trust & Savings Bank in the sum of one hundred thousand dollars with accrued interest.

"You are Mr. Raynor Lanier?" he demanded.

"Yes."

"Take it."

Lanier took it. "Better back up to the fire before starting back through the snow," he suggested hospitably.

While the cowboy warmed himself, Lanier read his mail. Tom Harmon watched him with lazy interest. Ever since Harmon had changed his mind and declined to resign he had remained on at the Big House, for he was much more comfortable there. Moreover, he knew his employer lacked the courage to throw him out; that Lanier was merely giving his foreman time to think the situation over in the hope that presently his hard resolution would soften. For a few days following their heated interview an unpleasant silence had obtained between them—a condition which bothered Mr. Harmon not at all, for he knew Raynor Lanier was secretly anxious to reestablish harmonious relations at the earliest opportunity. Harmon decided that the opportunity should be forthcoming; now that Landrum had filed his suit he knew Lanier would again broach the subject of his, Harmon's, co-operation in coming to amicable terms with Landrum.

Consequently, after the departure of the cowboy who had served the summons, Harmon queried companionably:

"Well, son, what's the good news? Don't hoard it. I know it's good news because you don't look near so sulky as you been the past week."

"I haven't been sulky."

"Don't lie to me. You been sulkier'n a mean mule an' I've had enough of it."

Lanier sighed. "Don't pick a fight with me, damn you," he protested. "Fighting will get us nowhere and, besides, we have plenty of time to fight later if we feel like it. I have here a letter from Janet. She says to give you her love."

"Which the same marks a high point in the history o' the Harmon family. When you answer send her mine."

"I shall not. You're her enemy. Don't be a hypocrite, Tom. Until you consent to play the game with Janet and me you're outlawed from our affections."

"You're takin' in a lot o' territory with that statement, young man, but let it pass. As you remarked a moment ago we got plenty o' time left to fight in. We can be friends clear up to the day before Sam Gorton sells your cows at public auction to satisfy the jedgement Landrum's bound to get agin you—unless you do something about it."

"There isn't a thing I can do and you know it."

"I admit you've done everything but try."

"I did try. I had everything fixed to make everybody happy and you spoiled it. So I'm through."

"You give up, eh?"

"Why attempt to do the impossible in such times as the present? A ranch is a frozen asset and no individual or bank will loan money on a frozen asset now-a-days. I've written every bank and moneyed individual I know and there's no hope."

"The trouble with you, Ray, is that you're so close to the woods you can't see the trees. *That's* why I refuse to play the game with you an' not because it'd break my heart to pass up the job o' removin' Landrum. Now, listen to me. There ain't no doubt but you can borrow twenty-five thousand dollars from the government on a first mortgage on part o' your ranch. That's what Joint Land Stock banks are for, an' the interest is only six per cent. You pay it off in forty years an' nobody bothers you. Then there's them cattle loan companies that represent the government Intermediate Credit Bank. They get money from the government at four per cent an' rent it at seven, the difference bein' their profit for placin' the loan an' lookin' after it for the government. You hock all your cattle to one o' these outfits for enough to pay off Landrum. A little later you git the loan of twenty-five thousand on your ranch, which gives you operatin' capital for next year; if you have to you can sell enough fat steers, even at a loss, to reduce your cattle loan an' keep it sweet. As long as you keep it sweet an' make annual reductions as per contract you won't be bothered."

"I tried that cattle loan outfit in San Francisco and they declined with thanks. And why not when every calf that's dropped is a liability instead of an asset?"

"There's other loan companies," Harmon persisted, "in Arizona, Utah an' New Mexico. Go see them. Lots o' times a lender'll refuse a borrower if the application for the loan is made by mail, whereas in a personal interview maybe you outgame him. You might meet up with some feller that'd take a shine to you—figger you a smart, clean, capable young feller they could take a chance on. In makin' a loan them fellers also take into consideration as assets the good health, integrity an' ability of the borrower. How do them money-lenders know you ain't older'n Kansas City an' liable to die off next spring instead o' livin' an' workin' out the loan? Try givin' 'em additional collateral in the shape of a life insurance policy for say a hundred an' twenty-five thousand dollars. You're only twenty-eight an' term life insurance would be pretty cheap for you. Hell's fire, boy, you ain't done nothin' yet. Use your head for thinkin'. You know blamed well Landrum's goin' to have a jedgement agin you in ten days, but he ain't goin' to try collectin' on it until you've fed them cattle all winter an' looked after 'em. You know blamed well he won't grab 'em until just before they start calvin', so you got a heap o' time on your hands. Once you've took Landrum's gun away from him you can sell him your lake lands just the same—an' for a lot more money. Right off then, you can retire your cattle loan an' start livin'."

"I couldn't repudiate my deal. I made him a price, he accepted and stands willing to close, provided I can guarantee him against you."

"He's told you he repudiates the deal until you can guarantee him against me, hasn't he? Your promise went for all of your employees. Me, I ain't no employee of yours no longer. I'm just a guest at your house until I can fork a horse an' drift out o' here. It's up to Landrum to kill his own snakes. My row with him is private an' he ain't playin' fair to expect you to control my private opinions. So it seems to me you could, in honor an' after takin' his gun away from him, ask him half a million for them lake lands."

"Oh, I've thought of all that. But it seemed to me that if I traded with him now I'd be playing the game with Janet and placing her in position to be able to hold him up for at least half a million."

Lanier sighed. "She's a lone woman, Tom, and I'd prefer she should have the half million rather than I. A man can get along somehow, but it's different with a woman."

"Son," Tom Harmon pleaded, "Felix was right. He raised you a gentleman. You save yourself an' let Nature take her course regardin' Miss Janet. I've thunk this matter over a lot an' I've come to the conclusion you both got to sell out together an' at the best possible price—an' not attempt no squeeze plan on Milo Landrum. That ol' wolf won't be squeezed—an' he's still got another ace up the sleeve of his vest. You're still livin', ain't you? An' you're still liable to sudden an' violent death, ain't you? Now, you listen to me, because I'm givin' you an ultimatus. You get into your car an' start driftin' over four or five states for a new cattle loan. You keep goin' until you get it. If you come back here licked, I'll consider playin' the game with you, but not until. You got to work this job, son. Do you get me?"

"I do," Lanier retorted, and his voice was filled with rage. "Is that your final say-so?"

"You bet—an' this is your final do-so."

"I accept, Tom. You look after my affairs here while I'm gone. I'll pay your customary wage while you're doing it, of course."

"No, sir, I'm off your payroll an' I'll stay off, but I'll look after the ranch free gratis while you're gone. Vamose! You can be in Alturas tonight, leave your car there an' take a train out at midnight."

"Is Milo Landrum safe from you until my return?"

"I give you my word he is. I'll not be held responsible for the rest o' your help, however. You see Big Foot an' his people an' the Sphinx twins an' put 'em on their honor before you go. I don't trust none o' 'em."

"I'll do that immediately," Lanier answered and drove down to the ranch buildings to interview his men. No sooner had he left the house than Tom Harmon limped into Lanier's bedroom. On the bedpost Lanier's holstered gun hung by the belt, so Harmon removed the weapon, flipped out the shells and substituted six blank cartridges. Then he limped back into the kitchen and called up Lee Elkins at the county seat.

"Lee," he pleaded, "I want you should do Ray Lanier a big favor."

"That," said Elkins, "would be my delight."

"You're the district attorney. Sam Gorton's the sheriff. The day before Christmas Ray an' Sam had a ruckus in Modoc City. Sam got the drop on Ray an' took his gun away from him an' cuffed him. It was Sam's idea to take Ray over to the county seat an' try him for assault to commit murder on Milo Landrum an' for carryin' a concealed weapon without a permit."

"Yes, I heard all about that. The sheriff reported

245

to me and asked me to issue a warrant for Ray's arrest. I refused and suggested to Gorton that hereafter he had better mind his own business and not bother me."

"Well, now, Lee, you got to look at this thing from Sam's p'int o' view. While Sam's busy dustin' off Milo Landrum, Miss Corliss, his nurse that you met here, slips Ray her little gun, with which he holds up Sam, gets his own gun back, an' Sam's. Then he possesses himself o' Sam's keys an' beats it for home. Sam an' two deputies foller in a car, only to be held up unexpected on the road by Ray, who relieves all o' the possee o' their weapons."

"Sam didn't tell me about that."

"He wouldn't. He's afraid he'll be laughed out of office next election if that news leaks out."

"What do you wish me to do for Ray, Tom?"

"Ray Lanier'll arrive in Alturas about five o'clock this evenin'. Slip the word to Sam Gorton. Sam's itchin' to lay hands on Ray but dassen't come into Lonely Valley to get him. You tell Sam to lay for Ray at the Alturas garage an' get the drop on him the second he steps out of his car."

"Tom, there'll be a shooting scrape as sure as death and taxes."

"There won't. I've loaded Ray's gun with blanks."

"What else do you want me to do, you lunatic?"

"I want you to issue a warrant for Ray's arrest, on Sam's complaint, an' have Ray chucked in jail."

"He'll only get out on bail."

"Not if you an' the judge do the decent thing. He'll have to stay in jail all night, but in the mornin' he'll be clamorin' for trial. You see that he gets it. He won't hold it agin' you for issuin' the warrant; he'll figure you had to, in your official capacity, so you can make good with him by havin' him tried first thing tomorrow mornin'."

"But the judge is his friend. He'll only impose a nominal fine."

"You see to it that the judge is his enemy. The sheriff's been man-handled an' the law defied. It's the judge's business to uphold the law, an' while he can do it by imposin' a nominal fine in the case o' some ordinary person, he just can't do it in the case o' the sheriff. The judge has got to be hard-boiled an' sentence Ray to a month in the county jail."

"Good God, Tom, are you crazy?"

"Yes—like a fox. While Ray's in the jug he can have his meals sent in an' I'll have a good bed an' his own sheets an' blankets sent over to him. You can keep him supplied with books an' newspapers. What that boy needs is a good rest an' absolute safety from Milo Landrum's killers until I'm ready to talk to Milo an' point out to him the error of his ways. You know all about the jam he's in with Milo?"

"Yes."

"Well, I got a notion I can save him, but I got to have time to do it. I'm plannin' to do a job Ray wouldn't let me do if he could stop me, but it's just got to be done. Ray, he's too clean for dirty work like this."

"Any killing in this job you refer to?"

"None, except maybe by accident an' I'll try to avoid that. I can't tell you over the telephone but as soon as you got Ray sentenced I'll visit you an' tell you in person. If you don't approve you can fix it with the judge to get Ray out of the jug right off. Now, don't ask me no more questions. If you're a friend o' Ray Lanier's you'll do what I ask of you. You know me. I'd die for the boy."

"I'll do it," Lee Elkins promised. "It sounds crazy to me, but I'll do it."

"Bully for you," Mr. Harmon murmured and hung up.

CHAPTER TWENTY-FIVE

WHEN RAYNOR LANIER RAN HIS CAR INTO THE Alturas Garage that night, one of Sam Gorton's deputies came over, leaned in over the door and said: "Hello, Ray. Glad to see you. Your presence here saves me a long cold trip out to Lonely Valley. I have a warrant for your arrest for carrying concealed weapons without a permit from the sheriff and for resisting arrest. Here's the warrant. Read it and you'll see everything's regular."

Lanier perused the warrant. "This is regular," he informed the deputy. "I know Lee Elkins' signature, so I'll go peaceably. Here's my gun."

He handed it to the deputy and the latter then escorted him to the local hotel, where Lanier had dinner and called up Lee Elkins. "Do I have to sleep in jail tonight, Lee?" he queried.

"Of course not. I'm sorry to have had to issue the warrant. I refused at first but finally decided to issue it; otherwise Gorton will always be laying for you to bring you in without a warrant; if we get the job over now it will be out of our way. I've made a deal with Sam. He is to permit you to put up at the hotel tonight with his deputy to guard you and your trial has been set for ten o'clock tomorrow morning."

"How did you know where to lay hands on me?"

"Talked with Tom Harmon over the 'phone."

"Oh! Well, don't be too hard on me when you have to prosecute me tomorrow morning, Lee."

"Suppose you decline to make it hard on me by pleading guilty. Because you are guilty, Ray, no doubt about that."

"Very well, Lee, I'll plead guilty. The judge is a friend of mine but he'll have to fine me something in order to make good with Gorton. After all Sam's the sheriff, although I think I could whittle a better sheriff out of a chunk of sugar pine. Thanks, Lee. Good night."

Promptly at ten o'clock Lanier appeared, with the deputy sheriff, for trial. When the judge instructed him as to his legal rights and asked him if he was represented by counsel, Lanier grinned amiably and replied:

"Your honor, my legal rights are safe in your custody and in these hard times I decline to go to the unnecessary expense of having legal counsel. I manhandled Sam Gorton, resisted arrest and carried a gun without first having secured a permit from the sheriff. I plead guilty and cast myself upon the mercy of the court."

His Honor flushed a little, coughed and said: "Then you are casting yourself upon the mercy of a court not at all disposed to show you the sort of mercy I am certain you expect. Mr. Lanier, it seems to this court that you are bent upon sustaining the reputation of your family for triggeritis, for making your own law and holding yourself above the law of the state. In this instance you flouted the chief peace officer of this county. You drew a gun on Sheriff Gorton and that is an offense which, while possible of interpretation as a misdemeanor in the case of one who wears no star upon his breast, must be regarded as a near-felony in the case of the sheriff of this county. The dignity of the sheriff's office and the dignity of this court indicate for the two offenses to which you have pleaded guilty a punishment much more severe than this court ordinarily would inflict. You are a young man of culture and education. You know better. Also, you are a warm personal friend of mine and the district attorney. For this very reason, if for no other, this court may not show you the mercy you have, impliedly, asked for, and which, doubtless, could be covered by a fine. It is the sentence of this court, therefore, that you be confined in the county jail of this county for a period of thirty days. Owing to the fact that, because of your recent very severe illness, the sentence does not carry hard labor, and accordingly I request the sheriff (here he eyed Sam Gorton savagely) to permit you to have all of your meals sent to you from the hotel, and to sleep in a bed and under bedding furnished by yourself.

"This court desires to provide to Sheriff Gorton justice and punishment for your crime against his office but it will deprecate rough treatment. The court is dismissed and the sheriff will confine the defendant in the county jail forthwith, that he may commence serving his sentence immediately."

Amazed and indignant, Lanier leaped to his

feet. "May it please your Honor. I have some very important business matters to attend to and I would appreciate very much the privilege of attending to them first and serving my sentence afterward. I ask that sentence be suspended for thirty days and that in the interim I be admitted to reasonable bail."

"Reasonable bail?" the court almost shouted. "Mr. Lanier, this court will be the judge of the reasonableness of any bail that may be set—and your request is denied. You do not come into court with clean hands. In fact, you were wearing a concealed weapon when you were arrested last night. Sheriff, remove the prisoner."

The prisoner was duly removed. An hour later Lee Elkins visited him in jail. "Lee," he raged, "what the devil sort of frame-up is this? I thought you and the judge were my friends."

"My dear man," the district attorney replied soothingly, "we are. That's why you have been sentenced to thirty days in the bastile. It's a good safe place for you, and we both love you so much, Ray, we wanted to put you where Milo Landrum's killers cannot get at you."

"What rot? I'm in no danger from him and even if I were I'm amply able to protect myself."

"We know that. But still His Honor and I both think that in the event of Milo Landrum's sudden demise by violence, the county jail provides you with a cast-iron alibi, so you might as well make up your mind to like it. I've brought you some good novels and the newspapers and every afternoon I'll come over and play dominoes with you. Your man, Skunk Tallow, will be over with your bed and bedding late this afternoon. Meanwhile, do not ask me any questions because I'll not answer them. You are in the hands of your friends, so please do not embarrass them. Remember they are public servants."

"Tom Harmon had something to do with this," Lanier raved.

"He did. In fact, he suggested it. I talked with him over the 'phone a little while ago and he told me to tell you not to worry, that the money to save your cattle from Landrum would be forthcoming and for you to take a nice long rest and leave everything to him. He said he had to get you out of his way, otherwise you'd be sticking your finger into the machinery and gumming it up."

"The dirty, double-crossing hill-billy. When I get out of this jail—"

"You'll probably kiss old Tom on his alabaster brow and hug him. I've brought you a Bible. Read the twenty-third psalm. 'The Lord is my shepherd, I shall not want. He leadeth me beside the still waters—' That must refer to Lonely Valley Lake."

"Get out—and do not come back," Lanier cried. "You three fools have ruined me."

Lee Elkins got out, laughing as he went.

CHAPTER TWENTY-SIX

RAYNOR LANIER HAD SCARCELY CLIMBED THE grade out of Lonely Valley, on his way out to try to secure a loan, before Tom Harmon set his right foot gingerly on the floor, flexed his leg and stood on it. He grimaced with pain, but walked up and down the room nevertheless, although he limped sadly. Ah Fong came in and watched him.

"I'm limberin' her up," Harmon explained. "It hurts but I can stand that for a while."

He limped to the telephone to summon to the Big House the Sphinx twins and Skunk Tallow. They were to come up in a light truck and bring certain tools with them, including crowbars and picks. When they arrived, Harmon, dressed now for protection against the bitter cold, climbed into the truck with them and directed Skunk Tallow to drive to the boathouse. Here the tools were transferred to the speed boat and presently they were roaring down the lake.

During the winter the water level in the lake was at its lowest point, and the water was not flowing over the top of the dam, a condition of which Harmon was fully aware. Not until spring when the snow in the mountains melted would Lonely Valley creek become a roaring river filling the lake until the water flowed deeply over the dam, and thus rendering impossible the effort for its destruction.

Harmon led his men, armed with picks and crowbars, over the crest of the dam and down to its lower end.

"Felix Lanier did some work on a tunnel here some twenty-five or thirty years ago. I don't know how much he accomplished, but whatever work was done must have been started from the lower end of the dam. This here spot's just about the place I'd start a tunnel, so we'll pry them big boulders aside an' see if we can discover the old workings. I got a great curiosity to see how much work Felix done before the court enjoined him from proceedin' further with property that didn't belong to him!"

Two hours' labor uncovered the mouth of the ancient tunnel—an aperture about five feet wide and five feet high. Tom Harmon went into it with an electric torch, after allowing time for the foul air to leave the tunnel, and he carried the end of a steel tape-line held by one of the twins. Fifty feet brought him to the face of the workings. They had been well timbered but the long years and the dampness had rotted them so badly that Harmon could pick them apart easily with his fingers.

When he came out, he measured fifty feet over the top of the dam from a point just above the mouth of the tunnel. "About thirty-five more feet to tunnel," he decided, and paced off the width of the dam. It was approximately sixty feet. "Got to drive a T-head chamber across the face after completing the main tunnel," he reflected. "Fifteen feet on each side. Got to have an ore car and run a light track from the face well down the creek, to carry off the waste and dump it. Three eight hour shifts. Got to house the crew comfortably and feed 'em." He counted up the total number of hard rock men, timbermen and muckers he would require. As for the camp for them, that matter was readily solved. There was a forest service station within a mile of the dam—a snug, three room, log house with a lean-to kitchen and an equally snug log barn. On October first, after danger of forest fires was past, the ranger moved out of that country and would not return until spring was well advanced. So Tom Harmon decided to house and feed his tunnel crew in that station. In all probability nobody would ever know about it. At any rate, Harmon made up his mind to occupy the station and talk about it afterward. Provided the lake did not freeze solid he could run down daily in the speed boat and keep in touch with the progress made on the job.

The following morning he and the twins drove over to the county seat and Harmon purchased iron cots, mattresses, blankets and a long list of staple groceries. Leaving the twins to get these purchases back to the ranch and down to the forest ranger's station by boat, Harmon proceeded to Reno. He desired no local hard rock men for the task he contemplated and he knew he would have no difficulty finding plenty of unemployed miners wintering in Reno. While in Reno he ordered also and paid for in advance his fuse, a dozen cases of dynamite and thirty thousand pounds of black powder—this upon the advice of a powder expert he had employed. The force of dynamite exploded in a confined space is mostly downward, but black powder explosive force is upward. It has tremendous lifting power. The dynamite, being a faster explosive, would set off the black powder.

This shipment of powder he had hauled in trucks from Reno, for he did not dare risk shipping such a quantity of explosive by rail to the county seat and transporting it thence by the ranch trucks to Lonely Valley. News of such a shipment would be certain to be bruited about and news of it would certainly reach Milo Landrum. The ranch trucks, therefore, came through the county seat and Modoc City very late at night and nobody was the wiser. Fortunately the lake did not freeze over and, a ton at a time, the powder was transported to the dam by the speed boat.

On the day the mining operations were completed, the last can of powder delivered at the dam-site, stored and covered with limbs cut from the adjacent timber, and the men paid off and sent back to Reno, Raynor Lanier had completed his sentence in the county jail. To him here came Lee Elkins. Lanier refused to receive him, but the district attorney was not to be denied. He forced his way into Lanier's cell and sat down on the single stool the cell afforded.

"You look well," he announced. "You've gained weight. A trifle pale, of course, but a few days out in the wind and sun will restore your wonted color. And, by the way, the judge and I think you should not immediately return to Lonely Valley. It's still dangerous for you there, and Tom Harmon suggests that you continue on from here about the business you left Lonely Valley to prosecute a month ago. While he feels certain he can save you at the last minute he says you may not be agreeable to the means he will employ; that you might prefer to save yourself by your own efforts."

"Tom's a fool but on occasions he can think rather straight. I do prefer to save myself in my own way, if that be possible, so I agree to the judge's terms."

"Tom says that unless you succeed in securing a loan that will satisfy Landrum's judgment, you are to remain away until he, Tom, wires you to return. You are to keep him informed of your address."

"I agree to that. I'll agree to anything that will get me out of reach of my fool friends."

At eight o'clock the following morning Sam Gorton came to his cell, unlocked it and said: "You're through here. Beat it."

He stood just outside the door, glowering at Lanier, while the latter packed the bag that had accompanied him to the county jail. "Going to give me back my gun, Gorton?" Lanier queried when the bag was packed. "You needn't load it for me. Without cartridges in the chambers it isn't a deadly weapon—no deadlier, indeed, than a monkey wrench; it's mine and I want it."

Gorton handed him the gun.

"Suppose," Lanier suggested amiably, "you now issue me a permit to carry it—loaded. My life is in danger and for that reason I deserve a permit."

"Beat it," the sheriff answered. "You don't get no permit from me."

Lanier buckled the empty gun around his waist and stepped out into the corridor, at the end of which he could see Lee Elkins waiting for him. As he started down the corridor Sam Gorton could not resist kicking him severely under the coat-tails to accelerate his departure. The next instant Lanier had turned on him and led with his left, which Gorton dodged, only to connect with a right uppercut, a stiff, short-arm jolt that came from just above Lanier's hip and had all the weight of his hundred and eighty pounds behind it. The sheriff fell over against the barred cell and reached for his gun; Lanier grasped his arm, wrung it and the pistol dropped to the floor of the corridor. With a kick Lanier sent it sliding down the concrete surface, then proceeded to cut the sheriff to strings and ribbons. He stretched Sam Gorton on the floor, sat on him and pounded him into insensibility. Then he joined Lee Elkins.

"You saw the sheriff kick me, didn't you, Lee?" he demanded happily.

"Certainly—and I shall be very happy to testify that you defended yourself. When Sam comes to me for a warrant for your arrest I'll tell him to go get you without a warrant. That will induce him to forget the mauling you gave him. Your car's outside the jail and I've paid your garage bill. Make yourself scarce. Head out of town as if you were bound for Lonely Valley, then circle the town and go to Reno. You can't be extradited from Nevada for assault and battery, even on a sheriff. Goodby and good luck to you."

CHAPTER TWENTY-SEVEN

RAYNOR LANIER HAD BEEN GONE FOR A month.

One day a stranger motored over to Lonely Valley and sought Tom Harmon down at the barns. "My name's Donaldson," he announced, "and I'm an inspector for the Southwestern Agricultural Credit Corporation. We loan money on livestock and your Mr. Raynor Lanier has applied for a loan on his cattle. I've been sent up to inspect the cattle and count them; I'll also want to ride over the ranch and investigate feed conditions. I understand Mr. Lanier has a permit to graze ten thousand head in the Modoc National Forest and if that be true, of course, he has ample summer range. However, I can investigate the permit at the forest ranger's office in Alturas on my way back. If I report favorably on the cattle and the feed conditions Mr. Lanier will be loaned the money he requires. He assured me you would give me all the aid possible in my investigation."

Tom Harmon scratched his ear in some perplexity. "We got all the cattle in fields, feedin' them hay," he announced, "an' owing to about eight inches o' snow all over the ranch I reckon you ain't goin' to have an opportunity to investigate the winter range conditions. However, we got seven thousand acres o' flat meadow under free irrigation an' lots of it an' we cut a ton o' wild hay to the acre. Some o' the stacks has been fed but I reckon you could count five thousand tons on hand if you cared to. But we ain't got no summer range. Mr. Lanier's grazin' permit in the Modoc National Forest has been revoked. The chief ranger called up yesterday an' told me about it."

"Has Lanier been violating the rules of the Forest Service, Mr. Harmon?"

"No. Somebody else wanted his grazin' permit an' that somebody had pull enough to reach clear into Washington an' get it. Such things are done in this country once in a while, although the Department plays fair when the Congressmen an' Senators let it alone. The chief ranger an' the District Forester feel pretty badly about it an' both are makin' a protest agin the revocation o' Lanier's permit."

"Dirty work, eh? Well, without his summer range, Mr. Lanier would be embarrassed for feed; he might have to go to the expense of shipping his cattle elsewhere and paying far more for his summer range. Cattle must be regarded as raw material; feed makes them into the finished product. We never loan on raw material. We must be assured of the finished product, otherwise our collateral may die of starvation or have to be sold at a loss to prevent a total loss. I'm sorry but I'll have to report adversely on this loan. We are making very few loans on a steadily declining beef market, but this Lanier loan, on the surface, appeared rather attractive, even in these hard times."

"Oh, well," Tom Harmon replied easily, "your company has charged Lanier for the expense of your trip up here to make the inspection, so you might as well go through with the job. We'll ride over the ranch today an' look at the cattle; tomorrow I'll have the riders out an' we'll bunch 'em in fence corners an' count 'em. I'm tellin' you this loan *is* attractive, provided Lanier gets his grazin' permit back—an' I got a notion he's liable to. Everything else bein' O.K., if we get our grazin' permit restored the loan can go through, without delay."

To this plan Donaldson agreed.

When the inspector had left the ranch, Tom Harmon motored in to Modoc City and went into the telephone office. The woman who managed the little exchange had known him all her life and greeted him cordially.

"I want a private pow-wow with you, Tillie," he announced. "I'm bristlin' with suspicions an' I want 'em verified."

The manager led him into her private office. "Tillie," said Harmon, "I've known instances where the local telegraph company sprung a leak. You ever been solicited to let the same thing happen in your office?"

The manager nodded, smilingly.

"Regardin' Ray Lanier's business?"

Again the manager nodded.

"Him an' Milo Landrum's in a tangle an' Milo's just got to know things," Harmon went on musingly.

"Well, he didn't succeed in getting me or my two girls to betray Ray Lanier, Tom."

"I knew he wouldn't. Make you a nice offer?"

"A hundred dollars, cash in advance."

"For listenin' in on local or long distance calls?"

"Both, Tom."

"Want to do me a favor, Tillie?"

"What is its nature?" the manager asked cautiously.

"Make a deal with Landrum. Take his hundred dollars an' every time I put in a call from the ranch you switch a line into Landrum's office so he can listen in. I believe in feedin' the curious."

"You old crook!"

Mr. Harmon's bland smile appeared to admit this impeachment. "Go on, Tillie," he pleaded. "It's no crime when you got my permission to do it—an' the telephone company don't pay you so much you can afford to cast away a hundred dollars. I figger this deal's legitimate."

"I'll do it for you, Tom, but you cannot pay me for doing it."

"Tillie," Harmon replied, "you're as sweet as the warm spring rains that start the grass growin'. I'm obliged to you. You're a real neighbor. You needn't take up Milo's time with my local calls; in fact I only want him to listen in on one long-distance call. He'll figger he's got his hundred dollars worth right there."

"Call me personally when you wish to place your long distance call," the manager suggested, "so I can handle the wire myself. This office closes at nine o'clock nightly, but I am always here until nine fifteen."

"Is Landrum in town now?"

"I saw him at noon on the porch of the Mountain House."

"Then he's in his office now. Call him up and make your deal."

The manager telephoned Landrum and Tom Harmon heard her say: "This is Matilda Barnes of the telephone exchange. I've been thinking over that matter you suggested and if it is still of interest to you on the same basis it can now be arranged."

She listened a moment and hung up. "He's delighted, Tom. Say's he'll drop in with the cash late this afternoon."

"Good news. I'll be puttin' in a transcontinental call four or five days from now. Thanks, Tillie, until you are better paid—which don't seem possible."

He returned to Lonely Valley and laboriously picked out with one finger on Raynor Lanier's typewriter a long letter to Janet Corliss, which he sent to her by air-mail, Skunk Tallow taking the letter in to the post office at Modoc City that night. Four days later he received a telegram which the Modoc City telegraph operator relayed to him over the telephone. It was from Daniel P. Magruder and read:

*"Please telephone me Schuyler 7-6707
tonight Stop If you place call after nine P. M.
you get cheap rate."*

Tom Harmon was pleased. He felt morally
certain that Milo Landrum had received a copy of
that telegram and would await eagerly the
privilege of listening in on the requested long
distance telephone call. He was convinced of the
soundness of his conjecture when, half an hour
later, Tilly Barnes called him up from the
telephone office.

"Hello, Tom," she saluted him, "I hear you're
going to talk to New York tonight."

"I am," he assured her. "Be sure you're on the
job an' alone in the office."

At nine-twenty that night he got Magruder on
the wire. "Hello, Mr. Harmon," Magruder began
briskly. "Can you hear me clearly?"

"You bet."

"Has Mr. Lanier returned to his ranch?"

"No, he's stayin' away a while longer. This
country ain't any too healthy for him. That's why
he's left matters in my hands. You got my letter?"

"Yes. Mr. Harmon, my client will sell that dam-
site at the western end of Lonely Valley Lake for
three hundred thousand dollars. We cannot
consider your offer of a hundred thousand. As
you know, I have dickered with the Laniers,
father and son, for years and you ought to know

by this time that my client is a most obdurate person. I think my client might sell cheaper to somebody else, but the price to Mr. Lanier is three hundred thousand. We both know the land isn't worth three hundred, but what my client is wishful to charge you for it is a price based on its strategic value, plus an ancient animosity."

"Well," Harmon admitted, "it'd be worth three hundred thousand to Raynor Lanier if he could raise the money. Would you take a hundred thousand cash an' a first mortgage at six per cent on the seventy-five thousand acres that'd be drained as soon as we can blow out that dam?"

"I'm sorry," Magruder replied. "My client insists on all cash."

"Well, that cooks our goose. Lanier can't interest that much cash capital. If your client would accept his terms I figger he can organize a company an'—"

"Yes, he'd have to do that. I hear he's personally in a bad way financially. I understand a man out your way—Lanning or Lamson or some such name—has a judgment against him for something in the neighborhood of a hundred and sixteen thousand dollars and that a writ of execution has already issued against the cattle on which this Lanning or Lamson man holds a chattel mortgage; that the cattle are to be sold shortly at public auction."

"You got the straight o' that," Harmon admitted

ruefully. "Lanier can't meet that judgment, so he'll have to let Landrum take the cattle. However, if the skunk thinks he's goin' to live long enough to enjoy the profit on that deal, then all I got to say is that he's an optimist."

"If there's a bare chance that Mr. Lanier could organize a company that could get two hundred thousand dollars capital together as a first payment *I might* induce my client to listen to reason. Certainly there would be ample security in a first mortgage on the lake lands when drained."

"He'll have to move fast to do that, Mr. Magruder. I'm afraid he won't have enough time. Landrum'll buy those cattle in at a price that'll leave a big deficiency jedgement against Lanier, an' right off there'll be an attachment on the lake lands to satisfy this deficiency jedgement."

"Well, why doesn't Lanier incorporate all his holdings immediately and place all of the stock in the name of some trusted friend? Then he'd be execution proof. There are ways of doing these things."

"That's what I suggested, but he says Landrum would have him up on an order of examination to inquire into his assets and it just ain't in him to lie under oath."

"Listen carefully to me, Mr. Harmon. I wish to see that dam-site disposed of and promptly. As Donald MacLean's attorney that worthless piece of land has been a nuisance to me for forty years.

I've had a bushel basket full of correspondence about it; I could never get anywhere with a deal. Now, if Lanier will consider incorporating all of his holdings I think I may be able to get him a loan here in New York, for half a million dollars, with the stock as security. I do not promise it, because real money is mighty scarce these days, but at seven per cent, with collateral easily worth four times the loan, it *might* be done. With such a loan Lanier could pay my client cash for the damsite, pay Landrum's judgment and have some operating capital left. Also, he could show his bank a mighty fine statement and thus increase his line of credit. I'd want twenty-five thousand dollars for my efforts in putting through such a loan. The time is short, of course. Has Lanier done all in his power to raise a loan with which to pay off Landrum's judgment against him?"

"Doggone it," Tom Harmon replied, "he had a loan all arranged with the Southwestern Agricultural Credit Corporation. Their inspector was up here an' counted the cows an' approved their quality an' the winter range, when up jumped the devil. Lanier's grazin' permit in the Modoc National Forest was canceled, so that put the crusher on the loan. They won't make a loan to anybody in this country that hasn't got ample summer range."

"How long before those cattle go under the hammer?"

"Two weeks exactly."

"Pretty quick work will be necessary. Better get in touch with Lanier and have him incorporate his holdings, and in anticipation of his doing that I will start work on the half million dollar loan, although I tell you frankly I have no hope of obtaining it in time to save Lanier's cows—and he'll need those cows to help pay off any loan I may be able to negotiate for him. The situation is pretty desperate, but—you never can tell."

"Couldn't you cut your fee some," Harmon pleaded. "Five per cent is plumb immoral."

"Couldn't possibly cut it a nickel. The job's worth it—and Lanier is up against the gun."

"Well, will you get your client to wire Lanier an option on that hell-fired dam-site for ten days at three hundred thousand dollars?"

"I shall not. The first man to get here with three hundred thousand dollars gets a deed to it."

"Well, you see what you can do at your end an' I'll work my end an' let you know what luck we have. Thanks for your interest. Goodby."

Harmon waited a moment and then heard a telltale click as a local telephone receiver was hung up. "Well, Milo, you certainly got an earful o' information that ain't so," he soliloquized. "Now we'll see how you act on it."

He loosened his six-shooter in the holster and stepped out into the dark street, hesitated a minute, then made his way over to the Mountain

House, where he engaged a room for the night. He was too prudent to drive home to Lonely Valley in the dark, for, in the terminology of gangdom, he knew his "number was up."

As he was about to get into the ranch car in front of the Mountain House the following morning a chauffeur-driven limousine containing Milo Landrum and three men unknown to Harmon rolled down the street and turned east on the road leading to the county seat. Harmon noted a steamer trunk and a suit-case on the trunk-rack in the rear.

"I believe," he decided, "that dear old Milo is bound for distant parts—New York, in fact. I'll verify this suspicion."

He walked over to the telephone office and telephoned Lee Elkins at the county seat. "Lee," he announced, "Milo Landrum is headed your way, with three men I suspect are his new body-guard, a steamer trunk an' a suit-case. I think he meditates a long journey, so I wish you'd engage somebody to hang around the railroad station an' find out where the skunk buys a ticket to. Call me up at the ranch and let me know all about it."

About one o'clock Elkins telephoned to inform him that Landrum had purchased a ticket for New York. Immediately Harmon telephoned to Magruder and informed him of this. "He'll call on you with all his tradin' instincts standin' up like the hair on the back of a wild boar. We got him hooked. I've done my part, now you do yours."

Three days before the Lanier cattle were to be sold at public auction the telegraph agent at Modoc City called up Tom Harmon and read him a message that had just been received. It read:

"Dear Tom: I have just banked a certified check for three hundred and fifty thousand Stop You are a darling Stop Uncle Dan and I flying west this afternoon

Janet."

The effect of this message upon Tom Harmon was remarkable. Within half an hour after its receipt he was at the wheel of Raynor Lanier's speed boat skimming down Lonely Valley Lake with eight men. With feverish haste these men fell upon the cans of powder and carried them into the tunnel prepared for them. At the upper end of the tunnel a T-head chamber had been cut and smoothly lined with concrete to keep out the drip of water coming in between the huge blocks of lava. The entire tunnel had been similarly treated and such water as entered it from the bottom was running off in a little channel cut in the floor of the tunnel and covered with planking. Over this planking tarpaulins had been spread and on top of these the men emptied the cans of black powder and tamped the T-head chamber full. At the head of the tunnel they piled their dozen cases of dynamite, attached fulminating caps to half a dozen sticks and ran these wires down the mouth of the tunnel. Then they piled more black powder over the dynamite.

They were three full days loading that tunnel, and when at last the job was done they filled in the mouth of the tunnel with rock, spliced the wires running from the fulminating caps to a single wire which was drawn up over the north wall of the gorge and carried along the lake shore. As each reel of the fine wire was stretched Harmon, following along with the speed boat, tossed a new reel ashore, to be spliced on. They had the wire stretched twenty miles up to the Big House on the evening of the day that Sam Gorton mounted the steps of the County Courthouse and sold Raynor Lanier's cattle to Milo Landrum, who must have flown back from New York to be present at the sale.

The following forenoon Raynor Lanier came home, driving in his car from the county seat. Affer putting his car in the garage he came into the house through the back door and found Tom Harmon comfortably toasting his shins before the log fire in the living room.

"Welcome, Little Stranger," Mr. Harmon announced cheerfully. "I hear you been to a lot o' places, includin' thirty days in the county jail. How did you find the service in Sam Gorton's hotel?"

Lanier stared at him bleakly. "Thanks for

attending to my affairs during my enforced absence, Tom. However, now that I'm home there will be no further necessity for bothering you with them. This time you're really fired and for two reasons, the lesser of which is that I can no longer afford the luxury of a foreman. I'm practically down in the nester class now. Skunk Tallow will drive you in to Modoc City."

"Can't I even stay for lunch?" Harmon pleaded tragically.

"If you're hungry—yes. But you're not welcome, I assure you. What was the brilliant idea that moved you to put me in jail?"

"I was tryin' to do a few things for you, things I knew you wouldn't do for yourself, an' I had to have you out o' the way while I was doin' 'em."

"If you had succeeded I could afford to forget that thirty days in jail. Landrum bought in the cows yesterday. Cost him fifty-two dollars a head. The loan on them was fifty dollars a head, so it seems Landrum isn't going to have a deficiency judgment against me, after all."

"I seen to that, Ray. I had a friend o' mine there to run up the bids on him. The cows were a bargain at fifty-two a head an' I figgered Landrum had to have 'em. They were just another trick he had to take in his game to ruin you."

"But your man didn't have any money."

"No, but Landrum didn't know that."

"Suppose Landrum had quit bidding at the last

274

bid your man made and permitted the cows to be knocked down to him?"

"In that case, Ray, I reckon we'd have been embarrassed, that's all."

"Well, you used your head well, for once in your life." Lanier could not forego a twisted smile. "I suppose I'll have to forgive you that jail sentence in view of your action in saving me from a deficiency judgment."

"That's mighty generous o' you, son."

Lanier winced at the all too apparent sarcasm. He glanced away and observed that the table had been set for luncheon and that there were four places. Also Ah Fong had set out place plates and the best napery and glassware. There was a huge bowl of violets in the center of the table.

"Hum-m-m," Lanier remarked. "Pulling off a party in my absence, eh?"

"We expected you to be present."

"Whom do you mean by we?"

"Wait an' find out," Harmon replied with asperity—and even as he spoke there came faintly to them the prolonged shriek of an automobile siren far up the grade. "They're comin' now," Harmon added, "so you won't have long to wait. Meanwhile, if I was you, I'd go wash my face and hands an' mebbe my neck an' ears, an' comb my hair. You might ha' noticed I'm wearin' a white silk shirt an' a black necktie an' my Sunday pants an' shoes."

Lanier stepped out on the porch and gazed up the grade. A small coupe was rolling down it to Lonely Valley and at sight of him the driver sounded the siren furiously; he saw a hand fluttering out of the window.

He dashed back into the house. "I think Janet's coming," he cried to Tom Harmon. "At least the car resembles hers."

"*It is* Miss Janet, fool," Harmon shouted. "Go make yourself pretty."

Both men were waiting on the veranda when the car pulled up under the porte-cochère. Janet Corliss thrust her head and shoulders out the window and cried:

"Well, am I welcome?"

For answer Lanier leaped down the steps, opened the car door, lifted her out, held her, suspended, at arm's length a moment, then drew her up to him and kissed her.

"That's a heap friendlier'n his goin' away kiss," Harmon yelled, "but still there's room for improvement. I never did see such a bashful fool. Howdy, Mr. Magruder. Pile out an' in. I'm Tom Harmon an' this here's the boss o' the rancho, Ray Lanier. Ray, remember your manners."

"You're both welcome," Lanier assured them as he shook Magruder's hand. "Do come in. Tom, remember your manners, and put Miss Janet's car in the garage and after that bring in my guests' luggage for them."

"Not until I've kissed him," Janet cried, and leaped into Harmon's arms. "You dear old schemer, I'm so glad to see you again."

"We meet," quoth Mr. Harmon, "in a mighty sad hour. I've been fired."

"What?"

"Fired, dismissed, discharged, given the air, informed that my room's better'n my company. However, the boss has relented long enough to let me stay for lunch."

"Tom, you're jesting?"

"I'm not."

Janet turned on Lanier. "Is this true, Ray. Have you dismissed Tom?"

"I have," he replied, "but without prejudice—at least, not very much—not nearly so much as I had. I can't afford him now. I can look after what cows I have left."

Harmon nodded owlishly. "I'm coupled in the betting with King Alfonso. We've both joined the ranks o' the unemployed."

"No, you're not, my boy," Daniel P. Magruder assured him. "I'll buy a small ranch and put you in charge of it."

Lanier flushed darkly. "You might have spared us this embarrassing moment, Tom," he said. "And out here in this cold spring weather is no place to discuss it, anyhow." With a wave of his arm he indicated the open door. Janet entered first and ran back into the kitchen, from which arose at once a strident shriek with elements of delight in it. Tom Harmon cocked his wild eyebrows and laid his head in a listening attitude.

"Ah Fong," he announced, "is pleased—for some reason or other."

"Well, Janet, what brings you back to Lonely Valley so soon?" Lanier inquired as Janet returned to the living room and he stepped forward to remove her fur coat.

"Oh, Uncle Dan's feet began to itch. He's heard so much about Lonely Valley he was seized with a sudden yearning to see it. Business was quiet in his office, so he suggested we come out and visit you. I gladly agreed. I had no idea you might require cheering up."

"Well, you're mighty welcome, both of you. And I could use a moderate quantity of cheerfulness just now. Landrum got my cows—at a bargain even on the present low market. The calf crop goes with them."

"Has he removed them from your ranch?" Magruder inquired.

"No, but he will tomorrow, I daresay."

"He gave you quite a hard financial poke, didn't he?" said Janet sympathetically.

"Well, I'm out of debt and I'll recover from the poke, although I'll never look the same again. Janet, you will occupy your old room. Mr. Magruder, permit me to show you to your room. Luncheon will be served in about forty minutes."

Tom Harmon came in with the bags. "Reduced to the grade o' bell-hop," he complained. "Ray, I never suspected you'd rob me o' my best years an' then throw me out in the snow."

"Will you be good enough to cease your vile complaining," Lanier cried sharply. "If you had played my game instead of harkening to your own base instincts, you wouldn't be out in the snow today, I would still be the cattle king of Lonely Valley and possessed of sufficient working capital to enable me to carry on for the next five years, regardless of the price of beef. For the second time I assure you I think you're more than a little insane."

Harmon set down the bags. "Oh, shucks," he murmured and thrust his finger in his mouth, after the fashion of an embarrassed child. "I plumb forgot to tell you I settled with Milo Landrum over the telephone this mornin'. An' Milo's pleased—so pleased, as a matter o' fact, that he accepted my invitation to come out here this afternoon to discuss with you the purchase o' them lake lands. Of course he ain't goin' to pay you no such price as you asked, but at that I expect he'll be reasonable. I got a notion you ain't in no tradin' humor this afternoon, so I reckon you'd better leave the tradin' to me. Before I get through with Milo you're goin' to have your cows back at their cost to Milo, he's goin' to abandon that grazin' permit he took away from you an', as the poet says, all will be merry as a marriage bell—if I may be permitted," he added elaborately, "to bring up such a delicate subject."

Raynor Lanier leaped, caught his foreman by the throat with both hands and choked him and shook him and rushed him all over the room. When finally he let the foreman go he said:

"Tom, if you do that I'll not throw you out in the snow."

"I don't guarantee it," Harmon gurgled, "so in consequence I'm wearin' my long-legged an' long-armed winter underwear. However, you leave it to me an' I'll do the best I can."

"I didn't think Landrum would have the courage to venture into Lonely Valley, Tom."

"Oh, I told him he could bring his bodyguard an' that you'd put on your coyote-skin coat an' go out an' set in his car with the bodyguard while him an' me discussed business. He wanted assurances an' I give 'em to him. He's bringin' out ten thousand in cash as settlement in full for the pain an' suffering he caused me, an' I'm to sign clear of all claims agin him."

"If you'd done that three months ago—"

"Couldn't," Harmon protested. "I was thinkin' of your honor. Remember, Felix complained to me just before he died that he'd made a mistake by raisin' you a gentleman. Well, I ain't got no such handicap, besides which I'm older'n you an' almost three times as smart."

"Tom, in heaven's name out with it. Don't feed me news in driblets. What the devil have you been up to?"

"Ain't been up to much 'ceptin' I been tryin' my best to fix things so's this foreman's job o' mine could be made permanent. You ain't got no idear how hard I've been thinkin'. I reckon I've used up a gallon o' bromides tryin' to cure my headache."

Ah Fong opened the door leading to the kitchen. "Somebody want you on telephone, Ray," he announced.

It developed that Milo Landrum wished to speak to him. "Lanier," he announced, "your man Harmon says he's willin' to be good an' not stand in the way of a trade between me an' you. How about it? Do you guarantee him?"

"He won't harm a hair of your head, Landrum. It will not be necessary for you to come out with your bodyguard. You'll be absolutely safe. You have my word of honor for that."

"I'll be out at two o'clock an' I'll come alone—that is, I'll leave my bodyguard down the road a piece in case you shouldn't be able to make some of your help behave. If anything happens to me it's goin' to be just too bad for you an' your men."

"I'll meet you half a mile from the house and remain with your men as a hostage, a guaranty of your safety. Harmon told you that, and now I give you my assurance. You'll find me waiting in the

281

road and if anything happens to me, you and your bodyguard will have to go through machine gun and rifle fire to get out of Lonely Valley. I think we understand each other."

Despite the unstable condition of his affairs, Janet's presence brought to Raynor Lanier a feeling of happiness that had not been present since he had seen her last. Janet, too, was in good spirits. Magruder had little to say during the luncheon, seeming content to listen and appraise Raynor Lanier; a move which the garrulous Mr. Harmon considered he might follow with profit.

At a quarter of two o'clock Lanier excused himself and walked down the road from the house, turned and proceeded along the road that led up the grade until he came to a little clump of stunted firs. The Sphinx twins awaited him here. Lanier gave them their orders and walked back about two hundred yards, where he waited until two cars came rolling down the grade. The first was a coupé driven by Milo Landrum and contained no other passenger; the second was a limousine, with a tough looking chauffeur and three bleak-eyed men passengers. When this limousine stopped Raynor Lanier opened the door, stepped in and sat down on one of the jump seats. He lit a cigar and stared out with mild interest at the foam crested wavelets on Lonely Valley Lake.

Landrum paused long enough to satisfy himself

that Lanier was in the limousine, then pushed on up to the Big House. Tom Harmon opened the front door and hospitably invited him in; he even helped Landrum remove his heavy fur coat and begged him to seat himself in front of the fire.

"Well," Landrum announced briskly, "let's talk. Ain't no sense leavin' Lanier an' my men settin' out in that car in this raw spring weather. I take it Lanier's agreeable to any trade you may make for him."

"Right as a fox," Harmon murmured. "You brought the deed an' a check for two hundred and fifty thousand dollars with you?"

"I've brought a deed an' a check for one hundred thousand with me."

"But that wasn't your deal with Ray."

"Harmon, time an' tide wait for no man. When I was ready an' willin' to do the right thing, you blocked the deal, so I had to go ahead an' take possession o' Lanier's cattle to pay my judgment against him. Since I talked with him I've bought that dam-site from Donald MacLean's heir, a woman by the name o' Janet Corliss, so it looks like I'm holdin' cards an' spades, the four aces an' Big Casino. Lanier's holdin' Little Casino."

"Sort o' looks like you're holdin' a nice hand, Landrum. Mind showin' me the deed Miss Corliss gave you?"

"I never bluff, Harmon." Landrum handed him the deed and Harmon noted that it had been recorded the day previous. He handed it back.

"Lanier's down to about three thousand head o' cattle an' he's shy on operatin' capital," Landrum continued. "Them lake lands ain't worth a cent to him now, because I can block him forever from drainin' them. However, I'm willin' to be generous an' give him a hundred thousand for the land."

"Before we get too deep into that discussion," Harmon suggested, "suppose you settle with me."

With a grim smile Landrum handed him ten one thousand dollar bills. "Thanks," Harmon murmured. "I'd be willin' to get shot once a year for that much money. We're square, Landrum, so now we can take up Lanier's business. To begin, no price that you're willin' to pay is acceptable. Ray's made up his mind he ain't goin' to sell them lake lands to you or nobody else. They been in the family for a long time an' he's got so attached to them the thought o' partin' with them fills his eyes with tears. He don't need operatin' capital. The boy's goin' to marry Miss Janet Corliss an' she tells me it ain't been so long since she banked three hundred an' fifty thousand dollars o' your money."

Landrum jumped as if snakebitten. "I don't believe it," he snarled. "You can't run no blazer like that on me."

"No? Well, take a look through that winder—up the hillside. You see a young lady an' an old gentleman walkin' down from the Lanier family cemetery? Well, the young lady is Miss Corliss, an' as you've done business with the old gentleman you know his name is Daniel P. Magruder. They're Lanier's guests."

Landrum paled and looked uneasy; Tom Harmon's plain features were wreathed in a sweet and tender smile. "You remember the night I had a long distance telephone talk with Magruder, Landrum? Well, that conversation was all dust in the air, for your benefit. I fixed it with Tillie Barnes to plug you in on our conversation. Here's the hundred dollars you gave her to betray me. Milo, you dear, sweet-scented murderer, we sold you a pup—now, now, don't reach for your gun. There is peace between us—an' I have the drop on you. Look around, Milo, an' see the vision o' sudden death behind you."

Landrum looked around. In the entrance to the hall that led from the living room down to the wing of the house in which the sleeping rooms were, Big Foot stood with a shotgun pointed at Landrum.

"Eleven buckshot in each shell," Harmon elucidated. "However, do not worry. Big Foot will not kill you unless you kill me—an' I know you're too good a business man to do that. Not on the home grounds, anyway. Well, to get back to business. Milo, you don't want Ray Lanier's cows. You never did want them except for a definite purpose an' now that purpose don't exist no longer. You've put yourself out of the running—ruined your own game. You figured you had to beat Ray Lanier to buying that damsite—an' you done the same, thereby provin' how nice you can be when the sperrit moves you. So now it'd be plumb foolish of you to try ruinin' Ray Lanier. You think you got him treed because you had enough political influence to have his grazin' permit revoked—"

"Yes, yes, I had it revoked," Landrum wheezed. "That's one poke he won't get over in a hurry."

"No? Milo, I do declare you're the most optimistical person I ever did see. Forty year ago old Donald MacLean scripped every water hole an' stream in the Modoc National Forest. It was the free range in them days an' he got control o' the water holes to freeze Felix Lanier off the range. But before he got around to that the government withdrew all that free range from entry an' included it in the Modoc National Forest. However, the MacLean parcels are still there, only now they belong to Miss Janet Corliss. Milo, I believe Raynor Lanier's got influence enough with her to have her fence all them water-holes an' creeks, so cattle can't drink at 'em. An' if she does that Lanier'll supply some gutful men to see that nobody tears the fences down to let the cattle in to drink. An' you know as well as I do that when a cow brute can't find water on the

286

range it'll drift until it can find it. Cripes, what a hell of a round-up you're goin' to have next fall!"

"I'll risk that," Landrum replied triumphantly. "The government will sue immediately to condemn those lands back to the public domain an' pay cash for 'em at an appraised value or exchange 'em for other lands not in a forest reserve or national park or national monument. An' the government never loses a suit like that."

"I know that. I ain't altogether a dumb fool. But Lee Elkins tells me the government moves kinder slow. It'd take 'em mebbe a month to prove they had to enter suit an' another month to get the complaint drawn. Then, after they'd hunted around four or five months tryin' to find Miss Corliss an' serve her personally with a copy o' the summons an' complaint the summer'd be gone, but—them fences would still be there. So they'd serve her by publication an' then she'd have thirty days after that to answer the complaint an' finally the suit would come to trial. Then the verdict would be appealed—why, Milo, I've told all that to the district forester an' he laughed fit to bust himself in two. He saw right off that if that deal went through the government wouldn't get a cent o' revenue from the Modoc National Forest this year, so he wired the details back to the Department of Agriculture an' the Secretary got busy an' looked into the matter o' the cancellation o' Lanier's permit, with the result that he's wired the Chief Forester in San Francisco that the grazin' permit will be took away from you an' give back to Ray Lanier, after which he hopes Miss Corliss will listen to reason an' exchange her water-holes for just as good land or better somewhere else."

Harmon paused and eyed Landrum almost sadly. "Now ain't all them Lanier cows goin' to prove an embarrassment to you with no summer range for 'em? An' anyhow, what do you want to be botherin' with cows for, when you ain't goin' to live to enjoy 'em?"

"How do you know I ain't goin' to live? You figger on havin' me killed, you figger on double-crossin' me, after I've paid you ten thousand—"

"Nothin' so coarse as that. Nobody on the Lanier payroll is goin' to kill you or hire you killed. You got Ray Lanier's word for that an' lemme assure you, that boy never breaks his word. But there's a man you little suspect an' he's right under your nose day an' night, who's waitin' to kill you the minute somebody telephones him you refused to sell Ray Lanier's cows back to him for what Ray owed you on that note. That means you got to sell here an' now or you'll wake up in hell."

Landrum was silent for fully a minute. "Well," he admitted heavily, "I guess you're right. I'm not lookin' for trouble. Never was, in fact."

"You been unfortunate in havin' a lot of it thrust

on you, Milo. Well, Ray ain't got the money to pay you for them cattle right now, but he can get it an' pay you the minute he gets his grazin' permit back, which should be in about a week. Meanwhile, I got here for your signature an agreement to sell, provided you're paid ten thousand dollars down to bind the bargain. Here's a fountain pen an' here's the ten thousand dollars."

"I won't trade on them terms."

"Suit yourself. You know the answer. You got to get your cattle off this ranch tomorrow. You got a place to put them?"

"No, I was thinkin' o' makin' some arrangement with Lanier to hold 'em for me a little longer—"

"Not a day after tomorrow. If your men ain't here to gather 'em by eight o'clock tomorrow I'm goin' to throw every head down in a field close to the lake. That field's full up with wild parsley, cows like it an' it always poisons them—"

"I'll sell on your terms," Landrum interrupted. "I don't want no more trouble than I got already," and he signed the agreement of sale and accepted the bills he had so recently handed Harmon.

"Thanks very much," Harmon murmured politely. "I guess that's about all the business we got to transact, Milo, old thug."

"Name a price for the lake lands," Landrum pleaded. "Damn it, I'm stuck with that dam-site, but I'm willing to pay a good price for the privilege of blowing the dam out and reclaimin' the lake-bed. Have some common sense, Harmon. Unless I blow out the dam the lake remains as is forever. I'll give Lanier half a million dollars. Now, that's an offer he just cannot afford to refuse. I'm holdin' a pat hand and you certainly know it."

"You look a mite pale an' peaked," Harmon evaded. "Can't I prevail on you to take a little whiskey? It might steady your nerves."

"I'd be obliged to you for some whiskey," Landrum panted.

"Just press the button on that little block o' wood on the smokin' stand in front of you, Milo. This leg o' mine's still stiff an' I don't like to move around much."

Landrum leaned forward and pressed the button. About five seconds later the sound of a distant and terrific explosion broke the quiet of the room; the shock of it caused the electric light fixtures and the pictures on the wall to shake and rattle. The windows rattled too, and something crashed in the butler's pantry.

"Good God," Landrum cried, "what was that?"

"It must have been an explosion, Milo. And it was quite a ways from here—way down the end o' the lake, I imagine." He crossed to the window and looked out. "Yep, it was down by your dam, Milo. Look! You can see all the white smoke in the world billowin' up over the hills. Milo, I'll lay you ten to one some low-flung enemy o' yourn has blowed out that high-priced dam. Wait a minute an' I'll tell you whether they made a good clean job of it or not."

Landrum stood at his side, staring. Suddenly a rocket arched high over the hills and burst. "There's the signal I expected," Harmon went on. "That rocket means the operation was a great success—that Lonely Valley Lake is disappearin' at the rate o' mebbe four million gallons a minute."

"You—you damned swindler," Landrum cried furiously. "I'll sue hell out of you an' Lanier an' that Corliss girl. I'll have damages on all o' you— I'll put you all through bankruptcy—I'll—"

"You'll be quiet, Landrum. Sue if you want to an' get a verdict for damages. I did that job an' I'm proud of it. Ray Lanier's as surprised about it as you are. So is Miss Corliss. He was in jail while I did the dirty work, so when you sue I'll confess judgment. I reckon the judge'll give you a verdict an' ten cents damages. You see, Milo, a feller can't be awarded damages unless he proves he's sustained 'em—an' as far as the judge would be concerned that quarter section o' yours was just plain land, with no value except for hold-up purposes. If the whole quarter section was to be blowed up you'd still be as well off as you are now. You can't damage worthless property, feller. But that ain't the only joke on you, Milo. When you pressed the button to ring for that drink you blew up your own dam."

Landrum steadied himself against an armchair. "What else do you know?" he asked. He was trying to conceal the hurt.

"You got a Chinese cook at your house in Modoc City. He's a cousin o' Ray Lanier's Chink, Ah Fong. Ah Fong's been a mite peeved because Ray Lanier's been so long about killin' you. He figgers Ray has lost face for not avengin' his father, so he took the duty on himself an' planted his relative in your employ. Not a hard job. When your white housekeeper quit, on account o' too many corpses dumped on your front stoop, you hired a Chinaman. Ah Fong paid that housekeeper to quit and recommended a Chinaman to take his place. It was the only way Ah Fong could get inside your bodyguard, an' he's only been waitin' to know the result o' my recent operations before telephonin' his relative to slip somethin' in your soup. Well, you've done everything I asked you to do, so now it's up to me to do you a favor. As soon as you get home you pay that Chinaman off an' send him down the road. Meanwhile I'll go get you that drink you need worse'n ever now."

"Never mind," Landrum replied in a very weary voice. "The jig's up an' I ain't got no further business here. So I'll go home."

"An' when you get there, dismiss your bodyguard. You don't need 'em no more, for of course, you'll behave yourself in the future. Indeed, Milo, if Ray Lanier dies before you do an' with his boots on, you're goin' to get the blame for it, even if you was in Europe when it happened."

He picked up Landrum's coat and helped the trembling man into it, opened the door for him, took him gently by the arm and led him down the veranda steps to his waiting car. They passed Janet and Magruder coming up. Harmon opened the door of Landrum's coupé and helped him in, closed it behind him and stood waiting while Landrum started his motor and ran it a minute to warm it up. Then he slipped in his gears and rolled slowly down the trap-rock grade to the main road. Instead of turning east at the intersection with the road that led up over the grade to Modoc City, Landrum's car crossed that road and went bouncing across the meadow that sloped steeply down to the shore of the lake. It gathered speed as it went—suddenly the watchers on the veranda of the Big House saw it give a tremendous spurt. Although it was late spring there were a few inches of frozen snow on the meadow and the light car rode it as it would a concrete highway. At about seventy miles per hour it shot out into Lonely Valley Lake in a great shower of spray; when the wheels sank in the soft bottom the car turned over twice and came to rest with its wheels uppermost in about three feet of water.

Tom Harmon leaned against an upright on the veranda and laughed softly, and Magruder turned on him, disgusted and angry. "Get some men in Janet's car and get down there immediately, Harmon," he commanded. "Do you want to let the man drown, imprisoned there in that closed car?"

"The men, with the exception o' Big Foot, are scattered all over the ranch on various jobs, Mr. Magruder. We'd need five or six strong men to roll that car over an' get Landrum out. Me, I got a leg that's still a mite stiff an' I'll be hanged if I'm goin' to wade out to my waist in that cold lake an' mebbe contract pneumony o' the lungs. That limousine yonder contains his chauffeur an' bodyguard—four men all told. Let them fish the old goat out o' the drink. They're paid well for waitin' on him an' I ain't."

"There is no necessity for hurry, Uncle Dan," Janet spoke up. "The man is dead. He was dead before he crossed the main highway and started over the meadow for the lake."

Tom Harmon eyed her pridefully. "Yep, Miss Janet, he up an' died on us. You told me once it was dangerous for that man to let his angry passions rise, an' I gave him more'n a well man could stand. He couldn't talk back—he just didn't have no verbal out, so he had t' take it an' make believe he wasn't hurt. His heart popped about half way down the grade; then, I reckon, his body fell over on the wheel an' somehow he shoved the hand-accelerator over—an' away he flew to the lake."

There was a light of impish mirth in his gray eyes as he met Magruder's horrified glance. "Mr. Magruder, you've just witnessed a miracle. You've seen a man die an' try to bury himself in a lake he killed four men tryin' to possess. You've just seen the good Lord bump off a human animal to save better men from committin' murder. Miss Janet, if you don't mind I'll run down in your car an' bring the boss back. He's in mighty bad company, although the twins are watchin' him."

As he backed Janet's car out of the garage and swung it in front of the house, he could see Landrum's men running along the lake shore toward the semi-submerged car. He found Raynor Lanier still sitting in Landrum's limousine, smoking serenely; the twins were hurrying up from their place of concealment.

"Come home, son," Harmon invited. "It's all over an' you've took all the tricks."

Lanier got into Janet's little car and the twins stood on the running board; thus they returned to the Big House, from the veranda of which they watched Landrum's men wade out to the car, smash in the floor boards and drag the dead man out. They laid Landrum on the shore and examined him, then the chauffeur came hurriedly up to the house.

"The old man's dead," he shouted to Raynor Lanier.

"Leave him where he is," Lanier ordered. "I'll telephone the coroner and he'll deputize somebody in Modoc City to come over and bring the body home. You and your friends may drive down to the ranch kitchen and dry yourselves out at the range. My men will guard Landrum."

"How do we know your men didn't kill him?"

"The coroner'll be the judge o' that," Tom Harmon took charge of the situation. "Twins, you come with me down to Landrum. He had ten thousand dollars cash in his pocket when he left here an' I got to make sure these thugs o' his'n ain't frisked him."

CHAPTER TWENTY-EIGHT

TWO HOURS LATER TOM HARMON RETURNED to the house. He came into the living room and backed up against the fireplace, for he was quite chilled. "Henry Eckert, the deputy coroner from Modoc City, come over an' took him away," he announced. "Henry was afraid the bodyguard would hold him up for the money he found on the corpse, so I sent the twins in to guard him. I let them have your car for the trip, Miss Janet."

Janet did not answer. She was at the window,

gazing out at the lake. "Don't talk to her," Magruder counseled. "She's been crying."

"About Landrum?"

"No, you idiot," Lanier spoke up. "She's been under a strain and now the strain is ended."

"An' she's relaxed! Well, so am I. So are you. Ray, all the trouble an' worry you're goin' to have from now on will have to be of your own makin'. I've tried to clean this mess up right an' I think I've succeeded."

Janet turned from the window. "Just what have you done, Tom?" she demanded tremulously.

"Well, I talked Milo into sellin' the cows back to Ray for just what they cost him. I got a sale agreement out of him, duly signed an' I paid him ten thousand dollars cash to bind the bargain, balance in sixty days."

"Where did you get ten thousand dollars, Tom?"

"Milo gave it to me for forgivin' him his trespasses an' promisin' not to kill him." He grinned at Lanier. "Now that Landrum's dead you'll get your grazin' permit back again—in fact, you'll have it back in a week. That'll enable you to put through that loan with the Southwestern Agricultural Credit Corporation an' pay the balance due Landrum's estate on them cows. The possession o' the cows, of course, cinches the calf crop for you."

"Thank you, Tom. What was that tremendous

explosion at the western end of the lake this afternoon?"

"While you was in jail, Ray, I rounded up some hard rock men an' completed the tunnelin' an' chamberin' under that dam. I had it loaded with thirty thousand pounds o' black powder an' some dynamite, waitin' to touch it off the minute Janet had sold her land to Landrum an' got her money. I had a wire run up here an' I got Landrum to touch the button an' blow his own dam out, which blew his heart out, too, I reckon. Anyhow, I hoped it would; a feller can't be ruled off for tryin'. With the dam out the lake drains—"

"Who paid for all that powder and the labor?"

"I did. I been drawin' down two hundred an' fifty a month for the past twenty years an' I don't spend nothin' except a few dollars once in a while for new overhalls or boots an' tobacco. I'll render you a bill when I get around to it. No hurry, however. You can repay me when you collect that seventy-five thousand dollars from the State Swamp and Overflowed Lands Trust Fund."

Lanier crossed the room and put his arm around his foreman's shoulder. "Tom, old horse, why did you do all these things for me?"

Mr. Harmon was terribly embarrassed. "Aw, shut up," he protested. "I ain't done nothin'."

"You've done everything," Janet corrected him, "and it's going to be a long time before I can forgive you for refusing to let me help."

"Out this way, Miss Janet," Harmon reminded her gently, "men don't take help from a lady. You don't know Ray like I do. He likes to roll his own hoop; he don't mind bein' favored by me, because I'm his hired man an' he expects me to do my duty. Besides, he knows I'm right partial to him, right or wrong—an' his father was good to me. When he was dyin' he sent for me. 'Tom,' he says, 'I've made one big mistake in life. I've raised my son a gentleman. However, you ain't no gentleman. You look after the boy an' when you see him havin' difficulty doin' things he don't want to do, you git back of him.'"

Harmon rolled and lighted a cigarette. "You see, Miss Janet, no Lanier could blow out that dam. The court had enjoined them an' the Laniers never cuss the umpire. So I blew it out an' I had to put Ray in jail so he wouldn't stop me. An' I had to handle Landrum an' act tough an' make him pay me for not killin' him, so I would have money to help Ray out." He gazed meaningly at Janet. "I just had to help him out, Miss Janet. Unless he could be got in the clear without askin' help from outsiders—"

"Am I an outsider," the girl demanded gently.

Harmon's eyes twinkled. "Not now, Miss Janet, not now. Remember, I owed you somethin', too. An' I wanted to pay you off."

"What does Harmon owe you, Janet?" Daniel P. Magruder wanted to know.

"A husband," Mr. Harmon shot back at him. "I been playin' cupid around this ranch until I'm plumb sick o' my job." He turned to Lanier. "Ray, have you asked her?"

"Not yet, but it's understood I'm going to. I thought I'd discuss the matter first with Mr. Magruder. He is, in a sense, Janet's guardian, occupying a position somewhat less than paternal and somewhat more than avuncular."

"Oh, take him, Janet," old Magruder urged. "Tom, his father was right. He raised the boy a gentleman, otherwise he'd help himself to whatever he wanted, and ask permission of no man."

"He is a dreadful slow-poke, Uncle Dan," Janet declared.

"Not when the road ahead of me is clear." Lanier went to the girl and drew her to his heart. "I love you, Janet. Will you be my wife?"

"Of course," she answered. "What else do you suppose I came out here for and brought Uncle Dan with me? It's his job to give the bride away."

At that moment Ah Fong entered, to see if the log fire required more fuel. He gazed upon the tableau, then bent an inquiring look upon Tom Harmon.

"Something doing?" he queried.

Mr. Harmon bowed grave affirmation.

"What' you think ketchum little dlink, Tom? One big bottle champagne on ice hab got. Long time all other bottle gone but I savem one for good news."

"That's a constructive idea, Fong. Trot it out. The boss is in no condition to give orders."

Magruder had discreetly retired to his room; Tom Harmon had departed for his own cottage down at the ranch proper, never again to make free in the Big House except upon special occasions, for he knew his place and took a pride in keeping it. Alone in the living room Lanier and Janet sat before the fire and, hand in hand, talked of the days to come. "Ah, sweetheart," he told her, "I never dared dream that this day would dawn. If you knew the number of reasons I had adduced as to why I shouldn't ask you to marry me—"

"I know them all. Tom Harmon and I have discussed them. They are pusillanimous reasons and long since outlawed by lack of usage in our more settled districts. In agreeing to be your wife I've picked a real job for myself. I realize that when I first met you, you were just a cattle baron.

"Now, together, we're going to start the long, hard job of building you into a land and cattle king. That will require time and hard work and worry, because we haven't quite enough capital, even after I throw my purse into the pot with you. And now, together, we're going to see Lonely Valley as your grandfather saw it first.

"Within a week we shall see Lonely Valley

creek meandering once more through the length of that fat land. While the years tiptoe past us we shall see the willows and poplars and sycamores grow again along the creek bank. In that valley, drowned for eighty years, the same trees will crowd again into shelter for our cattle when the snow flies. Nature will be slowly reseeding the valley to the native grasses, keeping pace with our slow operations, our gradual accumulation of cows to dot that little empire. We may be lonely, but we'll try not to be. Our friends will visit us. From time to time we'll visit them, and perhaps in five or more years we can play a little while Tom looks after the outfit. You're going to have worries and know the thrill of turning sharp corners, but that will be an assurance to me that you are not vegetating."

He sat there, thinking of Tom Harmon spending his savings to blow out the dam and set free at last that land that lay in bondage; of Janet giving her money to save him from financial worry, to sweeten his life a little; of Ah Fong's thwarted effort to kill the man who had planned to despoil the author of Ah Fong's income. Of Big Foot and Skunk Tallow and their tribe, so dependent upon him, so silently grateful; of the Sphinx twins hugging their secrets, content to serve in silence, indifferent that none should ever know the pride of their service.

His throat constricted, his eyes filled. "I have

been loved more than I have deserved," he murmured. "I have been forced to accept acts of love I would have rejected—but I'm glad now that they have been thrust upon me. I have—why, Janet, you've brought back my oil painting of Lonely Valley Lake."

Her fingers twined around his. "Yes," she assented. "I felt it belonged there—where we can both look at it through the years—and remember what drew us together."

He caressed her tenderly.

"Kiss me," he pleaded. "I'm away behind in my loving, despite all the love I've experienced today."

"Ah Fong is peering at us through the crack in the kitchen door."

"Who cares! All he wants is some assurance, so he can carry on. It's been a long time since I was a baby and climbed upon his knee."

Center Point Publishing
600 Brooks Road ● PO Box 1
Thorndike ME 04986-0001 USA

(207) 568-3717

US & Canada:
1 800 929-9108
www.centerpointlargeprint.com